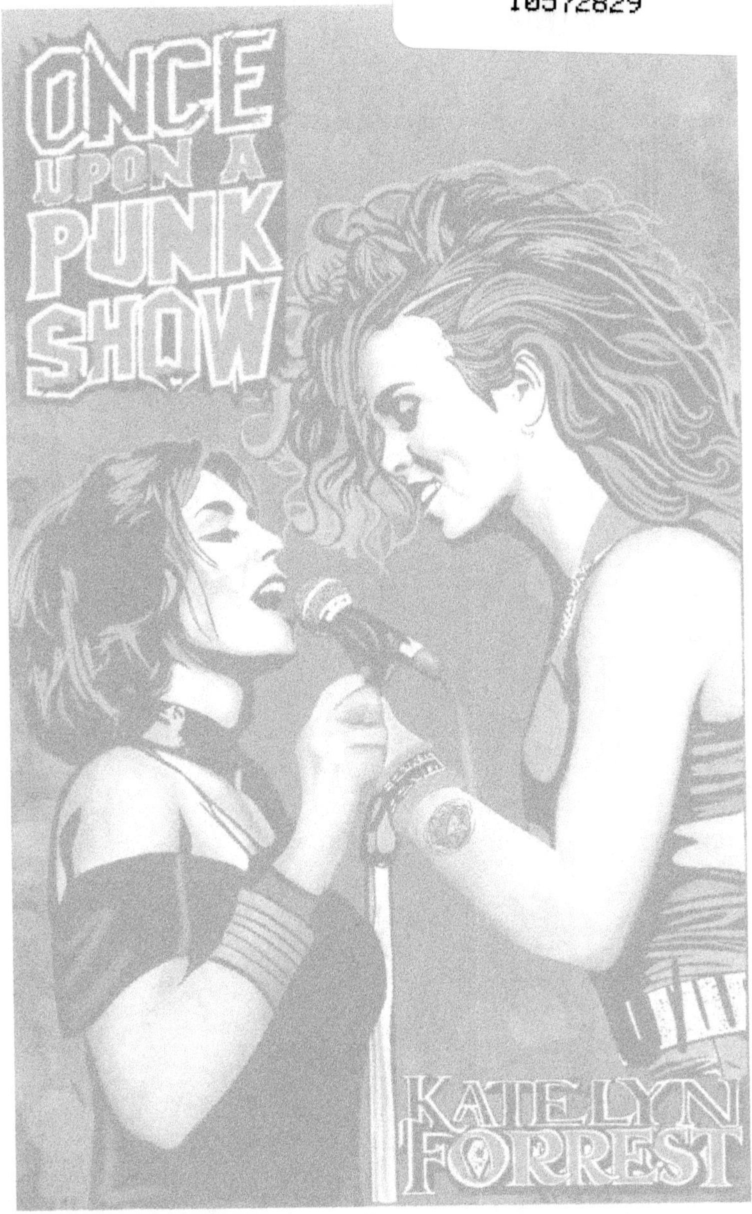
ONCE UPON A PUNK SHOW
KATELYN FORREST

Cover art by Lauren Sullivan

Paperback ISBN – 979-8-9990554-0-8

Ebook ISBN - 979-8-9990554-1-5

First printing 2025

Once Upon a Punk Show
by Katelyn Forrest

<u>*Once Upon a Punk Show*</u> Playlist

For those who need the right vibes to rock out with this book -
Search it on Spotify

"Juilia" – The Horrorpops

"Strawberry Milkshake" – Bad Waitress

"Pay Up" – Civet

"City of Angels" – The Distillers

"She Thinks She's Punk Rock and Roll" – Hands Off Gretel

"Nightmare" – Bad Cop, Bad Cop

"Volcano" – Kills Birds

"Double Arrows Down" – The Bombpops

"Fuck you" – Rumkicks

"Gimmie Action" – The Last Gang

"Hold On" – The Venomous Pinks

"Wicked Heart" – The Devotchkas

"Danse Macabre" – 18Fevers

"Sister K" – Fea

"No Love for a Nation" – Petrol Girls

"Rebel Girl" – Bikini Kill

"Strippers on a Sunday" – Bite Me Bambi

"Eat Slay Chardonnay" – NOBRO

"50 Shades of Fuck You" – Neighborhood Brats

"Seether" – Veruca Salt

"Who Invited You" – The Donnas

"BURN THE WITCH" – Pinkshift

"Red Sky" – The Hellfreaks

"Everything" – The Dollyrots

"Yellow Bellies" – Tilt

"Puncha Nazi" – Doll Skin

"Queer As in Fuck You" – Dog Park Dissidents

"C'mon" – Go Betty Go

Chapter 1 – Giulia

The hangover needled into my head before I realized I was awake. Under my pillow, I squeezed my eyes shut against the day. I was on stage last night. Then there were shots. Then... I'm not sure. One mosh pit blends into another after a while and yesterday's rum was not helping with my memory. A concert hall full of sweaty punks and veins full of alcohol left me feeling gross in a very specific way so I must have been at a show. I peeked an eye open. My hair covered my face. I blew it away and winced at the morning light. I sat up with the care of a bomb tech and untangled myself from the sheets. Once my bare feet were safely on the floor, I straightened out the shirt I had on. The band on the tee sucked as bad as the ex-boyfriend that gave it to me, but it was clean. When I put it on at least. Now it smelled like a hundred punks and a dive bar.

"At least I didn't pass out in my boots or jeans again." I winced at the sound of my own voice. Too loud.

I ran my hands through my coal black hair. It was stiff and crunchy, laying bedraggled near my shoulders. Shower. The world was going to make demands of me way too soon, but only after I had a shower. I stumbled across my bedroom and tripped over a boot on the floor. It was not mine.

"Shit."

From across my loft, I heard the shower come on. "Shit shit shit."

I crept over to the bathroom door. It was open a crack and steam was pouring out already. On the vapors, I could smell someone had opened up that fruity shampoo Angie gave me last Christmas.

"Um. Hello? Mr. One Night Stand?"

I heard a muffled voice say something back to me over the sound of the water spray.

"Ok, ok. Miss One Night Stand," I yelled back. "You were great. I think. Maybe. When you're done, um, go home!"

I darted away from the door before whoever was in there could say anything back to me. I scooped up pants, a hoodie, boots and went for the exit. I only slowed enough to check that my phone and keys were in the pants pocket before leaving my loft through the kitchen. I slammed the door behind me. I put on my pants while standing on the landing above my band's converted warehouse practice space.

I left my building and plodded down the cracked sidewalks of Apponaug, the closest neighborhood Warwick had to a downtown. It was the ungodly hour of nine AM. Rhode Island's morning traffic whizzed by me, paying the small pedestrian no heed. I kept the black hood of my band's sweatshirt pulled up over my head to keep the sun out of my throbbing eyes. I shuddered every time my filthy hair rubbed against my shoulders and back. With my In A Murphy Minute hoodie two sizes bigger than me and the hood up, I looked more like some kid skipping out of high school, not a grown ass woman.

If I got busted, it wouldn't be for truancy though. The city cops have busted up too many late night garage shows to not know exactly who I was. I was too hungover to give a flying shit even if they did roll up.

In the center of Apponaug, a parking lot opened up into two options. Coffee and donuts, with a long line at the drive-thru, were on my right and a liquor store on the left. My hangover yelled at me for even looking in the general direction of the liquor store. I shuffled across the parking lot to the Dunks, not caring that their coffee tasted like burnt ass. There was no way in hell I could walk all the way back to my car and then drive somewhere better. I needed something greasy, something sugary, and something caffeinated. And I needed it now.

Dunks had a line. Ugh. It always had a line. I grabbed a water from the cooler and drank it down right there in line, earning a look from the cashier. My hangover thanked me for the water though. I ordered a greasy as fuck egg and cheese and a wicked sweet coffee. I paid with a wadded up ten spot then shuffled over to wait with the other coffee zombies.

All the coffee zombies were sunk nose down in their phones. Except one.

She leaned against the pickup counter watching the whole place. My stomach backflipped she was so damn gorgeous with unruly black curls and a runner's lazy, fluid stance.

She caught me looking.

I flinched. I must have looked like death warmed over to her, but I couldn't look away.

The hangover beast in my head threw up a waking nightmare. What if she was the woman from my shower that I told to go away and got here faster than me? New rule, always look before kicking them out.

But this woman smiled, so I couldn't've pissed her off yet. She unfolded from her lean and took a step towards me. I held my breath.

"Order's ready."

A paper bag and a coffee held out for each of us.

I felt my cheeks burn. I snatched my food and got out of there before I could make any more of a fool of myself. I speedwalked towards home with an eye over my shoulder. The throbbing hangover said slow down but the raging embarrassment said hurry the eff up.

I sat on the loading dock behind my building and dangled my feet off the edge. The place was an industrial leftover of New England's milltown past, complete with the railroad fifty yard away out back. This one was converted into artist workshop space plus the odd loft I lived in. The hangover beast needed fresh air still but the food couldn't wait. The loading dock sat in the morning shade and the cool air helped clear my head but my food was going to get cold sitting out back.

Shit.

The asshole at Dunks gave me the wrong order. I was too busy gawking at that other woman and we swapped orders. I sighed with some dejected, yet colorful, curses. She was a bacon eater and I didn't eat pork. Of course, Dunks got the 'greasy as fuck' part of my order right, so I could not even pick off the bacon and still eat it. The bag wasn't empty though.

I pulled out a yellow apple the size of a softball. The fruit sticker on the giant apple had some sorority looking letters on it with "For the fairest" written around the edge.

The hangover beast growled. So I fed it. I crunched into the apple and my whole face felt tingly. The hangover beast was messing with me something weird. It was a friggin' delicious apple so I didn't let it stop me.

I ate the apple and drank the horrible coffee down to the dregs. Footsteps crunched through the dirt behind me followed by a sigh. Angie, my bass player, co-founder of In A Murphy Minute and my best friend since we were six and both new to America, sat down next to me. She gently took the coffee out of my hands and sniffed for any alcohol. I had no fight in me.

"What are you doing out here Giulia?"

"Watching the door." I still had to enunciate each word very carefully. The hangover beast entrenched itself quite firmly in my head still.

"Why?" Angie was careful with that question.

"There's someone in my shower."

Angie swore under her breath in a string of Spanish I knew was rather colorful. Swearing transcended language. "Do you know who we're looking for?"

I shook my head and it didn't hurt like it should. The apple calmed the hangover beast somewhat. I pulled my hood down further over my eyes anyways. "She might have left already. I think she was a she. She sounded like a she from the shower. I don't really remember though. Might have left while I was getting breakfast. Here. They put bacon on it." I gave the greasy sandwich to Angie.

Angie already knew what "breakfast" could be on mornings like this. She sniff-checked the coffee cup again. "So you have no idea who we're watching for-"

"Right."

"-and no idea if whoever you shared your bed with is even still there or not?"

I shrugged. "I guess."

We sat there on the loading dock and watched the front end of the building. The only person we saw was Lars, the blacksmith from the other end of the building, and he was arriving for the day, not leaving. The sun crept to the treetops. My hangover coiled around my head, a beast lulled to sleep but ready to eff me up if I poked it. The bad coffee tried to energize me and just managed to convince the hangover to swell up my brain only two sizes too large for my head instead of three. From her pocket, Angie fished out one of the minty toothpicks she carried around since she had quit smoking. She tucked it into the corner of her mouth and the faint spearmint scent drifted around us. Still, no one else left the building. Still, we sat.

"Why do you do this Giulia?"

"Because I can see the front door from here."

"Damnit that's not what I mean, and you know it."

I just looked at my boots dangling over the edge.

Angie looked up at the sky and shook her head. "You can't keep destroying yourself one groupie at a time."

"I'm not-"

"You don't even know who's in there."

"Well, at least I know it's a girl this time," I said.

"And you told me yourself that's 'cause you walked in on her in the shower. Not because you remember last night. That's not a one night stand. That's a problem. Why do you do it? What do you feel inside doing this?"

I did not want to answer her. Angie was asking things I did not want to hear. I stared at my feet for a long moment.

Angie shook her head in defeat. "Sometimes you make me wish I still smoked."

"I don't feel anything," I whispered.

She put her arm around me and I leaned into her shoulder. I doubt I knew what I wanted to hear from her. Angie could not know what words to say, but her presence said enough.

I could not bear to hold myself up, so I leaned on Angie. After a while she helped me stand. "Let's go evict last night's paramour."

We stood and I shuffled after Angie. The world was too bright, too loud, too much of everything. Eating that apple and getting something in me turned my senses up to eleven. I stood shaky on my feet, but I was ok if I didn't turn my head too fast or look up at the sun. I figured Angie thought I was still drunk. I didn't do much to convince her otherwise. She diverted to her Civic, parked off to our left, and rooted around the glove box. She found a box cutter with a sticker bearing her family's cafe logo on the side.

"Let's go." She tucked the box cutter in her back pocket and we crossed the street.

Angie led the way via the back door and I just plodded along in her wake. My stomach made flip flops around The Fairest One apple I ate. The wide central hallway was empty with all the bay doors to the studios closed on either side of us. The distant clang of Lars' hammers drifted our way. No one else stirred. The fourth door on the left had 'In a Murphy Minute' and "G. Cesari" spray painted across the face of blacked out windows. It was my handiwork when I first moved in.

Angie crept in the practice space. It had high ceilings covered in cheap as hell foam sound dampening. Graffiti and stolen show posters covered three walls. The fourth was one big whiteboard I scrawled out half complete lyrics on. Angie's boyfriend, Jin-Wei Kwok, kept his second drum kit here for practices. Her brother, Ricardo 'Punk Ric' Zanetti, kept some amps and a steamer trunk full of crap here. The décor was curbside sofa chic. Tucked in among all that, there was a DIY silk screen set up and boxes of blank t-shirts for cranking out our own merch.

"Ah, no luck. Your paramour isn't on the scuzzy futon." Angie touched the back pocket of her jeans where the box cutter was waiting just in case. She sighed and walked over to the spiral staircase leading up to my loft. I stood there and watched her go up the stairs.

"I should feel bad about all this," I whispered. "I should feel relief. I should… feel."

Angie stopped halfway up the stairs. "You coming? I'm not evicting your lovers by myself."

I shook the thoughts out of my head. My fucked up senses made the head shaking a bad idea. I went over to the stairs and up to the landing with Angie. She tied back her hair and mustered up every bit of her height before pushing open the door and stomping into my kitchen. I slunk in behind her.

"Hey there, rock star," a woman called out from the other room. "I thought I heard-"

She stopped dead in her tracks when she saw Angie. The blonde was wrapped in my beach towel, drying her hair with my only other clean towel. She scowled at Angie. I sat at the table and stared at the dirty woodwork covered with debris and empty bottles.

"What the fuck is all this?"

"Clear out," Angie said with a flip of her head towards the door.

"You've got a girlfriend? Fuckin' A, you can't even kick me out yourself? You're just going to sit there?"

"I…Yeah."

"Come on, no need to make a scene." Angie made a placating gesture.

"I'll make all the fucking scene I want." Blondie stormed through the living room to the bedroom. Out in the kitchen we heard a constant litany of swearing. Blondie came out dressed with a purse and a pair of sneakers under her arm and got up in Angie's face.

"You need to keep your woman on a leash, asshole."

Angie pushed Blondie's waving fingers aside with one hand but I saw the other twitch near to her back pocket. "Just go," she said with a calm I doubt she felt.

Blondie wheeled on me. "And you, you drunk bitch, you weren't even that good in bed. I could've had a better time by myself." She wound up for a hard slap across my face.

I leaned away from Blondie's slap and dodged it more by random chance than any real intent. My stomach cramped up. I felt like a guitar string wound too tight.

Blondie's slap caught nothing but air instead of my face. She lost her balance and slammed her hip into my table. She let out a wordless sound of surprise. It slurred right back to anger. She picked up an empty bottle sitting out on the table and channeled all the rage and disgust with me into a trajectory right into my wall. The glass shattered on the brickwork. Angie flinched, but then went towards Blondie. My hookup was already leaving though. She slammed the door behind her and stomped her way down the stairs. From the practice space there was a crash of toppled cymbals.

"Damn. Jin-Wei's gonna be pissed." The tension deflated out of Angie. She slumped against the wall and eyed me. My friend looked sad.

Angie came over and led me by the arm through my flat to my bed. She poured me into it and pried my boots off. "Sleep it off, Giulia," she said as she tossed a blanket over me. "We'll be over later to gear up for tonight's show."

I closed my eyes against the day. I heard Angie and the sweep of broken glass. She came back, thinking I was asleep, and put a bucket next to the edge of the bed. She opened up the drawer to my nightstand and took out the hip flask of rotgut I kept there. I did not move. There was another one under the corner of my mattress just in case.

The hangover fought a short and victorious battle against my consciousness. Sleep was just about to grab hold of me when I heard Angie was still in the room.

"You can't keep doing this, Giulia. You can't let your demons kill you before you even realize they're following you everywhere."

The distinction between falling asleep and passing out was a very hazy one. I drifted along the edges of one or the other but the shuffling about my apartment kept me awake.

"Go away Angie," I said into my pillow. "Let me pass out in peace."

"It's not Angie. It's Jin-Wei."

"Wha? When did-"

"Decent under there?"

"Yeah I-"

He yanked the cover off the bed. I yelped at the sudden cool air. I bolted upright, too fast for my still buzzing senses. I doubled over and wanted to heave as nausea slapped me hard. "Fucking hell!" I said between clenched teeth.

"I drew the short stick today," he spoke with the barest hint of any accent. None of us in the band spoke English as a first language and he had the most proper English of the lot of us. My own Italian accent came out when I swore. I swore a lot.

"I brought the Giulia Kit." He pressed two aspirin and an antacid in my left hand, a to-go cup of coffee in the right, black as sin.

I grunted my thanks and gulped them down, one after another. I closed my eyes and let the triumvirate do their magic until I did not feel like there was a badger trying to claw out from inside my forehead. Jin-Wei sat on the bed near me and waited with unbreakable patience. He was always the easiest of the band to deal with when I was hungover. Angie mothered me. Ric got grouchy.

"What time is it?" I asked.

"Three thirty."

I swore.

Jin-Wei nodded. "Ric wanted to wake you up a half hour ago. You've been passed out all day."

I groaned again, eloquent as always, and flopped back on the bed. My drummer grabbed my hand and pulled me back to my feet, though. He guided me to the bathroom and I shuffled along after him. Jin-Wei was not one to be swayed when he made decisions. I knew from experience if I refused to shuffle along, he would drag me along.

"I'll tell the others you're up," he said. "Take the time to clean up. You smell like the bottom of last night's bottle."

"Hey! I... can't actually argue that one."

"See?" he cracked a smile. "Momentum has you acting human again already. We'll all be downstairs." He slipped out, closing the door behind him.

I sighed to the pounding in my head. If I looked as crummy as I felt, I definitely did not want to look in the mirror yet. I cranked up the shower to searing hot, discarded the grimy clothes and jumped in.

It took twenty minutes to scald off the residue of my hangover and last night's show. Once it rinsed down the drain, I felt human and brave enough to look in the mirror. My skin looked a bit reddish from the hot water but healthy enough, my eyes were bloodshot as hell and my hair dripped down to my shoulders. I had some cuts on my knuckles and a wicked purple bruise on my ribs under my left arm. I felt it out and winced. The fucking thing was new and I had no idea how I got it. I sighed, my best guess was the mosh pit. I usually remembered stage diving, even if I was majorly blitzed, so I ruled that out. If I was not looking top notch yet, it was still a vast improvement over the sticky, ashen drunk that got into the shower.

Annoyed that my one night stand had used my last clean towels, I was still damp when I went to rummage through the hangers in my closet for something to wear. I closed my eyes and trailed my fingers along my closet and chose one at random. It felt right to do that. I put on my orange In a Murphy Minute tee, the one with the black clock logo. Everything went with jeans and Doc Marten's so I pulled back my hair and decided that I was kitted out well enough to face the day, even if the day was half over.

I left my loft and went down the spiral stairs into the practice space. Jin-Wei was decked out in one of the vintage bowling shirts that straddled the line between the punk world and his day job. Today it was blue. He was packing a box full of cables. Angie had a sleeveless top on to show off her full sleeve tattoos. It was the same color red as the stripe dyed into her hair. She was moving boxes of merch by the door to load up in her brother's van. The tinny sound of Ric's unplugged guitar filled the room as he fired through one of his solos. He still had on his cafe shirt and paid me no attention. I was not sure if he ignored me on purpose or was lost in the music.

"Hi guys." I waved to the room. I felt like a sack of potatoes thrown through a dryer and I would bet solid money that I sounded the same. I had a bit of spring in my step though. My band was here and I was going on stage in a few hours. In my chest, my heart raced in anticipation of the stage high.

"'Bout damn time," Ric said. He slid into the first chords of "The Bucket."

"Ricardo, was that really needed?" Angie stopped and gave her brother a look. They had one of their unspoken sibling conversations.

He threw up his hands and went to pack the guitar in its hard case.

"I had a rough night. It happens," I said.

"A lot," he muttered over his guitar case.

"I'm here now. I am ready to go. Can we move on with our lives?"

Ric stopped and closed his eyes. He breathed in and out for a moment. The tension in his shoulders sagged. "You're right. I'm glad you're feeling better and I'm glad you're ready to go."

Angie handed me a box of t-shirts. "We're only going to The Vault tonight so there's no rush. You didn't miss any of the heavy lifting yet."

"We're playing The Vault?"

Ric rolled his eyes while he walked his packed up guitar to the pile going to the truck. "You forgot? Or did you kill that brain cell last night?" He wandered out to the van in a huff.

I looked at the floor and shuffled along with my merch box. "I thought we were playing in Providence..."

"Two nights at The Vault," Jin-Wei said. "Providence is next week then Fall River. The week after that we start our New England tour. You remember that, right?"

He meant well, but Jin-Wei and his infinite patience made me feel like a grade school kid being scolded by the principal. A knot of anxiety opened up that empty hole inside of me. My chest felt hollow. I felt like I was going to collapse in on myself. Jin-Wei waited me out. With that fucking patience. After two years of dating him, Angie swore she could read him like an open book. All I saw was the look you gave to a misbehaving puppy that did not know better. I saw pity, the kind you gave to that puppy when you knew it would never learn and keep fucking up.

I turned away.

Angie bit her lip. She was holding something back. She was sad. She looked like she was about to reach out to me. That was worse.

I was not ready to face this, not now, not before going on stage tonight.

"Yeah, I'm good. Just had my calendar on the wrong page," I said. Angie reached out to me, but I shrugged off her arm and carried my box out to the loading dock for the short trip to The Vault.

Chapter 2 – Eris

A pair of hard operators with rough hands dropped me into a folding chair with enough force to rattle the metal legs against the concrete. The hood over my head smelled like wet dog and a heavy rope bound my hands behind my back. The goons knew their business. The rope tied into a damp sailor's knot was magically warded. I worked the rope back and forth, but my skin was red and raw. I gave up to bide my time.

"So my reservation's ready?" I drew chaos from the Void and laid the charm on thick. "I'd like a table by the window, if you don't mind."

"Cut the snark," a rough accent growled. A heavy fist slugged my shoulder like a brick wrapped in beef jerky.

"That all you got?" I kept a straight face and popped my shoulder back into place.

"Ah, Eris. *Mien Ketzchen*. It does not have to be this way," a new voice said.

"You do not get to call me that. Not anymore. Not in a long time."

The hood came off my head. I could not resist taking a big gulp of fresh air. Well. Fresher air. Old warehouse was marginally better than wet dog. My eyes blinked in the dim light just to see a dingy room and less than friendly company. They stuck me in the corner of a rough looking storage room at the center of everyone's attention. There were shipping crates labeled in Chinese, some with Cyrillic letters, and they were tossed about with vaguely nautical supplies. Someone moved the stacks in a recent and sloppy job. A window in the corrugated steel walls just showed me it was dark out and nothing else. A path snaked through the packed pallets. The faint echo of the sea drifted into the room.

I glared at the five people staring down at me in a loose semi-circle. That look had shriveled better men than these. I suspected being tied to a chair made my glare lose some punch.

"You show respect." The biggest goon with the same accent and heavy hands stepped forward and puffed up his chest in front of the others. He reeked of wet dog. With a gesture from the man in the middle, he stepped back.

"You stay on your leash, *oborot*." I said to the posturing oaf. The Russian stank of werewolf. His silent counterpart to my right looked crammed full of steroids. Magical or mundane, he at least smelled better, but the non-*oborot* goon was just as much of a problem to me.

"Play nice with Dimitri, Eris. We want to be friends here." Wodanaz stood away from me in the center of things, aloof with a lieutenant on either side. The German thunder god embraced modernity more than many of us old time deities. Wodanaz wore a designer wardrobe in black and silver. His black hair was slicked back for a proper Euro trash look and his ancient spear slung across his back. My heart held a special spite for my ex.

The tall black woman to one side of Wodanaz was Something-or-other Alessandra, a Caribbean water deity punching above her weight class since she started working with Wodanaz. The redhead woman covered with Celtic ink on the other flank carried a lot of high tech gadgets. I knew the Tuatha De Dannon so she was no deity, just an underling with magic toys.

They did not matter. I kept my eyes locked on the one who did.

I rattled the chair I sat in. "Because this is playing nice, Wodanaz?"

"Merely precautions given our history, *ketzchen*."

"Why don't you come over here and I'll give you some precautions?" The sarcasm danced off my tongue. I leaned forward but stopped short. The muscled one pressed a thick blade against my neck. The edge was dull, but inconvenient. I stayed put.

"We could still be great together," he said. "Do not dismiss me and what we do here out of hand."

I channeled the cold heart of the Void into an icy glare. The water deity lieutenant frowned behind him.

Wodanaz sighed and waved the Celt forward. "Do it O'Shea."

She stepped forward with a device in hand. It looked like a cold iron brand sticking out from an aluminum tattoo gun. Electronics were grafted into the top and an LED blinked green. O'Shea held it away from her body. Cold iron was the antithesis of most magics, but especially O'Shea's Celtic magic. Just having that brand out in the open sucked ambient magic out of the room.

"Last chance, Eris," Wodanaz said. "The great Greek Goddess of Chaos does not need to be brought low. Us old time gods need to ally together in solidarity."

"Fuck. You." I reached for the primal chaos at the root of my soul. It crackled at my fingertips bound behind me. Alessandra's warded rope binding my hands made the magic slip through my fingers, like trying to hold onto a quicksilver egg yoke.

"The modern world has made you uncouth, *Ketzchen*."

O'Shea, the Irish witch with the tech, leaned across my left. Being so close to the cold iron itched like termites buried under my skin. The device whirred to life. Chaos magic began to creep around the warded bindings. Another moment and I could free myself and escape...

Then the needle touched skin on my bicep.

The shock was akin to a titan's strike and stole the breath from my lungs. My body jerked like a tangled puppet to get away from O'Shea and her cold iron. I pushed and the world turned sideways when she fell to the floor. I kicked out with my unbound feet. The folding chair collapsed on top of me. Alessandra winced and the *oborot* inched away. An ugly keening sound filled the room.

It was me. My voice. My lungs stretched to breaking in agony.

The screams evolved into words.

"Fuck!"

Then they evolved into good words.

"You limp dicked harpy spawn! The years have made you daft if you think you can get away with this." The full goddess visage fell over me and rage turned me into the booming voiced deity the likes of which Homer wrote epics about. "Release me Wodanaz or by the very heart of primal Nyx, I swear I shall see your end."

Wodanaz stood above me and smirked. His people went into a frenzy.

"Don't just stand there," Alessandra barked. She shoved the witch aside and held me down herself. My cheek ground into the gritty concrete floor. The *oborot* took a kick to the chin getting my feet under control. His buddy held my arms. O'Shea's gizmo came to life like hummingbird wings bringing down the pain. Any pretty curse words left in me melted into screams while O'Shea traced lines into my skin.

I caught flashes of Wodanaz's arrogant smile while I struggled against the pain. Screams tapered off into exhausted snarls. O'Shea finally called out "Done!" and the lot of them backed off like I was a live bomb. The *oborot* and his partner clenched their fists in a vague macho way. O'Shea turned her back and stowed the cold iron tat gun in a wooden case covered with druidic wardings. Alessandra was smart, backing off slow, never breaking eye contact like I was a rabid dog set to bite.

I struggled to my feet at the center of the formation and tried to feign nonchalance. Alessandra drew upon the elemental magic ambient in the room and bundled it into a ball of water hovering between her hands. She looked to Wodanaz, but he shook his head. Alessandra stepped back but kept the magic at her fingertips.

The warded bindings biting into my wrists crumbled to ash. Flecks of dead magic and burned hemp rope floated to the floor. A wicked smile spread across my lips and I reached for my magic.

"You have made the last mis—"

Nothing. Primal chaos was out of reach

Panic stole my breath. The cold iron ward carved into my skin pierced my spirit with the dead numb chill of nothingness. my arm felt like a hunk of dead weight tied to my shoulder. The ward was a wet blanket smothering my connection to primal chaos. The barest thread wove its way through the damage to my aura. A sense of dread pricked at my spine. Withdrawal pains crept in already and made my good hand twitch.

Wodanaz laughed, a hearty sound that echoed though the warehouse. "You should have teamed up with me *ketzchen-*"

I spat at his old pet name for me.

"-the first time I asked you. My offer was genuine."

"Ha," I laughed without mirth. "Your offer was a vague and vain attempt to rekindle a flame that died long ago. One that died because of your own arrogant obsessions and tremendous personal failings."

Darkness fell across Wodanaz's eyes. A crackling smell of ozone filled the air. "You never should have left me back in Italy."

A pulse of magic came across the thread I could still touch. Barely there, but I grabbed for it. Wodanaz wrapped himself too tightly with his emotions and he leaked magic into the room. The ancient thunder god created chaos for me. I hid my smile behind a sneer.

"Go fuck a wrinkly old hell spawn. You're mad," I said. "You have been a corrupted asshole since the Renaissance. Why do you think I left you?"

"I am trying to bring magic back to *Mutter Erde!*" Wodanaz laid his accent out thick with his anger and German words slipped into his English. "*Die menchen* will thank me for what I do! The old gods should be the first to offer up an allegiance to me. You remember what it was like. Humanity revered us. It shall be this way again!"

"You are a forgotten god," I spat. "How much of that humanity you covet so very much even knows the Germans had gods?"

Wodanaz stopped, then he shook with rage. I knew too well he resented those of the old pantheons who were remembered by humanity. The color in his face turned unhealthy shades of vermillion. Crackles of electricity sparked in the corners of the room. He took his spear in his hand, the weapon and icon of his godhood, and stamped the butt against the floor. Fissures formed in the concrete from the strike. Every move he made sent waves through the primal chaos. A smile at the edge of my lips slipped out.

Alessandra saw this and narrowed her eyes. "Boss, she's bating you."

"Do not presume to speak among your betters," I said to her. "You are nothing more than a drunken sailor's imaginary heartthrob with delusions of grandeur."

"Humanity will see what we can bring back to them," Wodanaz yelled, giving his lieutenant no room for a comeback.

"You are a footnote in the history books, Wodanaz. A leftover. An Odin wannabe."

Wodanaz screamed and the thunder god threw magic around the room with blind rage. O'Shea vanished. The *oborot* backed away looking for cover. As a water deity, Alessandra was in a bad spot at the center of Wodanaz's lightning, but tried to talk some calm into her boss. I stood my ground and the smile finally broke free of its cover. The chaos Wodanaz created in the fabric of his own plans seeped through the crack in the cold iron ward etched into my skin. I latched onto every scrap of energy that broke through. My soul swelled with the surge of chaotic energy. My knees buckled from the sudden rush.

Alessandra proved observant to what I was doing but Wodanaz's tantrum held her in check. She shouted to her people over the cacophony that Wodanaz created in his anger. The *oborot* struggled to keep a humanoid form thanks to the surge in ambient magic. O'Shea stayed gone. The human muscle was bold and stepped forward, his serrated hunting blade held out before him.

I shook my head.

I released the chaos held within me, 'Escape' the only desire in my heart.

I blinked out of the warehouse, Wodanaz's cursing echoing in my head.

My eyes opened at the end of a dim hallway. My breath echoed in my head, a rhythmic, pounding pulse. The veins in my head ached like a hangover worthy of Diyonosis. I looked up at movement ahead. Some foot traffic crossed the end of the hallway, but no one saw me appear... wherever I was.

The pounding in my head resolved into a booming baseline that rattled the building. The hallway walls were covered album art. Brooding punks in dirty shirts and carefully spiked hair. Band stickers formed part of the wall's structural integrity featuring names like Birds of a Feather, East Bay Kitsune, The Harmnones, and The Pat Buchannan Button featuring the Hanging Chad.

The chaos magic dropped me in the back of a concert hall.

The trickle of chaos fed through the crack in the cold iron ward grew into a steady thread of magic, thin, but enough to keep me functionable in this place. I held out my hands in front of me and the withdrawal tremors settled to a steady ache in the back of my head. A raw chord from a barely tuned guitar came from ahead of me. A couple punks pushed past and I realized I stood between the bathrooms and the rest of the venue. They looked like they knew where they were going, so I followed.

I walked out on the edge of a packed house. A thousand bodies pressed against the stage where a band bounced around to a lively and loud punk rock beat. A circle pit created a vortex swirl in the middle of the crowd. Fury and music beat against my ears.

I leaned against the wall and felt the tension roll out of my muscles. The barely controlled chaos of a punk show fed that trickle of magic and put me at ease. Wodanaz still hunted after me, no doubt about that. When he latched onto an idea, he was like a dog with a bone. It turned him into an asshole. His idea of bringing magic and the old ways back to humanity was not a bad goal, but Wodanaz was bitter with humanity. His name was a footnote between the Romans and the Christians. I got fed up with his attitude during the Italian Renaissance.

The band on stage was good. I had no idea who they were and they sounded pretty raw. Newbies perhaps, since the night seemed early still. Raw was chaos. Good for a punk band and good for the goddess of chaos.

A large part of my soul wanted to enjoy the show, but the world still felt muted, like a wet blanket pressed between me and the world thanks to that bitch O'Shea and the ward etched into my skin. I pushed up my shirt sleeve and touched the skin with my opposite hand. The ward felt cold, like ice cubes under the skin. This was a new feeling. After five thousand years, new grew hard to come by but for once, I did not welcome the novelty. The… thing… on my arm left me with barely enough magic to… to what, exactly? What would happen to an immortal deity when torn away from the magic that flowed through her cells?

The Greeks did not die like some pantheons of old gods, but without the magic, was I mortal now?

I shuddered at the great unknown. I feared that my cells would realize they had not aged since civilization was still a new concept. Wodanaz's endgame and rekindled obsession with me still floated the open question of why. His people would be after me regardless. What's-her-name Alessandra came from a tier that hardly counted as a pantheon, but back in the warehouse, she twigged that I was trying to escape when no one else did. I would have to be careful of that one.

I knew they would find me eventually. Again. Some power in their possession pulled a signal from the noise and would lead them straight to me. For all I knew, O'Shea's ward would do it. I needed a game plan to survive this mess.

Too bad plans ran counter to my nature as a chaos deity.

I closed my eyes and tried to rub the tension out of my temples while the venue bounced with energy around me. It was pointless and I harrumphed. Off to my left, at the back of the venue, I spied a bar.

I pushed my way through the crowd. Even with the band on stage, a steady stream of patrons hit the bar for cheap beer. I found a seat at the end of the bar and paid for a drink. It was not good beer but it gave me something to do while I processed my thoughts and soaked up what chaos I could from the horde of punks crowding the venue.

Trying to come up with a plan and make proper decisions, ate away at what little magical reserves trickled in past the ward. O'Shea occupied the number one spot on my shit list now, may the ravens devour her unburied soul.

I placed my hands on the bar in front of me. The tattoos on my wrists faced upwards, a Magic 8-Ball on the right and a twenty sided dice made up of little triangles on the left. Normally they danced across my skin with lazy motion and answered questions when I needed to be pointed in a random direction to feed the chaos inside me. Thanks to the cold iron ward, there was not enough ambient magic in my body to keep them moving. They were lifeless and dull on my skin.

"I swear by Zeus' groady sack, I will kill O'Shea for this," I told the dregs of my drink.

Chaos would provide a way out, one way or the other, not that I had any other options.

Eyes closed, I spun around on the bar stool. When I slowed to a stop, I opened my eyes, facing away from the stage. A large poster, done up in bright colors with 'TONIGHT!' scrawled across the top with a marker, was the first thing I saw.

The Vault presents LIVE

In A Murphy Minute

With The Camorri Trio

The Bludbunnies / The Providence Hooligans

A obligatory photo/album cover of the headliners sat underneath the text. Standing in the front of the four-piece formation, In A Murphy Minute's lead singer looked out of the poster at with piercing eyes and the smallest smirk that said, "I know you're looking." I was taken aback by the power of the woman's eyes. She looked familiar. Cover her hair with a loose hoodie. Trade the rocker stare for 'I just got caught looking.' The woman from Dunkin's.

Marked by Chaos twice in one day.

There is a strong woman, Eris thought, even if she does not know it yet.

The thread of chaos sneaking past the cold iron ward felt stronger when I looked at this woman's picture. The primal chaos that fueled my being had decided that this woman would play some part in whatever was ahead of me whether anyone liked it or not. Fighting a direction provided by primal chaos was difficult on a good day, but nearly impossible with such low levels of magic to work with. So be it.

I turned back to face the stage. The crowd spread out across the venue. The band on stage was winding down and the mosh pit dispersing for a breather and a drink between sets. I waved the bartender over for another drink before the upcoming rush.

"She is out there," I said to my empty glass before it was taken away. "Somehow, she is the path forward."

Chapter 3 – Giulia

I caught my breath from the melee in the mosh pit. My adrenaline was still jacked up but it had nowhere to go now. I drifted with the crowd to the back of The Vault to the bar area. The Vault was a bank in its previous life and the bar kept its bank teller look. I pushed to the front and waved to the bartender.

Without the chaos of the music and mosh pit, the demons were in the back of my head whispering sweet nothings. Again. I drummed my fingers against the bar. The bartender was screwing around with some other woman's drinks down at the other end.

My tequila finally showed up and I knocked it back in one go. I felt that sweet burn down the back of my throat.

I needed another.

"Giulia! Where the fuck've you been?"

I turned and saw my guitar player pushing his way to the bar. Ric, the older of the Zanetti siblings, looked pissy and annoyed. That was the face he usually gave me lately. My tequila hit my bloodstream and I swayed a bit. I needed more if I was going to deal with him.

I did not get it.

Ric grabbed my shirtsleeve and pulled me away from the loving embrace of the bar. I shuffled my feet along after him. Some other punk kid, barely old enough for a fake ID, slid into my spot at the bar just as I left it.

The house speakers played an old montage of 70s UK punk while The Bludbunnies broke down from their set up on stage. The murmur of the sweaty crowd and the noise of so many people shuffling their feet grated on me without the music turned up loud enough to hide it. I trailed Ric through the crowd to the backstage door. A Vault staffer waved us through.

In the wings just off stage, the rest of In A Murphy Minute was gearing up to take the stage. Angie dropped what she was doing and ran over to me. Jin-Wei came over to stand between her and Ric. Manny, the Zanetti's cousin, ignored us while he played roadie for us.

"You had me worried," Angie swept me into a hug then held me at arm's length. The Bludbunnies rushed back and forth past us. Their lead singer, Tish, kept lingering near Ric, but caught the bad vibe from us and left us alone. There was a pool going for when they would hook up.

"She was at the bar," Ric said. "Took a while to catch up with her from the pit."

Angie made a face.

I sighed to myself. Angie was being protective of me again like I was some porcelain doll that could get trampled by some big baddie. I let it go. She meant well.

"This place is epic tonight." I made a wide gesture to the crowd roaring for the band on stage. "There's—"

"There's something chaotic in the air tonight," Jin-Wei interrupted.

"Exactly. I got carried away in the pit."

"Well you're here now. That's what matters."

Everyone around us in the wings cheered The Bludbunnies for a kick ass set. I drifted away a couple steps from the rest of the band. Ric said something. I did not really hear it. I stood right on the edge of the stage. The lights were dark and Manny led the crew as they scrambled to swap out the drum kits. I closed my eyes and took in the energy of the crowd.

"Let's start with 'This is Where I Belong," I said.

"But we have 'A Long Day's Fight' on top of the set list," Angie protested.

I started to speak but Ric cut me off. "Giulia's always right about this stuff. Whatever else she does," he snapped, "she's never wrong with set lists."

In the stage dark, I walked out to my mike. Manny and the Vault crew were not ready for us yet but worked around me. The crowd murmured in anticipation. Without the stage lights, they mistook me for more of the Vault crew. I closed my eyes. This was my calm before the storm. The peace of it settled over me. I grabbed hold of the certainty that surrounded me.

"This is where I am supposed to be," I said just above a whisper.

Maybe the mike picked up on my words. Maybe the crowd full of punks noticed me on stage. Someone out there started cheering.

For me.

Angie walked out on stage. In the dark, the low pulse of her bass hummed across The Vault. She started the intro to 'This is Where I Belong' low and slow. The crowd stepped up the volume. I wrapped myself in its warmth. I smiled and laughed into the mike. Jin-Wei layered in his drums with a crash of cymbals like this was something we actually planned. The beat grabbed hold of me. The crowd became part of my soul. I held on to the mike stand and fought the urge to dive headlong into the song.

Anticipation was a thing of beauty. Make them want it. Make them need it. Make that crowd fucking beg you for your offering.

Angie stepped up the tempo. Jin-Wei followed with a double crash. Ric dove in with a vicious pick slide. When my heart was about to burst, we nailed the intro in a flash of light. The Vault crew knew this song and turned on the spectacle for us. I crooned the opening line and let myself go to the music.

I ended the song breathless and full of energy. My lungs had three seconds to catch up with air before Ric launched us into '(I Don't Live in) Massachusetts.' He punched through rapid fire chords. This song made use of his lightning fast fingers. I took the mike and tossed aside the stand. I leapt and flailed with the music. I became a one woman mosh pit. I belted out the lyrics with a ferocity that welled up from deep within. I poured out an offering to my people before me.

I was alive.

The show was a blur of kinetic energy. I dove off stage in the second song. I bought the mike with me and I screamed the chorus with the crowd. Ric pulled me back on stage for the third song. Arms draped over each other's shoulders, we sang out the first lines of 'Under the Greenwood Bridge.' I shared the mike with Angie for our cover of 'Rico Suave' and we crooned to the crowd together.

I stood in the middle of the stage completely jacked the fuck up on the stage high. There was something in the air that night that was messing with my head underneath it. An undercurrent of energy in the room that I never felt before but could not quite pick out from the stage high. Angie drifted over and put a hand on my shoulder. "Giulia, are you ok?" I heard her yell over the wild cheering. My face must have shown something was odd. Angie's protective streak usually ran towards kicking asses alongside me.

The human contact brought me back. I nodded and made a crank-it-up gesture. Angie's eyes said she was not going to drop it, but the spirit of the stage was infectious. She could not ignore the wild chaos of the Vault either. Her bass guitar slid into a holding loop with the rest of the band. I turned towards them and like a symphony conductor, I brought them all into the next song.

I let the song take me over again. I hit all the right words to 'Cleanse the Mind.' I changed our encore songs to 'Half Step Off' and 'A Noise in the Crowd.' The crowd got nutty for another encore and we obliged. We drew it out and dropped a full half set. The Vault staff practically dragged us off stage to stay legal with Rhode Island's zoning laws about midweek live shows cutting off at eleven. One of the staff plugged in a phone on shuffle to keep the music up and keep it legal. Last call for the bar was still a ways off.

Offstage, the congratulations were a blur. I felt like I was floating six inches above the floor from all the energy and adrenaline pumping through me. All of In A Murphy Minute was swept up into a suddenly crowded backstage. Tish, from The Bludbunnies, swept me up into an excited embrace and then I was mobbed. The other bands, staffers, groupies and people who snuck backstage surrounded me like I was some celebratory idol and they could share in a piece of the night. The tide of people pulled me in a different direction from the rest of my band. I caught a glimpse of Angie and Jin-Wei laughing and smooching. Ric found Manny and a lot of groupies.

Someone in the blur pressed an unopened beer in my hands. I wanted it. Bad. The stage high was falling. I felt the ache in the back of my throat. My fingers tightened around the neck of the bottle.

No.

I pressed it into some other hand in the crowd. I did not give two flying shits who got it, I just knew I wanted it too much to have it. It ended up in someone else's hand without me ever seeing what it was.

I ducked the worst of the crowd to make my way to the backstage ladies' room. I loved The Vault, but backstage was the one and only civilized bathroom in the place. I still had to weave my way through a hallway full of people, but they were of the "Let's hang out and chat where we can hear each other" variety. I beat the post-set rush to the bathroom.

On the return trip through the backstage hallway, weaving through the men and women flirting with each other, I saw something out of place.

Rather, I saw someone out of place.

All of a couple minutes went by since my last pass down the hallway and leaning up against the wall like she owned the place, a familiar woman stood looking right at me with a half smile perched on her lips. She was gorgeous, catlike slim with sun touched skin that spoke of Mediterranean shores. Her hair was a chaotic cascade of curls pulled over one shoulder, the same jet black as her eyes. An apple blossom scent hung about her, noticeable even over the stale beer and sweat of the bar. There was no way this woman was there when I passed by before. I would have noticed. I became very aware I was a hot mess, covered in stage sweat. My swagger faltered in a flare of self-consciousness. She caught my eye before I could slink away.

"Hey there, rockstar."

She looked at me like I was the only person in the world. Her midnight colored eyes held my gaze and would not let go. Her voice was a velvet caress.

"You have a good choice in breakfast," she said.

Was I drunk? That made no sense.

She laughed and the crystal sound made my stomach flip flop. "I saw you this morning at Dunkin' Donuts. Our orders got switched. That was a bad ass show. I am glad we crossed paths a second time today."

I smiled, but it was a nervous thing. She saw me hungover as fuck right after a one night stand and now I felt out of my league just standing there near her. Something in the air felt thick between us. It sent a jitter through me.

Not now, I thought, don't let go of stage high.

"I'm glad you liked the show," I got out. "We laid out a pretty good offering on the altar of punk rock tonight."

I made her smile despite my ham fisted words. My stomach tied itself in knots.

"I like your choice of words, rockstar. This kind of place is a perfect temple," she said. "Would you like to come have a drink with me at the bar?"

My brain skipped a beat. "I... I have to catch up with my band."

Shit. Why did I say that?

The woman frowned and uncrossed her arms. "That is unfortunate. I thought we could have a lot to talk about." She leaned in close to me and my breath caught in my throat. "There is something in the air tonight, Giulia, and I can sense it in you."

"What did you-"

"But I don't want to keep you from your band, Giulia. I will be at the bar if you change your mind." The woman shrugged and started to walk away. She turned back and tossed something to me that I caught out of the air by reflex. "By the way, you dropped that."

She did not turn back and melted into the crowd. The apple blossom scent followed her.

"Damnit, why did I say that?"

No one else in the hallway listened to my question or gave me an answer.

I looked down at what she gave to me.

A yellow apple, same as I ended up with at breakfast.

I shook my head. Who the hell carries fruit to a concert?

My stage high was starting a slow spiral down. She's just fucking with you, the voice in the back of my head whispered. You're a disheveled mess, why would she want you? You're not good enough for her.

I crunched into the apple.

Fuck. I wish my mind would shut the hell up sometimes. A lot of times.

The apple was amazing even if packing fruit to a punk show was friggin' nuts.

My feet carried me out of the backstage hallways and into the crowd, weaving in and out of the dwindling press of people. The Vault bar stayed open after the show ended, but a lot of people cleared out right away after the midweek concerts. I ducked fans and ignored well-wishers. She said she was going to be at the bar and I was intent on finding her.

She was facing the bar with her back to me. I stopped in my tracks, nervous again. The voice in my head was whispering poison to me. I told it to shut up.

She still wants to have a drink with me.

You don't know that, it said.

She's out of your league, the poisonous voice in my head said.

"Bullshit," I said aloud. "I'm a fucking rockstar."

I ditched the apple core and pretended I was on stage. I walked up to the bar with my head held high. I slid into the barstool next to the woman, but I could not look at her yet. My hands were shaking with nerves as I signaled the bartender for drinks. Two shots showed up in front of me. I knocked them both back and that special tequila burn quieted the yammering self-doubt in my head. The alcohol made my stage high feel farther away, though. My stomach did flip flops again. I waved the bartender over for two more shots. With great self-control, and only a little bit of self-loathing, I only sipped my tequila this time. I peeked over the rim of my glass and saw myself in the mirror behind the bar. Still a mess. I slid the other drink over to the woman next to me and finally looked up at her.

She smiled at me and I felt like I was going to melt into a Giulia-shaped puddle.

"Why'd you give me an apple?" I said. It was a pretty stupid opening line.

"Oh, it's a thing I have a habit of," she said.

I must have made some sort of face.

"Titans below, I am sorry," she said. "The mysterious stranger bit comes to me too easy. It is too comfortable for me. I felt a connection, and after we had crossed paths to see you a second time... in my life, that kind of thing means something."   "I... s'ok. Seeing you at Dunks was the highlight of my morning." Fuck, why did I keep trying to remind her about how I looked like crap on my hangover walk.

"Ok. Let us start over." She closed her eyes and nodded with a serious look on her face now. When she opened her eyes, she had a smirk on her face. "Hello Giulia Cesari, I am Eris... Katsopolis. Since we have never met before, it is a pleasure to meet you."

Eris held out her hand. There was a Magic 8-Ball tattoo on the inside of her wrist. The opposite wrist was inked with a twenty sided dice. When I took her hand I felt a jolt like someone slapped me in the face with a case of Red Bull. A surge of energy shot up my arm and spread through my body. I felt keyed up, like someone took my stage high and poured it over my head. Eris smiled again. I did not have a good poker face.

"Wow. Um. Hi."

I was a fantastic conversationalist.

"I am beginning to think that you're not just being coy, Giulia."

"About what? And how did you know my name?"

"You are the main attraction here. People came from all over to see your band play, Giulia, to see you on stage. Did you know there is a group that drove down from Canada because they could not wait for you to play any closer?" Eris shrugged. "Learning your name just took a bit of asking around. No magic involved. It is on the back of the album."

I relaxed as much as I could around someone I was so attracted to. It was a relief Eris was not being a creeper. "Right, right. Sorry. I'm... kind of keyed up right now."

"And you have no idea why?"

"I know why. The stage." I felt a very femme wistfulness slide into my voice. "But there's more tonight. Something... I dunno, something in the air. Cheesy as that sounds."

"My name is not familiar to you at all?"

I wracked my brain. Alcohol, the stage high, unadultered lust, and whatever that energy that slapped me upside the head all fought amongst themselves to see who could screw up my thinking the most. There was no way I was impressing Eris. What was she playing at anyways? She sure as hell was mysterious and confusing. And hot.

Eris eyes darted to the inside of her wrist at her tattoo. She took a quiet sip of her drink. "Nothing about magic?" she raised an eyebrow at me.

"Like some Gandalf shit? Were you named after one of his friends?"

Eris laughed out loud. It was a hearty laugh. It was a beautiful laugh. I wanted to run from her and kiss her all at the same time.

"I am sorry, Giulia," she said between the laughs. "I do not mean to be rude. This day is full of surprises."

"You found me first," I said.

Eris reached out and placed her hand on mine. I could not help the grin on my face. She leaned in closer to me. The scent of apple blossoms was intoxicating. "How about we get out of here? Together. I am sure there is an all-night diner or somewhere we could go with something we could do."

I jerked back in surprise. Of all the things I could have possibly expected her to say, this was nowhere on the list.

"I guess if you do not want-" she stated.

I absolutely wanted to. Eris had my emotions all tangled up in a big mess and the tequila made me not give a flying rat's ass. Something in the air about her made me feel... comfortable? Happy? Energized? Like I was that dude from that movie at the front of the boat on top of the world? Some screwed up mess of all of the above. I took her hand and pulled her to her feet. I fought back a swoon. A swoon! She was going to make me into a swooner. I felt like a dork. But, damn, she was beautiful. My friend alcohol prepped me for bad decisions tonight but there was no way that Eris counted as one, right?

"Yes."

I grinned like an idiot until I saw the rest of In A Murphy Minute over in the thinning crowd. Manny was with them and they all had packed up boxes of merchandise. I could tell they were looking around for me and they were heading right for us. They knew the bar was the first place to start looking.

"Shit. We gotta go."

I grabbed Eris' hand and pulled her into the crowd. There was a small sound of surprise from her as we sped off through the crowd. I slowed long enough to throw money at the bar with our abandoned drinks. We dashed through the people, running even though no one was chasing. I found us an unused and poorly lit corner near one of the emergency exits. I stopped and slumped back against the wall. No one noticed us. Probably.

Eris had a question written across her face. I looked down at my hands and knotted my fingers together. "I saw my band. I really was supposed to meet up with them."

She laughed her kissable laugh again and I felt a lot less guilty about ditching everyone.

I laughed with her, because Eris laughed that kind of laugh.

"So what would you like to do?" I asked. "We could-"

Eris reached a hand behind me and pulled us together. A smolder burned in her eyes as she pulled me in. Her lips touched mine and we kissed. My knees felt weak and the wall held me up. Her kiss was feather light and the hand at my back was strong. This was too fast, it was too much. But how is it any different than Blondie last night? Or that drummer Wes? Or that bartender in Fall River? Or that sorority redhead down at URI? Or Sound Guy Jose in Hartford? Or... or... or... or... there is always another or.

Because I pursued them.

This time, she pursued me.

Was this a bad idea?

No one who made me feel this good with just a kiss can be a bad decision.

But didn't I plan on making bad decisions tonight?

Eris broke the kiss and looked at me with a quirky little smile. The light from the bar behind Eris shone through her curls. Her apple blossom scent hung in the air between us.

Over her shoulder I caught a glimpse of Angie on the edge of the crowd. She caught my eye. Crap! We were busted. Angie just shook her head. I thought I saw a smile. I hope I saw a smile. Maybe it was wishful thinking. She waved us off and turned back to the crowd.

"So..." Eris whispered to me.

My stomach did a flip flop inside of me. I was sure that I looked like some sort of grinning idiot, but could not help myself. I felt too comfortable there with Eris to care. The air between us felt charged. I took her hand in mine. Our fingers twined together like it was the most natural thing on earth.

"Let's get out of here."

Chapter 4 – Eris

Giulia grabbed my hand. We dashed outside into the cool night air.

"My place is just down the block," she purred into my ear.

I took her hand in mine and kissed it like a courtier of old. "You read my mind rockstar."

We ended up on the steps outside her loft above her band's practice space in the converted warehouse she called home down the street from The Vault. I stood behind her and pressed my body up against her. I kissed the side of her neck below her ear. Savored the scent of her hair. I felt a shiver course though Giulia. She fumbled the keys to her door.

"Not helping."

I ran my hand down her arm. The thin trickle of magic left to me sparked between us. Goosebumps prickled on Giulia's skin.

"Was not trying to," I whispered and kissed that same spot again.

The key took and we burst into the loft. I kicked the door closed behind us. We stopped and gazed at each other. Giulia reached out and took my hands in hers. I leaned my damaged left arm away slightly to hide that mess of a magical ward Wodanaz and his team of assholes tagged me with. My tiny thread of magic latched onto Giulia and buzzed between the two of us. Magical tension and sexual tension bleeding into each other.

In my head, I frowned but would not let it show on my face. The magic of primal chaos and random chance led the two of us together twice now. It started this. But the magic was greedy now, searching for more of its own kind. Giulia must have an affinity for it. No surprise there. The punk rocker steeped herself in chaos with every performance.

It is dangerous to be around me right now, I thought. *I need to stop this. For her sake. I need to get out of town. Out of Rhode Island. Back down to DC-*

Giulia must have felt the magic too. She looked at me with energy sparkling in her eyes and a lazy, lusty smile played across her face. Giulia was gorgeous and the vitality she showed on stage back in The Vault was my magnet. I did not think that her innate chaos, and all the trouble following me, would latch onto her. I hoped not. Because I wanted this, Titans below, I wanted her. Standing inside of Giulia's loft, I felt like we had done this a thousand times before.

Thinking about leaving made my stomach turn and an ache creep into my head behind her eyes. Chaos withdrawal. When I opened myself to the primal forces for a decision, they were tough to fight. Without enough magic inside me to burn off, I was not sure I could fight the whims of Chaos. I felt the shakes coming on.

Giulia saw none of this, thank mother Nyx.

She wrapped her arms around me with a flurry of motion and kissed my lips with a hunger. Giulia's kiss tasted of cinnamon, citrus and a hint of smooth tequila. My mind said this was a bad idea but my body gave in. Giulia leaned into me and pressed her body against me. Up against the door, I let her. Giulia trailed kisses down the side of my neck.

I bit back a moan. Coherent thoughts fizzled away.

Giulia reached under the hem of my shirt and ran her electric touch against bare skin. I broke the kiss long enough for Giulia to pull my shirt over my head and catch a breath. The cool air of the loft sent a shudder across my skin. Giulia placed a kiss on the spot on my neck just below my ear and danced a feather light touch along my curves. My knees just about gave out from the anticipation. I grabbed Giulia by the butt and held her close.

"Bedroom. Now," I whispered.

"Oh is that not helping?" Giulia kissed that spot again. I moaned into her hair. Giulia slid her hand down the back of my jeans.

"Will it help better over here?" Giulia kissed the same spot on the other side. "Good thing I'm not trying to help."

"Bedroom. Please," I said, but my words trailed off into a moan thanks to Giulia. I ran my nails up the small of her back along her spine, leaving a slow trail of magic. It crackled between us again. Giulia felt it. She shivered into me.

"Bedroom. Now," Giulia agreed.

I tried to find words but Giulia turned my brain into mush. Some sort of wordless agreement came out of my mouth. Giulia kissed it. She grabbed me by the hand and we flew across the loft, through the kitchen and a bedroom I saw only as a blur. Giulia stopped at the foot of the bed. She wrapped her arms around me with a kiss that penetrated my soul. We tumbled onto the bed. With a flurry of limbs, we got naked. I tried to go on the offense but gasped and melted into the mattress at Giulia's touch. Giulia had the easy mind blowing touch of a longtime lover. Eventually, I was able to give as good as I got.

We were lost to the world for hours.

Giulia drifted off to sleep curled up against me but my own slumber was elusive. My brother Hypnos had no messages for me this night. My mind was troubled now that I could think straight again. The power of random chance brought us together. Heeding that power kept my magical reserves steady, but only just barely thanks to the ward in my arm. In addition to the fantastic sex, every ounce of magical energy should have recharged. More often than not, sex created chaos. The whos, the wheres and the whens of sex tended to be spontaneous. Even if the intimate event was scheduled into some kind of To Do List, sex itself was an instinctual act, reactionary amongst the people involved. Chaos fueled me and sex was steeped in chaos.

I leaned over and kissed the top of Giulia's sleeping head. Her hair was a tangled mess and I could not help smiling. But it was a short lived smile. Sex that good should have given me a chaos fix to last a day, easily. Instead, I felt the withdrawal shakes a half step away already.

It is that order stained ward, I thought.

I slipped my right arm out from under Giulia. My lover stirred, but did not wake up. I probed the raw ward that marred my left arm. I bit my tongue to keep from yelping out and waking up Giulia. The ward hurt with anything more than the lightest pressure. The skin on my arm felt properly dead to the touch.

I snuck out of bed and padded across the room. I paused by the window and saw the first, purplish, hint of dawn in the distance. Marathon sex ending with a sunrise made me think of better, ancient times. If it was not for the threat of Wodanaz hanging over my head, it would be the perfect morning. Either way, I could have killed for a kylix of Ismaros wine like back in the old days. Or Scotch. The Scottish knew their alcohol.

In the bathroom, I turned on the light and shut the door so it would not bother Giulia. I got the first good look at the ward in the mirror. The cursed thing was a swirling knotted pattern shot through with angular lines. The lines were coal black on red, raw skin. My arm looked like it was halfway between a burn and an infection, neither being good.

It sure was not Greek magic. I recognized a bit of Celtic in the knotwork elements of the ward. That made sense since Wodanaz had that Irish witch do his dirty work. Knowing how Wodanaz thought back when we were together in the Renaissance, I suspected there was something chemical or alchemical about the ink as well. The rest of it was unfamiliar. And when you got to be five thousand years old, unfamiliar like this was rare and unsettling.

I watched myself in the mirror trace out the knotwork of the ward. It hurt. Sweat broke out on my brow but I forced myself to trace the whole thing. Celtic magic based itself on binding the natural world together. If I could undo the knots, it would undo the bindings and unravel the ward. But I frowned at the thought.

It seemed too simple a solution.

It made sense, but I knew better than to place all my trust in logic when strange magic was involved. That tidbit of binding theory was the extent of my Celtic magical lore. No obvious solution seemed at hand. If I snuck back into the bedroom and found my pants, I could find my cell and call up some backup. I mentally scrolled through my contacts. I did not know any of the Tuatha de Dannon well enough to trust with a consultation. There was too much bad blood between the old Irish gods and some of my Greek cousins. Annona Augusti would help if she could, but she was Roman and would know even less of Celtic magic than me. The local Scott family vampires disdained witches and the Rhode Island kitsune made for bad business. Chaos and tricksters together caused collateral damage and I needed to lay low until this was solved. If Wodanaz was running a big operation in the area, it's likely any of the major local players would have a whiff of what was going on. I had not been in the country, let along New England, long enough to know who to trust in this and Annona's intel probably did not extend this far outside of Washington DC.

I shook my head just once in the mirror.

I needed my magic back. It was not just a desire or convenience, but a fundamental need for my cells to function. With the ward separating me from primal chaos, I felt withdrawal creeping up on me near constantly. I felt sick to my stomach. A headache like needles jabbed into my sinuses. Without a magical fix, I would not be able to see straight soon and vomit away with convulsions. My heart rate jumped at the mere thought. I thought about sneaking back into bed with Giulia for another round of glorious fucking while the sun came up. It was a great thought. A fantastic thought even. I blushed in the mirror thinking about all the things we could do. Again.

No, I could not fuck away my problems.

Not with the looming threat Wodanaz presented.

So I needed my magic back if I was going to keep breathing and I needed to keep breathing to get Wodanaz to fuck off and if I could get Wodanaz to fuck off, I could get back to my new lover. I latched onto the simplest solution and avoided the irony that the goddess of chaos was using logic to get out of a tough spot.

Giulia left her razor on the edge of the bathroom sink. I took it and broke the plastic sheathing holding the triple blades together. I took a single blade and held it near the skin of my arm. I tried to relax my muscles. The ward throbbed with each pulse of my veins. The tip of the metal barely touched the lines of the ward. It was going to hurt. There was no way around it.

I closed my eyes.

The edge of the razor stabbed into my skin. The dead seeming flesh roared to life, shooting white hot pain down my arm. I fell to my knees and clung to the sink to keep from crashing to the floor. I swallowed the scream in my throat. The razor stuck in my flesh, golden ichor oozing from my veins and down my arm. My vision faded around the edges. Incoherent Greek curse words happened between clenched teeth, desperate to not wake Giulia.

Unconsciousness crept close tinged with fear. The ward's stranglehold on my magic meant the fabric of my being was in question and immortality was a heavy thread in that fabric.

In that moment, I feared a true death for the first time.

With a burst of movement, I grabbed the razor and slashed through the ward. The blade sliced though skin like a tangled spider's web. My legs gave out. A tidal wave of primal chaos slammed into me. I lost myself in it and passed out.

Chapter 5 – Giulia

I rolled over in bed and snuggled up closer to the warm body next to me. The morning sunlight shone bright through the windows and the sheets were crisp enough to be right out of a laundry commercial. We shared a single pillow. I almost touched my nose to hers. Eris flashed a smile warmer than that morning sun. She ran her fingers through my hair. I kissed her lips and her apple blossom scent danced around us. Together, under the covers, I felt energized and relaxed, ready to take on the world but with no reason to ever leave Eris' side in my bed.

"Good morning," I said to her.

Eris ran her hand down my body. She grabbed me by the ass and pulled us closer together. My breath caught in my throat. I wanted to laugh in delight but Eris stole a kiss. I melted into her. My heart felt fluttery while the rest of me felt hot. I caressed her breast to restart where we left off last night.

Eris gently rolled me on my back. Her kiss lingered before she leaned away and looked deep into my eyes.

"I am sorry, Giulia."

I moved to kiss her again but she leaned back ever so slightly. I caught the ghost of where she was.

"I don't understand," I said.

Eris caressed my cheek. Her touch was light and her hands strong. "You have to wake up," she said. Eris' smile seemed sad.

"What? It's my-"

"Your phone is ringing."

"No it's not. I-"

"Shhh." Eris touched my forehead and I shot upright in my bed.

The day outside my window was that special kind of New England dreary. My skin prickled with goosebumps from sleeping the whole night on top of the covers. I was all alone in my bed.

And the fucking phone really was ringing.

I found the green button to take the call.

"It's Giulia... Oh Kevin... ... ... Seriously? ... ... I don't fucking care... ... That's a you problem... ... You knew I was taking the time off for my band... ... Fine. I'll message someone, but for fuck's sake tell Jeff to pay some friggin' attention to the schedule."

Kevin was the assistant manager at Demo's Music, the place I worked. It was an old school record store that carved out a niche by selling obscure or collectable music. Tourist season was flush with New Yorkers eager to spend their money so the store kept surviving. The owner, Freddie Demonstra collected misfit staff like we were trading cards, saying he needed people who appreciated the store to properly work in the store. Most of us were in bands of some sort. Personally, I think Freddie hired us to give the store a

High Fidelity vibe. Couldn't be a quirky music store without quirky staff.

Freddie didn't quite pay enough, but he was an ex-roadie so he understood the band life and let us take time off to play shows. I scraped by. Sorta. My loft came with the practice space I rented for the band. The Zannettis and Jin-wei chipped in. The loft wasn't exactly a legal rental space so the building owner let me live up there on the sly. Landlord got paid, I didn't have to crash with a half dozen roommates. Win-win.

But a "quirky" staff getting paid just barely enough to get by wasn't always good for things like "scheduling" and "show up for work on time." Whatever. I had hangover days too.

I tapped out a bleary-eyed email on my phone to a couple of the other Demo's crew. Henri or Eloise or one of them would bail out Kevin. Or not. Wasn't my day to care.

Email sent, I tossed the phone onto my bed. It flashed with unread messages. I flopped back onto the bed. The blankets next to me were cold. I had the bed to myself for a while. I frowned.

"Eris?" I whispered to my quiet bedroom.

No answer.

I called out her name louder.

Some ancient pipes in the walls rattled.

I eased out of bed. My body was sore in about thirteen different places. Some of those sore places were proof of all the fun I had last night, but some were thanks to a bad night's sleep once we were done. I rolled the stiffness out of my right shoulder while I picked around the floor for clothes to wear. I found a tank top that did not smell like old feet and slipped it over my head. It got paired with some UConn sweats an old "not quite boyfriend but better than a fuckbuddy" once left behind.

Another hangover brewed in the back of my head. An empty feeling made my heart ache.

I padded into the kitchen and opened up the fridge for a breakfast beer. The bright light from inside my appliance jabbed at my eyes. I slammed my eyes shut and the pounding in my head was strong enough to make me dizzy. I peeked through my eyelashes and fished out the first thing that came to hand without looking. I got a bottle of water instead of the beer that I wanted and it was probably better that way. My head felt like it was kicked around by the Brazilian football team. I went to the bathroom medicine cabinet to fight it back with some aspirin.

My bathroom was a mess. Well, a different mess than usual. A razor blade sat in the bottom of the sink. It was covered in some thick, golden liquid, like someone doused the sink in honey. I touched a finger to it then took a sniff. No idea. It held a vaguely citrus sweet scent to it and stuck to my fingers. I wiped my hand off on my pants and saw the sticky stuff covered the counter and floor under my feet.

"Fucking crap, why would someone explode a bottle of honey in my bathroom?"

The sticky sweet smell was lodged in my head now. The whole cramped bathroom smelled like a bad dessert now. I was not quite convinced that the crap squelching between my toes was honey, but my brain did not want to wrap itself around this mess. Too many questions, and not enough painkillers, in my system.

I did my best not to make eye contact with my reflection. Catching the briefest of glimpse at the wild combination of sex and hangover hair was more reflection than I needed.

Aspirin. I rattled the bottle, afraid it was empty. Something click-clakked against the plastic. There was no empty space on the counter that was not covered in sticky crap to put my drink down on, so I juggled it and the child proof pill bottle. The last two pills tumbled out into the sink.

"Shit!"

I dropped the plastic pill bottle, spilled half the bottle of water and shot my hand into the sink to catch the aspirin. I missed and the razor sitting in the bottom of the sink sliced into my finger from tip to knuckle.

The razor edge was sharp and the cut was clean. My nerves were still slow from all the drinking in my recent past. I held up my hand and looked at the blood oozing out. The golden sticky junk was all over my hand too. I watched a drop of blood mix with the crud.

My nerves woke up.

A stab of pain shot into my hand. The mixture on my hand moved. It went back towards the cut. The mystery honey was pulled to my wound like a magnet. I tried to shake it off but it clung to my skin. The sticky fluid was in my cut. It burned under my skin. My body soaked it up, wanted more. I grabbed at my finger, my hand, my arm as the burning spread through my veins.

Out. Out. I needed it out. I dug at my skin to get it out. My nails tore more skin. More ways for it to get in. The burning spread up to my shoulder. It hit the veins in my neck and exploded up through my head. The pulse in my ears turned to hummingbird gunshots. I felt a pop in the back of my brain. Sounds bled into colors. I smelled purple. I heard the goosebumps on my skin.

My breath stopped.

My empty flesh fell to the floor.

I tasted time.

My lungs came back with a scream.

I felt the sound waves bouncing off the tiles in the room and hammering me into the floor. The shit that soaked into my veins burned like salt in an open wound. Or drain cleaner. The burning spread to every cell in my fucking body. I couldn't even double over in pain because it came from all sides. There was no direction to pick. I laid there on the scuzzy bathroom floor. My body vibrated and twitched in pain. The wiring in my head got all fucked up. I tried to move but all I managed was a flop to the side. My arms were nothing more than ten pounds of wet noodles attached at the shoulder.

As my cheek pressed into the cold tile, my breathing fell into short gasps that rattled in my chest.

I am going to die here, I thought.

I wished I had cleaned the floor.

I waited to die. My brother would be pissed if he ever found out on the other side of the country. Angie would be sad but not surprised. Ric and Jin-Wei would be strong for her. I lost religion too long ago to think I'd see Mom and Dad again.

"Just get it fucking over with," I said. I tasted the sounds of my own voice, a gravely mush.

I tasted footsteps coming from the rest of my flat. I tried to move toward them but my nerves have all burned away in fire. My muscles did not respond. Face still on the floor and eyes wide open, I could not move.

A pair of feet crossed into my field of vision. They were mannish feet in sandals with wings on the side. I definitely did not recognize the feet. What kind of fucking hipster wears bird sandals?

Whatever. *If he helps me off the fucking floor so I can die somewhere clean, he can do whatever the hell he wants with his feet.* I still could not move.

The voice muttered in a language I did not recognize. His voice sounded like fresh squeezed fruit juice.

"*Skatá.*"

The sound of a swear was universal.

I felt a hand on the top of my head. Some words were said and I blacked out.

Finally. I was dead.

...

Except I wasn't.

Sunlight creaked through the bathroom window and woke me up. There were no happy dreams this time, just a vague confusion that I was alive. I rolled over to stare at the ceiling. I wiggled my toes. Then my fingers. I lifted a hand in front of me.

My limbs worked. The razor cut on my hand that started all this was gone. I got to my feet. I felt... great? No more battery acid in my blood. I looked into the mirror. I glowed. I fucking glowed. Not in a neon lights or pregnant lady kind of way, but a youthful radiance I've never owned before. I leaned in towards the mirror and touched my cheek like a goober. No make up, not that I owned the level of product required to look like I came out of a tv commercial. I ran a hand through my hair. No post-drinking, passed-out-on-the-floor scuzz either.

"Hello?" I call out to my flat. I walked through the mess in the living room to the bedroom. Rumpled sheets were the only evidence I had great sex the night before and the hipster sandal dude who poked my head while I was dying left no trace.

Maybe I hallucinated him. I tasted colors, for crap's sake, so hipster feet were not that much of a stretch.

Maybe it was all a fucked up dream, I thought.

The air in the room left goosebumps on my skin, like the ozone in the air after a thunderstorm. I opened a window but it did not help. My fingers shocked on the metal window sill. The energy in the room made me feel uncomfortable. I rubbed the goosebumps out of my bare arms and dashed to my kitchen. I reached into my fridge without looking and pulled out a bottle of orange juice. I did not want that, but the act of not looking at what I chose felt so natural, I could not put it back.

Outside the kitchen door, leading down to the practice area, I heard something stirring. I went out on the balcony looking over the area strewn with musical instruments, amps, futons and clutter.

"Eris, you down there?"

I rushed down the spiral stairs to the floor without waiting for an answer.

"Who?" Angie stood near the bottom of the stairs packing a box of In A Murphy Minute t-shirts.

I stopped dead in my tracks. "Oh. Um…"

Angie rolled her eyes and went back to packing the box. We had a silk screen press set up in the corner to make our own merch to sell at shows. I went over to the clothes line strung up in the corner and started taking down dry shirts.

"I met a girl last night," I said without looking at Angie.

"Figured. I win the bet."

"What?" I turned back to her.

Angie shrugged. "Ricardo bet me it was a guy this time."

"You're betting on my sex life?" I gave her a look.

"Little bit, yeah. What? Don't look at me like that. I had to evict one yesterday."

I tried to grumble about that, but could not manage the ire. Angie supported me too much to not have a little fun, I guess. I cracked a smile.

"So what'd you win?" I asked.

"He covers a shift at the coffee shop next week."

I kept folding the fresh In A Murphy Minute shirts. A comfortable silence fell over us. All the new shirts I folded were special made with the cities and towns we were going to hit on the upcoming New England tour. I turned to Angie with an armload of shirts. She was standing there looking at me with a hand on her hip.

"Well?"

"Well what?"

"Were you going to tell me about that?" Angie said.

I stumbled and almost dropped the shirts. I put them in the box while I reached for words.

"I... well, last night. When she was here-"

"Woah. No way." Angie put her hands over her ears. "I don't wanna know the details of what you're doing in the sack."

"Then what?"

"Look at you," she gestured at me up and down. "Since when do you get all done up the morning after a one nighter? She give you a makeover last night?"

"Something like that," I felt the heat in my face and turned away so Angie couldn't see me blush.

We drifted back to the kitchen. That charge in the air still hovered around me like a static filled fuzzy blanket. If Angie felt anything odd about my flat, she did not show it.

"I got to go," she said. "Dozen things I need to do before tonight's show. Broke the E string during the last song yesterday and I can't find any more."

"I'll go," I blurted out. I needed out from here. There was an ache in my heart from waking up alone and an ache in my soul from creeping near death. Brooding around the house was a bad idea.

"You're a life saver, Giulia. Amina called out of the café today so Mom's stuck there and got me running up to Prov for more of those fancy Italian espresso beans and-"

"None of the stores in Prov sell the strings you like," I finished for her.

Angie gave me a hug and was all thank yous as she bustled out the door on her errand for her parent's café. The moment she was out the door, the silence in my flat that I normally found peaceful, became oppressive instead. I hurried through getting ready to leave the house. I went so fast I did not bother to tie my Docs. I had a long sleeve shirt in my hand, ready to put on because for all that I was pro naked sexy times, I rarely left the house showing so much skin. The sun was out thought and the breeze coming in my window was warm. I stuck with the tank top I had on. I balled up the tee and threw it on the couch as I left. A little notion in the back of my head said to let the world see my glow. Besides, Angie said I looked good today.

I rode my bike down to East Greenwich, a couple miles away from Apponaug and about as far away as I ever bothered with on two wheels. It had been a while since I rode anywhere and it felt good to stretch my legs like this. I bounced with energy when I first got my bike out and burning off all the weird energy I had pent up inside of me kept me from thinking about anything that happened to me this morning.

Angie's new strings cost me thirty bucks. I made sure to get some extras. In A Murphy Minute's New England tour started in a week and the only place I knew we could get more of Angie's perfect strings along the way was in Keene. If she was all out of spares, I did not want to gamble on one string holding out for six shows until we got to New Hampshire.

Wearing the tank top outside felt weird and uncomfortable at first. I felt exposed. Like everyone was staring at me. Like there was a giant, grotesque red flag on my back that everyone was going to point at laugh at. It felt wrong to ignore the impulse that said to go out bare armed and keep glowing.

I caught the guy at the music store low key checking me out. A woman shopping for drumsticks too. I stood a little straighter after that. I owned the look.

Sitting outside a Starbucks, jamming my body full of caffeine, I still felt weird, but not so self-conscious anymore. I had run out of errands to do though so I was twitchy and restless to go somewhere, do something. Angie would still be up in Providence, but maybe Jin-Wei and Ric were game for some time in the practice pit. I thought about biking back up to the Zannetti family café and waiting there for Angie for a late lunch. Mama Z would be happy to see me too. The café was back through Apponaug and a couple miles past that. Even with all the energy to burn, I did not know if I was up for that much biking on the day of a show.

My phone buzzed profusely.

It took four tries for the unlock patter to take. The smartphone's screen pixelated for a moment before I banged it on the table and it reset itself. I frowned. Something scrambled its little mechanical brain for a moment.

It felt like I did this morning.

My frown deepened and I had to physically shake the thought away. The strangeness that followed me around since I left the house was infecting my phone now. I called my little piece of pocket technology a fucker and I opened up my texts.

The phone flared to life and dumped a dozen texts in my lap all at once.

Angie was checking in on me with half the messages. I rolled my eyes at the phone but I tapped out a response anyways. She had protective streaks. I did my best to humor her. Smart phone virtual keyboards were the devil's own invention for anyone who had thumbs and with the phone acting all fritzy, I took four goddamn tries to spell the message right.

I scrolled through a mess of band stuff after that. Manny asked about merch for the night. One of the

Bludbunnies tried to gossip about Ric. Jin-Wei played master organizer.

The last number on my phone, I did not recognize.

And it had way too many digits.

The text was from an international phone number. That did not make any sense. Musicians in the scene and well connected fans could get my number, but they were mostly local people I had met before even if they were texting with unfamiliar digits. Who the hell was texting me outside the country? None of my grandmother's family back in Italy had been in touch since my parents passed away, and they would not know my number. My Italian was rusty from a lack of use, so it would be a garbled mess of a phone call anyways.

I brought up the message. The timestamp said I got it this morning while I was on the phone with Kevin and before I almost died on my bathroom floor...

I shook that thought out of my head. Avoidance was the way to deal with that one and maybe some drinking later. I just tapped on the message.

<<Heard you were dreaming about me, Miss Giulia. Sorry I had to leave. Find you @ show tonite. -Eris>>

I shot upright and scared the stuffing out of a pigeon creeping up on some patio crumbs. My pulse drummed in my ears and I felt a rush in my chest. She did not ditch me, not for real. My thumbs stumbled over the touchscreen to tap out a reply. The letters jumbled up as much as my thoughts did. I made a mess of the message, moving my thumbs too fast for my phone to keep up. I deleted the nonsense text and put the phone down on the table in front of me.

I resisted the urge to pace around the Starbucks patio and drummed my fingers on the table instead.

"Let's play it cool, Giulia. No need to say something stupid."

My phone sat there and blinked an accusatory light at me.

I glared at it. "You're not helping."

Not that my phone intended to.

<<Hi. Free all day before the show if you want to do something. I'd like that>>

"Oh god, that's desperate," I said. I deleted it as fast as my thumb could mash the button.

<<I'll wear something cheeky for you>>

Too eager. Delete.

<<Sweet. Looking forward to it. I'll play a crazy song for you>>

I hit send before I could over think it and tossed the phone back on the table. Was that still too eager? Song dedications, what was I, some 90s radio station? Such a fucking dork. I wanted that text back. I reached for my phone and hit the back button. Too late. My phone decided to actually work correctly on the first try for once like it was waiting to throw a monkey wrench into my day. There was nothing I could do to stop the text now. Electrons and cell phone signals could not be plucked out of the air.

I started to send Eris another text, but I stopped myself again. "Just stop being neurotic. She'll be there tonight."

It was easy to say "Let's not be neurotic" but it was a lot harder to do. I needed to stay calm. Mellow out. Keep from getting all fucking wound up. My thoughts drifted to the quickest routes to all the liquor stores between here and home. I tried to shake the thought out of my head, but it was persistent. I needed to get moving and stay moving to keep myself out of trouble. I felt great and wanted to hang on to it. I needed to burn all the energy pent up inside.

I left my coffee sitting outside of Starbucks and hopped on my bike and started pedaling before I could convince myself that drinking all day was a better idea. Instead, I thought of Eris waiting for me at the show tonight.

I grinned like an idiot.

Chapter 6 – Eris

All the healing magic and spells across all the traditions of the world had limitations. When a wound sat on the doorstep of those limitations, a needle and thread was all that was left. I laid out with my arm held over a stainless steel tray of surgical tools. I could not make myself look, even after thousands of years on the mortal plane. The pull of thread through the skin over my bicep was an unnatural feeling I never wanted to get used to. I sighed and turned my head away to read the book spines across the library walls.

My immortal skin was midway through being stitched together in the library of Gnosi Manor of Salem, Massachusetts. The Manor was old New England money in all the ways that Newport or the Cape with their seasonal New Yorkers were not. The Manor, along with the section of library shelf I currently occupied myself with looking at, pre-dated the concept of America.

"You're wearing out my needles with your immortal skin, Eris." The Oracle, Dee, applied stitches with care. She knew I hated the sight of them. Like me, Dee was far older than the Manor.

"I'll make sure to bug Hephaestus for some fancy needles next time I'm welcome in Olympus, Dee."

The Oracle tightened up the last stitch and waved me off. "You've just got me worried. Cutting off god-magic is power like I have not seen in millennia."

I sat up straight but avoided looking at the stitches still. "Really? Millennia? That is a bit much, Dee. Especially here in Salem, this place drips with magic."

"New magic," the Oracle said with a shrug. "Druids and shamans. Witches and reiki. Not our kind, Eris, not deity magic." The last was said in Greek to drive home the point to her stubborn friend.

"Point," I conceded. "I cannot remember when I saw the last shrine to Olympus that was not in some stuffy museum. But I refuse to believe that Wodanaz and his band of scruffy assholes will ever be the type of scruffy assholes to move mountains."

Dee sighed as she put away her medical instruments. "His judgement is clouded by his obsession. Wodanaz never got over St. Boniface slaying his last believer before his eyes."

"Exactly-"

"But," Dee held up a hand and interrupted me. "Your judgement is clouded when it comes to this thunder god. You still see him as the lover you once left. You do not see the strengths his centuries long obsession has built, corrupted those strengths may be. You can only see his failings."

I turned away from the Oracle with a harrumph. "He has got a lot of those."

Dee laughed. "You speak the truth.

My phone buzzed to life in my pocket. I snatched it out of my pocket and checked my text messages. Dee pretended she did not notice the obvious.

<<Sweet. Looking forward to it. I'll play a crazy song for you>>

"Someone special on your little gadget there?" Dee teased.

I shoved the phone back in my pocket. "Just a thing. I need to go to. Later. Back in Rhode Island. With a person."

"Oh please," Dee rolled her eyes. "I have known you since togas were in fashion. It is written all over your body language even if I was not an oracle."

I blushed but Dee spared me from any more awkwardness.

"I am going to make some tea," she said. "You have business to attend to."

The Oracle left the room out the far exit with that knowing smile her kind perfected long ago. I knew better than to do anything more than wait it out when my friend, or any other Oracle, got that way. I drifted over to the bookshelves again. I closed my eyes and ran my fingers across the gilded hardcover spines. I pulled a book out at random. The forces of primal chaos fed me a hit of magic. It pulsed through my soul and I felt it from my fingertips down to my toes. It was the tiniest sliver of magic fed into my soul but meant my body worked properly for the first time since the last run in with Wodanaz. Or at least close enough to normal.

I let out a sigh.

"I didn't think colonial American battle history was your thing."

I resisted the urge to throw the book at the owner of the voice. Instead, I put it back on the shelf with deliberate care and tuned around before opening my eyes. I never noticed the book title.

"Hermes. Why are you here?"

Across the room from me, the Messenger God sprawled out in one of Dee's leather armchairs. Hermes was a spindly, little guy but tried to take up as much space as possible with his sprawl. He looked like he mugged a Jimmy Buffet fan and stole his clothes. The Hawaiian shirt sported a tacky yellow and blue motif of ugly parrots. Hermes' shorts were too long for his frame and the winged sandals of his office laced all the way up to the bottoms of his shorts. A pair of goggles were pushed up over spiked hair, complete with frosted tips.

Hermes pretended to be shocked. "Just a little professional courtesy among Olympians."

I crossed my arms and gave the other Olympian a glare. I pulled at primal chaos to put magic at my fingertips. Hermes could be a shifty little shit when he was in a mood and I had no idea of his intents. I did not regret avoiding the whole lot of my pantheon as a rule of thumb, but in that moment regretted not keeping an ear on the gossip. Wodanaz had me a big jumpy and I wanted to be ready. My connection to chaos still felt sluggish. Like an aging computer, my body was ok as long as there were no frills. I bit my lip and let a frown tug at my lips.

Hermes thought the frown was meant for him and put up his hands. "I'm serious. *Deos* to *deos*," he said in old Greek. "No trouble."

"I have not laid my eyes on you in years, Hermes," I said. Hermes wanted to interject but I cut him off with a gesture. "And with the shit that has shown up in my life this week, I am inclined to assume the worst."

Hermes' eyes darted to the stitched up wound on my arm. Dee never got around to covering the threads with bandages. The stitches were black and ugly on my skin.

I leaned my left side away from him. "Spill it," I snapped.

The Messenger stood and made an ancient gesture of respect with his hands. "Olympian business, Eris. I swear it. Cyprus was a century ago. I have put it behind me, moved on. And I owe you one from Key West in '77 so..."

"Fine," I huffed. Hermes flopped back into the arm chair but I stayed on my feet near the bookshelves. "This better be good if you think it makes up for Key West."

"I got tapped to play Psychopomp today."

I spun around on my feet. "What? It has been-"

"-hundred fifty years, three months, two weeks and a day. Not since Kostas Samaris fell fighting the Turks."

School kids forgot that Hermes was anything other than the Messenger of Olympus. Hermes filled the role of the Greek psychopomp, ferrying souls to the afterlife and the shores of the River Styx. Thousands of years ago he had spiritual reinforcements to handle the workload, but if you were pious enough, important enough, and lucky enough, Hermes himself would escort your soul. Since Mercury and the Romans muscled their way into Olympus, demand for Hermes' services was low. The Great Underworld Merger of 1249 left demand on life support. In the modern day, the Greek pantheon survived off the energy from academic study and schoolchildren daydreams. True believers in the Greek religion were so few and far between, they all got the personal touch when they left the mortal coil. Kostas Samaris, the last one Hermes ferried, was a name everyone part of the Greek mythos kept close to the heart. A true believer passing on was big news. Greek fey and other mythics would get the personal touch from Hermes as well, but it took a lot of violence to put down a being with no natural end to their lifespan. Bad news regardless.

"Why come to me first?" Eris asked.

"She was one of yours."

I scrunched up my face in confusion.

"No one knew you had a paladin," Hermes said. "What?!"

Hermes tensed. The Messenger looked ready to bolt from Chaos' legendary unpredictable temper.

"I didn't take her," he said as fast as he could get the words out. "I swear I didn't take her."

I stalked over to where he sat and loomed over him before he could get out of the armchair. "I need details."

"Seriously. Relax. It's cool. It's all cool. I left her where she was."

"And where was that?" I said.

"Titan's sack, Eris, keep track of your own people."

I knew my eyes darkened with the depths of the Void. I leveled a finger at my counterpart. Magic crackled and sparked in the open air around me. "You do not have any say in affairs that are not your own. I do not meddle in your affairs and you have no sway over the tides of Chaos." My voice boomed through the room and shook the air.

"I get it, I get it. Not my place. Sorry." Hermes flinched. "I am here to help you."

"Speak," I snapped at him but returned some personal space to him.

"She's not far from here," Hermes said. "South. A couple hours by car. If that."

I gave him a side eye. That did not make any sense. I had been hanging around the region for a few weeks. It was hard to take three steps in New England without tripping over a fey from some pantheon, but Dee was the only Greek I ran across and only then because my friend lived here. Olympus refugees usually stuck to warmer climates more like our old home. In fact, until Wodanaz and his team of assholes inserted themselves into my life, I had not seen another full deity since DC three months ago.

"Who was she?"

Hermes rolled his eyes but did not mouth off for once. If he wanted to play these little games, I could humor him for a while. "I dunno. Like I said, no one knew you had a paladin. Hit or miss if you ever keep in touch with the gang."

I stopped glaring, but did not say anything to him. Hermes guessed this was prompting to go on.

"She was messed up bad, Eris. Strung out on some bathroom floor in a shithole loft like she was on the losing end of three rounds with Akhlys' deathmist."

"Just passed out on the floor?"

Hermes shook his head. "Ambrosia all over the fucking place like she was bleeding out, but, you know, human. Should have been a horror show of red, not golden."

"Was she hurt?"

Hermes shrugged. "Something in Sparta was rotten, but I didn't see anything that could have made such a mess. Coulda been someone else's ambrosia." His eyes flicked to the stitches on my arm.

I had the same thought. "Wait. What did she look like?"

"Short. Dark hair. Miscellaneous American skewing towards the Old World." he shrugged. "Not Greek, that's for sure, not that things like that matter in this day and age."

"Giulia..." I whispered.

"Ha! I knew it was one of yours," Hermes looked smug. "Chaos magic has that certain feel in the air if you can catch it fresh. I get the Psychopomp call, chaos in the air, and I mean in the air. That shit was fresh, like I stepped in it. I knew I should leave the paladin alone. So what's the deal, Eris?"

I paced about in a small circle. "Hermes, do not tell anyone."

"What for?" Hermes laughed. "There's a new player for Olympus, we can all get behind that. Well. Most of us."

"I am serious Hermes. This cannot spread beyond these walls and this moment."

Hermes laugh dropped away and he narrowed his eyes. He slowly got to his feet. "What are you playing at Eris? Are you screwing with me? I came here first as a courtesy to you and you're putting your foot down?"

I looked at him for a moment. My mind raced. I decided to take the risk. Actively making the decision drained the reserves of chaos magic within me and I fought to keep a tremor out of my voice. "Hermes, there are things in motion here that you are unaware of. Things under the jurisdiction of Chaos and Chaos alone that cross pantheons which need to be resolved quickly and quietly before anyone else gets drawn in against their will."

Hermes rubbed eyes with the heels of his palms and made a sound of frustration. "Your jurisdiction is too broad to pull that card Eris. Cross pantheon problems are all the Olympians' problems."

"No!" Something quavered in the back of my voice. "I cannot have any more collateral damage."

"You *are* collateral damage, Eris. By definition."

"Not this time, Hermes. Not this person."

Hermes stopped and his eyes widened. "No way. No way, you can't be saying what I think you're saying because-"

"Please do not go there."

"-that would mean your paladin doesn't know."

I looked away.

"Oh man, Eris." Hermes ran a hand through his hair, screwing up his spikes and almost knocking the goggles off. "I know you operate by a different set of rules than most of us, but... fuck! This girl doesn't know?"

"Her name is Giulia."

"Whatever the fuck her name is, this is seriously fucked up. Even for you."

"Hermes. Please. Do not relay this back to Olympus."

"I dunno if that's a good idea..." Hermes said.

I stood straight and adopted a formal posture. Even in a slacker's jeans and a tee, an Olympian's formal cadence was commanding and powerful. I spoke with the full weight of immortality behind my voice. "I swear by primal Nyx-"

"Hera's tits, you're serious..."

"-that I, Eris, Goddess of Chaos, Holder of the Golden Apple of Troy, will grant unto you, Hermes, Messenger of Olympus, Supreme Psychopomp of the

Greeks, a boon of your choosing at such time as requested by you. By the ambrosia in my veins and the very immortality in my heart, I shall do all within my power to grant you your desire if you so agree to my request. Until I grant you my leave, do not report of my paladin to anyone outside these walls."

An immortal boon was not something to be taken lightly. Hermes clearly did not like the implications but a free pass from me was a powerful thing to hold in his back pocket though. As he pointed out himself, my jurisdiction was large. Hermes dithered while I stared at him with piercing black eyes. A messenger dealt with information, and he was missing too much to make a wise decision.

"Do you accept?" I demanded. "Make your answer."

"...yeah."

"Say it."

Hermes adopted the god-stance three paces from me in the Oracle's library. He summoned his caduceus to hand and held the snake winged staff between us.

"I agree to your request," his voice echoed, "in exchange for a boon granted at a time of my choosing. No word of your paladin shall escape my lips to anyone outside these walls until you give me leave. So it is spoken."

Hermes rapped the butt of his staff on the floor three times. Each strike of the caduceus cracked like thunder.

The thunder faded, and the tension deflated out of me. I itched to be in movement and get back to Giulia. My eyes darted back and forth with indecision about what to do next. A twitch of withdrawal brewed in the back of my head. The chaos in my body burned off with every decision I made here. My body screamed for randomness. I looked to the polyhedron dice tattooed inside my wrist. The numbers were spinning.

Hermes cleared his throat.

I jumped.

"Yeah..." Hermes said. "I should go." He sounded like a one night stand caught trying to sneak out. "I mean. You obviously have... stuff... to do."

"I need to go back to Rhode Island," I blurted out. Making the decision to act burned at my soul but I pulled out my phone anyways. The screen blanked out. A surge in chaos around me burned out the battery. I could not call Giulia, but the twitch in my soul died down a bit.

"Okay," Hermes said. "Good luck with that."

Keys in hand, I left the library before he finished the sentence. Hermes harrumphed behind me. "Fucking chaos magic," he muttered, thinking I couldn't hear him.

Whatever. I got what I needed for the moment.

I passed through the kitchen on my way out when the Oracle grabbed my good arm and stopped me.

"Not now, Dee," I said. I tried to pull away but Dee held firm. "I have to go. Hermes-"

"-brought you news of someone you care about."

"Bad news. That is why I must be in Rhode Island. Now."

Dee's eyes glazed over the way an Oracle's did when they were Seeing. She shook her head and a small smile appeared. "It is only bad news if you let it become so. The power to choose-" The Oracle put special emphasis on that word -"lays here." She punctuated her sentence by jabbing me above the heart with her index finger.

My soul already burned at the edges. My body craved chaos. Choice was not a luxury I had right now. "Then may Nyx have mercy on us."

I was out the door and in my car without another word to Dee. The Oracle would understand, I told myself. My giant, borrowed Crown Vic with the DC plates stood out like a sore thumb in the narrow old streets of Salem. I gunned the engine and the V8 lurched through a red light. My chaos reserves trickled upwards a bit as I left horns and middle fingers in my wake. I stopped at the next red a few streets down. The onramp for 93 South, the quickest route back to Rhode Island, was to my right. I drummed the steering wheel against my will.

Even with my red light stunt, there was not enough chaos in my system to carry on. The punk show Giulia's band was going to play would give my system a jolt, but we were slated to meet before the show.

"Will not do to be drained fucking worthless when I find Giulia," I muttered. "I cannot survive a drive to Rhode Island this jumpy."

The light turned green.

I looked to the 8-Ball tattoo on my right wrist. The white circle with the eight inside it faded and that blue triangle spun in my ink.

A truck behind me leaned on its horn.

"Which way do I go?" I asked. 93 was the quickest route back to Rhode Island but the greater Boston area was surrounded by concentric rings of north-south highways. As long as I did not go east to the Atlantic Ocean, I would cross one of them eventually.

Swearing came from the open window of the truck. Motherfuckers punctuated with assbags and shitheads. In case I forgot I was in Massachusetts.

The swirling blue triangle inside my 8-Ball ink slowed to a stop.

I sighed, but did not have the energy to fight its decision.

The light turned red.

The Crown Vic lurched through another traffic violation and headed due west out of Salem.

During my time in New England, I stuck to the cities and major towns. I was surprised that less than fifty miles from one of America's most major cities, the suburbs dropped off into a rural setting real fast. The old Salem homes dropped off to cookie cutter subdivisions and they petered out into stretches of trees punctuated by old farm houses.

On an empty stretch of road, surrounded by new growth forests, I wondered when the hell I would find the next highway heading south. I kept glancing at the clock. With no way to let Giulia know my ETA, Chronos was my enemy. One of Massachusetts' jaunty white signs proclaiming a town line crept into view. A large black sedan and a neon sport motorcycle parked in the road. I slowed my car to a stop.

Andrea Alessandra leaned against the Lincoln radiating indifference. Her help stood astride the crotch rocket with no helmet on and his best "I'm a tough guy" face on. I did not know the one-off well enough to know if Alessandra's nonchalance was real or feigned. Wodanaz' *oborot* stood in the road next to O'Shea, the Celt with the brand. She had some sort of pendulum in her hands and looked nervous standing on the edge of the scene.

"Get out of the car, Eris," Alessandra shouted.

I humored them, mostly because I did not want to shout. I kept the driver's door open and leaned on it.

My glare was reserved for O'Shea. "We have unfinished business, you and I."

The witch stepped back.

"Yes. We do," Alessandra said, ignoring the fact that I had not been talking to her. "Run all you want, but we will find you. Wodanaz has made your power part of the plan, whether you give it voluntarily or not."

"Wodanaz can go get fucked by Cerebus' three pronged dick," I snapped. "How did you find me?"

Alessandra laughed. "Who do you think you're talking to, girl? Some Bond villain that's gonna spill the beans just 'cause you asked?"

I expected bluster from Andrea Alessandra so kept my eyes on O'Shea. The witch was the weak link. She tried to hide the pendulum she held in her hands. I looked closely. It was a quartz crystal with a leaf bound in copper to it. There was power in the pendulum. The leaf was chaos. Shit. The leaf was from the Golden Apple Lhassa, a relic from my past.

"Now, you going to come along nicely, or are we-"

I dove back in the car and mashed the gas pedal. The Vic left a streak of rubber in the road. The front end slammed into the bike and its rider's leg crushed between my Ford and the Kawasaki. He flopped onto the hood, incoherent in rage. I jerked the wheel to the right and the car skewed into the sedan, splitting the party and keeping the Vic between me and Alessandra and the *oborot*.

I jumped out of the car. Ignoring the biker clawing toward me, I leapt for O'Shea. The magic within me was still wounded but O'Shea stood on pavement. Irish magic flowed through natural soil. Just like her brand throttled my magic, O'Shea could not access the touch of Gaia through worked stone.

I threw a punch. O'Shea staggered and lurched for the side of the road and wild ground. I grabbed her arm and swung her back into the Vic. O'Shea hit the door and the side window cracked. I knocked her knee out from under her. She hit the ground and I took the pendulum from O'Shea.

Andrea Alessandra and her *oborot,* now in full were mode, circled the car. I thought better of this. I kicked the fallen mass of the Irish witch and jumped back in my car. I spun the wheel to the left, around the spilled motorcycle. The back wheels thumped over something or someone and I pointed the car west, leaving Wodanaz's crew behind her to lick their wounds.

Chapter 7 – Giulia

The door from the hallway to the In A Murphy Minute practice space opened and most of the band came in.

"Fuck. Why do I have to wake her up?"

"I took the last turn, Ric," Jin-Wei said.

"Yeah," said Angie "And I had to boot out the last groupie. Blondie was pretty pissed about it. At least Giulia should be up there alone."

"Fine," Ric grumbled. He started up the spiral stairs to my loft when I called out to them.

"Hi guys." They had walked right past where I was working on the silk screen press. None of them had looked left when they came in, expecting me to be upstairs. They all jumped.

"You're ... awake?" Angie said.

"Yeah… Why wouldn't I be awake?"

"Um… you're usually-"

"Passed out 'til dinner," Ric said. Angie cuffed her brother on the arm when he came downstairs.

"What have you been up to all day?" Angie asked. "Figured you'd be back in bed after getting the strings."

I looked at the pile I had worked up in the corner with me all around the silk screen set up and wondered why they were asking me that. "T-shirts. I made a new

batch with the upcoming New England tour cities on it."
I held up the shirt I just finished, a ladies tee, white
letters on red. I had started the dates with tonight's
Apponaug show up on the top even though the New
England Tour technically started in Providence next
week.

Ric even got over his pissy attitude to say he
liked what I did. In A Murphy Minute was in happy
spirits while we packed up and took the short drive
over to The Vault.

We got the shirts in Manny's hands and I had
nothing to do while everyone else took care of what
little set up there was. I checked my phone for any texts
from Eris. Nothing yet. I buzzed around the merch table
with Manny, arranging shirts, CDs and stickers. Still no
messages from Eris. I moved all the shirts to the right
side of the table and the CDs to the left. The only
message on my phone was junk email I trashed without
reading. I thought about moving the stickers out of the
center of the table and swapping them with the CDs.
Manny gently shooed me away. My phone was still a
silicone brick of inactivity. I sprung for pizza for Manny
and the band. I placed the order as fast as I could and
hung up the phone just in case another message came
in.

People started drifting into The Vault. The
Providence Hooligans were on stage tuning their
guitars. Wes Hayes tried to wave to me but he did not
register on my radar while I was checking my phone for
texts. The high school kid delivering the pizza was a fan.

The band came over for the food and the kid got one of the fresh shirts signed by the whole crew. I rebooted my phone just to make sure it was still working right. Tish and the Bludbunnies came over to help with the pizza and shoot the shit about the show. She kept flirting with Ric but he was clueless. Jin-Wei had this weekend in the pool for when they would hook up and was trying to be real subtle about nudging them together.

I missed all of it while poking away at my phone.

<<Prov Hooligans r on soon. Waiting for you @ the bar>>

I wormed my way through the growing crowd up to the bar. The Vault filled up faster than usual. Word had spread fast about the last show. I kept my head down and claimed a stool at the bar where I could see the front door. The bartender came over and I hesitated. I did not think I wanted a drink. I told myself that I should not want a drink. Yet. I kept my mind on just how fucking good the stage high was going to be. The crowd was excited and no one was on stage yet. I thought about Eris and her smile. The memory of apple blossoms filled my senses.

But she was not here yet. And the show was about to start.

I checked my phone again.

Still nothing.

I ordered a pint. I drank it so fast the carbonation burned the back of my throat. I kept drinking. My phone still had nothing.

<<Are you still coming?>> Send.

I waited all of thirty seconds for an answer that did not come. I growled at my phone and ordered another pint.

She must be driving, I told myself. She's got to be on her way, I insisted. I spun around in my barstool so I could watch the door better. I nursed my way through the second beer by the time the Providence Hooligans started playing. The crowd whooped and hollered. The Vault's bar hosted a constant churn of people looking for drinks. I was the only one parked on a stool waiting.

By the time The Bludbunnies hit the stage, I had a trio of empty pints on the bartop in front of me. Once The Camorri Trio came on, I started thinking hard about tequilla.

"Stupid technological bastard," I said to my phone. "You're a dick."

I grabbed the offending piece of tech and the most coherent message I could tap out to Eris was simply a single question mark.

The bartender came by again as the Camorri Trio wound down their set and I ordered another drink. He hesitated. I knew that look. He was about to cut me off.

"Come on man," I slurred. "You've all seen me drunk plenty of times."

He started to reach for a glass, but he stopped and looked to someone over my shoulder. It had to be Eris. I spun around in my stool and toppled over into Angie and Jin-Wei.

"You're not Eris."

Angie made a face. Jin-Wei raised his eyebrows. "Who is that?"

"I'm waiting for her. Here. At the bar. For the show. Because."

Angie rolled her eyes. "Groupie," she whispered to Jin-Wei. Whispering in a bar with a punk concert on stage still meant loud.

"She is not a groupie." I stamped my foot like a little kid throwing a tantrum. "We met the other day. She's coming tonight. She told me so. Look." I pointed my phone at Angie, but she just gently pushed it back toward me.

"I'm sure she did, but we have to go get ready for the show." Angie led me through the crowd to the backstage door. Jin-Wei threw some cash on the bar to cover my drinks then followed.

"But I need to be at the bar. I told her," I protested feebly.

"I'm sure she can figure out where you are," Jin-Wei said.

"Whaddya mean?"

Jin-Wei ignored me. Angie said, "You're going to be on stage in five minutes, Giulia. It won't be hard to spot you."

The crowd was riled up after a third wild set. By the time we got to the staging area, Ric was pacing around with an unlit cigarette between his lips. The people backstage were all high fives and cheering, but they were giving Ric a wide berth.

"Where the fuck have you been, Giulia?" he snapped.

I stood straight. Ish. The walls were spinning slowly out of focus. "I was-"

"Fucking hell, you're hammered."

"-waiting for my girlfriend."

Out of the corner of my eye I saw Angie shake her head slowly. Or maybe she was starting to spin with the walls too.

"She's coming," I said. "She told me she would."

"Then where is she?" Ric said. "Where is this mysterious girlfriend who definitely is not a groupie trying to get in your pants just like the last one? Huh? Where is she?"

"I was waiting for her." My voice felt small.

"Bullshit," Ric said. His accent got thick when he was upset. "You were fucking up."

"What?"

"Ricardo, that's harsh," Angie said.

Jin-Wei nodded. "Right or wrong, Giulia did not intend to get stood up at the bar."

Ric threw up his hands. "I'm tired of coddling her," he said like I was not standing right in front of him. He took the cigarette and poked me with it to emphasize his point. "You have a problem."

"Eris isn't coming." Saying it out loud felt like a punch to the gut.

"I don't give a rat's ass about your latest fuck, Giulia. We're going on stage in two minutes and you can barely fucking stand."

Angie and Jin-Wei felt a million miles away. My head was spinning and I was not sure if that was a literal fact or not. "You know about-"

"You're issues? Fuck, Giulia, everyone has issues, but we can stay sober for more than twelve hours."

"Ric... I..."

"You what? You're going to feel bad and then drink some more? You're just going to fuck things up for the rest of us. Do you hear that?" Ric grabbed my arm and pulled me to the edge of the stage wings. I stumbled over my feet and the wobbly floor after him. "Just fucking listen to that, Giulia," he said.

The stage was dark and empty. The house was packed full of people. I had to stop and refocus my head because I did not believe it was really that full. The Vault was one wall to wall mass of people. Rising from the crowd was a chant.

"Muuuuuurphy. Miiiiiinute."

"They're waiting for us, Giulia," Ric said in a low voice. "The house is turning away people at the door. Record labels flew in just to see us play. Isn't this why we play? A full house thrashing their asses off because we made it happen."

"I just can't..."

Ric swore and stormed back to the others. I followed after him. He whirled back on me pointing an accusatory finger at me. "Your inability to handle life like a fucking adult is going to ruin this for the rest of us. Your self destructive streak is going to get you killed. You don't see the excuses we make for you. We're the ones waiting for that phone call from some goddamn morgue or hospital because you passed out on the wrong floor or fucked the wrong person. You're issues-" he used air quotes "-are starting to screw up the people around you."

I felt tears welling up. It was embarrassing. Tough rocker chicks do not cry. Maybe the ones that drink too much do. "I never meant-"

"Just stop. Just fucking stop," Ric said. Angie reached out a hand to get him simmer down. He swatted it away. "No, Angie. Self-pity won't be any better for her than tequila." He turned back to me. "I don't care what you meant to do. Stop screwing up your life. Stop screwing up everyone around you."

His words started something smoldering inside of me. "You don't know what you're talking about."

"You know what? You're right. I don't know what's going on in your head. None of us do. You don't fucking talk to anyone not named Jose Cuervo or Johnny Walker anymore. You've cut us all out."

"It's not that easy."

"No shit? Really? I never noticed you take all your feels and horde them into something toxic. You're a goddamn performer. A singer. A. Fucking. Rock. Star. With a thousand people who want to cheer your name. They don't give a fuck about me no matter how many solos I drop. You're the face of this band and it lives and dies with your voice. They're here for you, Giulia. I've accepted that. Channel all that crap you're feeling inside of you into something awesome. Use it all.

"Pissed that tonight's fuck stood you up? Do something about it. Angry that I've called out your bullshit? Good! You should be. You're better than this. Last night was the best fucking show of our lives and those people out there want more and you're going to let them down! You-"

I snapped. I shoved Ric out of my way and stormed my way onto stage. A thousand voices, raised in excitement, swirled around me. Tears they could not see tracked down my cheeks. Ric was right. Everything he said was right and it felt like a hundred rusty daggers stabbed into my soul. I stopped at center stage and grabbed the mic. The band scrambled to get ready back in the wings.

There was no band on stage with me, no set list, no preparation of any sort. I was alone with my fucked up head, a microphone and a thousand screaming fans, hungry for the music.

I would bare it all to them.

I sang.

> *One day, we will see it eye to*
> *eye.*

I dropped into the first line of "Blue Eyes/Brown Eyes" half a beat slower than we usually played it. I let the crooning of my voice match the tears on my cheeks. Jin-Wei made it to his drum kit and matched my beat, leaning heavy on the bass and avoiding the hihats. Ric's guitar jumped in with a pickslide while he was still in the wings. He sauntered out on stage like everything we did was planned as part of some grand entrance. Angie walked out on stage with her bass hanging by the strap and a beer in hand. The song I started was one of Ric's songs to shine, full of string blazing solos. Angie hung out and finished the beer while her brother melted faces. She threw the bottle off into the stage wings. The crowd ate it up. I counted down with my fingers in the lead up to the chorus. They got the message and the Zanettis timed the jump perfectly.

Angie pounded away at her bass and abandoned her usual laid back stage presence. She whipped her hair around like an old school metal head and bounced around stage left. She locked eyes with me for a moment. I saw Angie's pent up frustration bleeding out on stage. Guilt cracked away a piece of my own walls. I stumbled over a line. Angie nodded to me. I tuned back to the crowd and jumped into the chorus at double speed. I fanned the flames. The rest of Murphy Minute caught up with me and set a blazing tempo through the song.

A human vortex formed on the floor of The Vault. It was a circle pit like I had never seen in the small venue. Like a pocket hurricane, the circle pit was a churning spiral of energy. It was the wildest crowd in the history of The Vault.

We did that, I thought. The four of us set a thousand souls into frantic motion.

A smile broke through the leftover streaks of tears.

I hit the end of the song and launched into "Law of Revenge" without taking a breath. Jin-Wei bridged the gap between the songs and the guitars caught up with me. I kept the tempo and tore through the song. At the end of the song I pointed to Angie and she leapt into "Goddamnit Another Song Title."

The Vault teemed with energy. The crowd did not want us to slow down and we were not about to anyways. Jin-Wei segued into the cover of "Rico Suave" and we hit "Three Chords Tonight," "Rhode Island Uber Alles," and "Sugar Skull" in rapid fire succession. Ric dropped into the opening solo for "Downstream." I motioned to him to stretch it out. There was a glint in his eye I had forgotten all about. He smiled and let his fingers shred through the strings.

I stood at the edge of the stage and laughed while Ric did his thing. I gave myself over to the stage high. It burned off hours of boozing and self pity. The air took on an electric touch that sparkled across my skin. I looked at the crowd before me. Ric whipped them into a frenzy. They reached out to me, fanatics at worship. They needed me.

I closed my eyes.

I jumped.

A dozen hands reached up to catch me. I rode across the wave of people. I tried to sing the words to "Downstream" while held over the heads of the fans, but I could not. I saw my band, the best people left in the world to me, playing their hearts out. We were knee deep in the craziest show of our lives and it was the happiest we had ever been. I was too happy to get any of the words out. I just laughed.

I held out the microphone to a nearby kid. He sang out the first lines of the song. A different woman sang the next. As I crowd surfed across The Vault, the song was sung by whoever knew the next line. The hands below me passed me along the edges of the churning circle pit and back up to the stage. With my feet back on stage, I caught my breath during the closing chords of the song.

That was when I saw her.

It was a one-in-a-thousand chance my eyes picked out Eris in the back of the crowd. My pulse quickened and my blood pounded in my head but there were no cliché spotlights out of nowhere like in a second rate chick flick. My eyes got tunnel vision. The crowd, the stage, my band, everything faded into the background.

Time stopped.

Eris waded through the crowd towards me. The crowd stood motionless. She sauntered into the mosh pit without a single jostle or bump. I stood there and watched her come towards me.

"Hey there, Giulia," her voice sounded like a whisper in my ear from across the room.

I forgot where I was.

I forgot there were a thousand fans watching me.

"Where were you?"

My question echoed through The Vault.

I forgot I stood with a live mic in my hand.

The crowd came to life before me again.

The band kept the music alive, but I could feel their looks on me without turning. This was no song intro they had ever heard before. A moment of panic seized me by the fucking gut. I wanted to run. I just spaced out and ruined our show. Eris still stalked through the people, in motion now, parting the crowd like Moses on a bender. She looked at me and shook her head. Eris did not want me to run. I knew this and something clicked around me. That spark in the air became a charge that crawled up my skin. The extra energy of the room became a turbo charge.

Fuck running.

I pointed to Ric without taking my eyes off Eris. I raised my hand like a conductor. He brought the tempo up in the lead. Jin-Wei dropped a bass drum beat and followed. I waved my hand back and forth to Angie. She stomped an FX pedal and loaded the room with reverb. That had nothing to do with what I hoped for but damn, it sounded good. In A Murphy Minute jammed like we were sitting around the practice space. The crowd sensed something special in the air and ate it up.

Eris stood near the foot of the stage then. My anxiety warred with my stage high. I wanted to burst. I wanted to run around in a circle and dive off the stage. I wanted to grab Eris and run away with her. I wanted to slap myself for thinking that so soon. I wanted to throw up. I wanted a drink.

So, instead, I sang.

Don't you know what you put me through?

Why weren't you here while I was waiting for you?

Eris reached up her hand. Not taking it never occurred to me. I gasped when our hands touched. There was a question in Eris' eyes. My answer was yes, whatever it was. I pulled her up on stage. We stood face to face with the mic down at my side. The stage lights bathed us in a purple glow. I did not know what was next.

"We keep singing," Eris said to me. She reached down and took the hand with the mic. We sang, trading verses.

> *You took my hand so now*
> *Let me show you*
> *Let me teach you*
> *Things that you can't unsee*

Break the fourth wall
Break the fifth wall
Show me what's out there
But only if I'm at your side

> *But will your heart*
> *But will your mind*
> *But will your soul*
> *Hold dear the sights we see*

In the dust of my last days
I know that I need this
Can you set me free?
Can you save me from me?

Oh what sights we have to
show you
If you'll just roll my dice
Take my hand once more
time
Take my hand again and
again

I'll take your hand
Please show me
Please teach me
Things I don't want to unsee

We finished the song and the lights went out. The low colors of The Vault's neon cast a shifting glow across Eris' face. She smiled and I felt something turn over inside of me. I grinned like a fucking idiot back. The crowd was already frothing for an encore.

"Hi," was the most eloquent thing I could manage to say.

"They're all watching us," she said.

I reached behind Eris and pulled her body against mine. My heart slammed in my chest. I stood on my tiptoes. We kissed. Eris wrapped her arms around me and stole my breath away.

The crowd whipped into a frenzy.

I grabbed her hand and we darted off stage into the wings. People surrounded us. High fives, power punches, claps on the shoulder, everyone wanted to congratulate us. I could barely pick out Jin-Wei and Angie over the heads of the crowd. I saw Tish and her band. Marty the stage manager dropped all pretense of keeping order to gush about the set. I saw Jean from the Camorri Trio, one of the Vault's bartenders, a half dozen roadies and a sea full of groupies. The faces became a blur I barely recognized.

Ric cut through the crowd. He bounced on his feet and scooped me up in a bear hug.

"That was amazing!" His words broke off into gleeful laughter.

He let me go and gave Eris the same treatment. She laughed right along with him.

Over the sound and fury of our own little crowd, we heard the chant start up.

"MurphyMinuteMurphyMinuteMurphyMinute-"

The staccato beat of voices calling out for us to play more songs hovered on the edge of control. They chomped at the bit for more. They stood before their alter and needed something to worship. The backstage crowd joined in.

Angie pulled Jin-Wei though the people to get to us.

"We going back out?"

"Fuck yeah we are," Ric shouted.

"What are we playing?" Jin-Wei asked. He looked to me. Both of the Zanettis turned to me.

"Why start planning anything now?" I said. I saw Eris break out in a grin next to me. Ric brimmed with energy.

"I'm going out there," he said. The crowd parted for him to grab his guitar and storm the stage. He plugged in and launched into a solo without waiting to even hit his mark. Angie marched out into the middle of the stage and gave a theatrical bow to roaring approval. Jin-Wei ran out behind her and scooped Angie up into a kiss to the tune of Ric's pick slide. They put on a show for the Vault and eventually got to their own instruments.

The whole world waited for me.

They needed me to walk out on the stage.

I floated on the stage high, one half of a sublime step behind myself. I looked down at Eris' strong hand held in mine.

"Do you want to come with me?"

She smiled. I fluttered. "'Course I do."

"But you don't know the songs."

Eris laughed and it was magic in my ears. "That didn't stop us before."

"Are you sure?"

I felt time slow for me and Eris. The world tuned out. I was in a circle along with Eris and all the sound and need out there drifted away as she looked into my eyes with her golden colored irises.

Eris reached out and touched the side of my head. It felt like a feather was tickled across the back of my mind.

"I'll manage, rock star."

Eris started out on stage. She had to turn around and come back for me since I stood there like a friggin' dummy. Her hands grabbed my arm. Her lips planted a kiss on my cheek. I felt a fire inside of me. I snapped out of my stupor. I felt the floor under my feet again.

We dashed out on stage to a roar heard across half the city.

Chapter 8 – Eris

All the songs had been sung. All the groupies had grouped. All the well wishers had wished well. We played that encore long after Asteria brought her stars out to play and the aurora of dawn tickled the horizon. Now The Vault was closed and only the last stragglers hung around the parking lot to watch the sun creep over the trees.

I perched on the edge of the loading dock and dangled my feet over the edge next to Giulia. My body buzzed with the raw chaos of punk. Giulia leaned into me. Her hair was wild but she hardly looked tired at all. She scooted closer to me. I could not help smiling as I slipped an arm around her waist. With her next to me, all the worries of my role as goddess faded. Only the happiness of me, Eris, remained.

"Giulia, that was amazing," I said. "It's been ages since I've done anything so... oh Olympus above, that was awesome."

"That song! I would have told anyone it was fucking crazy to pull that off. People are going to be talking about it forever." Giulia vibrated against me with joy and adrenaline.

And with the pure chaos magic from the altar of punk, the back of my mind reminded me. Magic bleeds off her, I thought. She stopped time twice already.

I shoved the ill timed thoughts away. There was time to be a goddess later. Right now, I wanted to just be a woman.

"It's the stuff myths and legends are made from," I said. The sparkle in her eyes gave me a flutter.

That voice in the back of my head nagged me again.

You don't have the faintest idea what the hell her deal is, it said.

I screwed my eyes shut like that would make my own thoughts go away.

You slept with her, my thought drilled into me, and then she woke up with magic thanks to your DIY surgery. Get the fuck away from her before you destroy her.

My tattoos itched to call on a bit of chaos and an exit. I realized the sounds outside The Vault were gone. The background hum of the city had vanished. I peeked at the world and darted my eyes around. A smoker across the parking lot had a butt hover in midflick. A car full of tired punks had its door stopped halfway through closing. Traffic out on the road was parked. Time had stopped.

Giulia had stopped time.

A chill rolled over my body.

"Bloody fucking hell," she said.

I cocked my head to the side and tried to play it cool. "Are you ok Giulia?"

"Holy fu-" The swear died on her lips and she about jumped out of her skin. Her heart raced with such a pounding, I felt it next to her. "The fuck is going on?"

She looked around at the world stopped in midstep. "I'm hallucinating. That's got to be it. The world on pause. The magical show. The amazing woman. My dreams are taunting me." Giulia looked into my eyes. I saw a sparkle of my own chaos in hers.

"I know!" she said. "I got drunk waiting for you and passed out backstage. Ric is going to be pissed. But since this is a dream, we should fuck again before he comes and wakes me up."

Giulia grabbed hold of me and kissed. Her tongue tasted of fire and lust. I lost myself to her in the space between heartbeats.

No. Not yet.

"Giulia. Wait."

She pressed herself into me. The fire in me did not agree with the words I just said. I could not have her if she thought this was a dream but, curse Aphrodite's every fiber, I wanted her so bad.

"Giulia. It's all real."

She jerked upright. I felt a chill without her body against mine. She looked around the time frozen world. I saw confusion. I saw fear. I saw someone who wasn't ready for this. A piece of my soul twisted. Why did I have to be a goddess right now? Why couldn't I be Eris for a few moments longer.

Giulia frowned and I hated seeing that on her face. "What the hell are you talking about?"

I placed a hand on hers. Giulia did not flinch but I sensed it was a near thing.

"It's magic. Real, bonafied, magic."

"Bullshit."

"I swear on my soul," I held her hand to my heart. "But it's not my magic."

"But then…"

I just looked at her.

"No fucking way," she said.

I nodded. "Relax your mind," I pointed to my temple. "And relax your soul." I pointed to where her hand laid over my heart.

Giulia looked skeptical, like she was going to accuse me of being a dream again. She closed her eyes and humored me.

The city rushed into motion around us.

The smoker across the lot finished flicking her butt. The car door thumped close. Traffic whirred to life again.

"Holy crap!" Her eyes went wide and she scooted away until her our knees barely touched.

Her voice was small when she spoke. "So this morning when I almost… that was real?"

I did not trust myself to speak so only nodded. My ambrosia should have killed her and it would have been my fault.

"And when I saw you across The Vault, time really stopped? It wasn't my brain going all super cheesey Lifetime movie on me?"

I saw a smile dance around the edges of her lips and my heart felt light.

"Oh it was cheesey, but that doesn't mean it wasn't true," I said.

Giulia scooted closer to me again.

"So you're a wizard?"

"Something like that," I said.

"Wow. That's... that's just fucking amazing. And I can..." Giulia scrunched up her nose. Her magic tugged at my senses and the city slowed to a stop around us. She hopped off the edge of the loading dock and staggered. I jumped down to grab hold of her and keep her upright. Time stuttered back to life around us. Chaos and time slithered on. The sounds of a world in movement rushed back into my ears. Giulia steadied her feet underneath me and waved me off a step.

"Shit, that's a mindfuck," she said.

I nodded and leaned against the building. Off across the parking lot, someone did a double take and stared at us a moment before shaking his head and moving on. I watched Giulia. She paced in a small circle. Nervous excitement or impending mental collapse? I chewed the inside of my lip. I had seen it go either way in the centuries since humanity forgot its magic.

"This... thing that I do, this stoptime. This is legit magic? And you know magic too? Cause you're a wizard. And we're not in some tequila fever dream?" she said.

The words "goddess" and "Olympian" danced at the edge of my voice but I glanced at the eight-ball tattoo on my wrist. Try again later. Shit. I swallowed it for later, but it stung to leave Giulia with the half truth.

Instead I lifted my hand and tapped into the power at the base of my soul. Magical chaos in its purest form coalesced around my hand. I spread my fingers wide. Purple sparks like static leapt across my digits.

Giulia's dark eyes shone in wonder. She reached out and touched the chaos in my hand. A crackle leapt from my skin to hers.

"It's warm," Giulia broke into a smile. "Tickles a bit too."

I drew the energy back into me with a closed fist gesture. The fancy hand motion was not really needed but pop culture made visual cues go over well with magical newbies.

Giulia held out her hands and scrunched up her face again. Stoptime stuttered around us and she jumped. "No sparkles for me?"

"Not all magic is flashy," I shrugged. "Magic manifests in all different flavors depending on the elements and traditions behind it. Chaos magic-" I flicked a sparkle to Giulia. She lit up with a smile and my heart melted a little. "-like we have is unpredictable by its very nature."

I almost said 'my nature.' Keeping secrets was tough because of that nature to begin with. Half said secrets could prove twice as difficult.

She stopped time around us again and looked around with more wonder this time.

"Teach me Eris," she said. "Teach me all about this."

I nodded. "If you'd like, we can go-"

"There you two are!"

I turned and silently cursed the timing of Giulia's bandmates. The bassist ran up and squeezed Giulia into a hug then turned and did the same to me. The guys followed without squeezing anyone but were all smiles. I could see they were riding the stage high. The guitarist bounced on his toes, unable to keep still.

"So you can't keep her a secret, Giulia. Not after that show," he said. "When are you going to introduce us?"

The drummer looked at the watch that did not exist on his wrist. "Hey look! I've got some time right now."

Giulia rolled her eyes but in a good way. She gave me a 'whaddya gonna do' shrug.

"Eris, this is the band. Band, Eris."

I gave her a nudge. The band protested her lackluster approach.

"Ok, ok." Now she hammed it up and channeled the spirit of some dead boxing announcer. "On bass guitar, my best friend since before either of us knew what a guitar was, my sister from another mister, Angie Zannetti. Standing next to her, on the lead six-string, her brother from someone other, the indominable, the irrefutable, Punk Ric Zannetti. Last we have the charmer, the smooth operator, the man with the sticks, Jin-Wei Kwok.

"And over here in this corner, we've got the mystery singer, the mosh pit mistress, Eris."

"Katsopolis. Eris Katsopolis," I blurted out the fake last name and shook hands all around.

"That sounds familiar," Angie said.

Jin-wei saved me from making another lie. "Eh. It's Rhode Island. Everyone knows a guy who knows a guy. Of course it's familiar," he said.

Ric and his sister bombarded us with questions, most of it for Giulia and she seemed happy to rattle off answers for her excited friends.

"Are you ok Jin-Wei?" I asked. "You look like you need to crash. Daylight is starting to happen. I'm feeling it too." That was not a lie. As a being of Chaos, I did not exactly keep regular hours, but after the roller coaster of disaster to excitement during the last couple days, rest beckoned me.

Giulia started to say something witty but Ric let out an epic sized yawn.

"This has been the most hardcore thing we've ever done on stage but-" he yawned again "-it's goddamn late. Or early. Whatever. And we still have to unpack the van. Padre needs it for deliveries today."

"I'll catch up with you guys," I said.

"Don't be a stranger, Eris," Angie said. Ric waved. Jin-Wei held hands with Angie as they left.

Giulia and I started across the parking lot. We slowed our walk to prolong the night.

"Giulia, I-"

"I want to see you again," she blurted out.

We got to my car on the far side of the parking on. It was the same, white Crown Vic with DC plates that I borrowed from Anonna Augusti when I came to America, now with bumper damage and a cracked window. She leaned against the side of it.

"I've never met anyone like you before," she rambled and shuffled her feet. "I mean, jeez, a wizard. Here. In Warwick."

"You really don't know anything about magic? I would be honored if you want to learn."

"No." she put out her hands to stop me. "I mean yes. I mean, that's not what I mean. Learning more about this thing... it is amazing. It's the sort of thing that doesn't seem real even after I touched it with my own two hands. But..."

"But?" I did not like the sound of that.

She shrugged. "It'd be nice to learn magic. But really, I don't want to presume that you..."

"Presume?"

She grabbed my hand in hers. Our fingers twined together with natural ease. "I'd much rather get to know you, Eris."

I closed my eyes and felt the tattoos on my wrists twitch. Primal chaos itched to throw me about and take my decision away from me. No. I pushed back. I wanted this decision to be mine alone but decision making was a zero sum game for me. Creating chaos balanced out the order of decision making and prevented me soul from burning out.

Giulia started to speak but I released chaos out into the world. She sensed something and spun around. Across the lot, a car backed into a post office dropbox. The Honda lurched and the bumper cracked into shards of plastic. Letters waiting for pickup spewed across the pavement. The man driving got out, swearing and kicking at his wheel.

Over near The Vault, one of the stragglers let up a cheer. A guy rocking one of the new Murphy Minute shirts held up a twenty he found on the ground. "Dunkin' Donuts, on me!" He tromped off around the block with his troop.

Chaos managed, I tugged at her hand. She tuned back to me. She smiled. I melted a little bit.

"Pick me up tomorrow." I took out a pen from somewhere and scrawled something the back of her hand. It said "Extended Stay Suites #307" with my phone number underneath. It was not far from here.

Chapter 9 – Giulia

My stomach flopped about like I was sixteen again. Eris waved to me as she drove off. Since I was so busy grinning like an idiot in the middle of the parking lot, I almost got clipped by a black Lincoln that left the lot after her. I flipped it off, but it was a half-hearted middle finger. I felt too damn awesome to care. My step had a bounce to it on the short walk from The Vault to my place. The cafe van was backed up to the loading dock. I pitched in moving the gear out so the Zanettis could make a pastry run for the café with it later on. The long day started to linger in the back of my head and I could tell the others were feeling it worse than me.

It was not our first rodeo though and we had gone through this routine quite hungover before. In A Murphy Minute was quick and efficient and in a short order the pile of gear moved from van to practice space.

"Lunch later?" Angie asked me around a yawn.

Her yawn was contagious. "Yeah. Diner?"

"You're making me tired you two," Ric said, also yawning. "I'm working later so let's go."

I waved to the Zanettis and they were gone. Jin-Wei puttered around with the accumulated pile of his drum kit. I gave him a halfassed wave goodbye. The giggly surge of energy I got from being around Eris abandoned me. Now between the long day, the show, and all the jumping around in stoptime, I felt I was on the wrong side of a kangaroo fight. My Docs clomped up the wrought iron spiral stairs towards my loft.

"Giulia, can we talk?"

I turned around and Jin-Wei stood at the bottom of the stairs, shifting from foot to foot. My bed was calling out to me so a sigh escaped. I regretted it and hoped Jin-Wei did not hear it. I turned around and sat on the stairs a few feet off the floor.

"Sure sure. I dunno how much I got left in me though."

He stood there looking up at me. Some thought tried to wiggle its way out of his head but he could not give it words.

"Are you ok?"

"Yeah," he said after a moment. "Yeah there's just something..."

"Oh crap. Look, it's been a long day, Jin-Wei. My bed is not far away and I'd really like to be in it right now. Can we do life changing confessions later?"

"Oh no. No. Please don't misunderstand." Jin-Wei paced around in a little circle at the base of the stairs. What the fuck was he doing? He was the calm one.

I sighed again and propped my head against the stair railing. "What's with the song and dance then?"

"I'm worried for you."

A hysterical laugh snuck out before I could stop it. "This is a first. Since when do Giulia Talks happen to me sober?"

"I'm serious Giulia."

I shook my head. "Angie is wearing off on you."

"What do you know about Eris?" he blurted out.

"Really? Are we really going here?"

"Humor me."

I threw my hands up in the air. "She didn't try to stab me with a beer bottle in my kitchen like the last girl I fucked."

Jin-Wei winced. I was pushing his buttons. He was all about steady monogamy so sometimes talking so bluntly about the groupies I took home still threw him off.

"What do you have in common? Anything... special? Or unique?" he asked.

"What are you dancing around? I'm fucking tired, just spit it out."

Jin-Wei just looked at me, indecision scrawled across his face. I crossed my arms to wait him out. Exhaustion grabbed hold of my senses though.

The drummer won the stare down.

"Look, we're new," I said. "We're just barely a thing. You know how it goes, wild fucked up brain chemistry. You saw what we did on stage. You were there. You were part of that glorious set. If that doesn't merit a proper date, I don't know what does."

"That's all you know about her?" he drew out his question.

I counted off on my fingers. "Likes punk rock. Likes me. Incredibly hot. Gave me her number. And... other stuff." I let him think whatever he wanted on that one. I could not tell Jin-Wei about magic.

"Can you be careful with this one, Giulia?" He held something back again.

"Eris isn't some fling," I realized I meant it when the words crossed my lips.

My friend was concerned and it was bothering me. My fingers twitched for a flask I was not carrying.

"Just... be careful. Make sure she's all you want before you make any commitments. We worry."

I got up and stumbled into a tired, friendly hug. "You're sweet when you worry. I'll be fine."

"I'll hold you to it," he said.

"Go home. You look like you need sleep as bad as me."

I plodded upstairs and barely kicked off my boots before I hit the mattress hard.

My phone chirped a sound that was too damn happy for me at this time of day. I groaned and checked my message to make the sound go away.

<<Are you almost here?>>

"The fuck?" I said aloud. Then I noticed it was almost noon and it had been six hours. I was just about late to lunch with Angie.

<<Almost>> I texted back.

Of course I was not anywhere near the EG Diner. I bolted out of bed and got ready in record time. I left my front door all of a minute later wearing the first mismatched clean thing I found. I grabbed my bike and pedaled through Apponaug heading south. Midweek lunchtime traffic was light but a mile down Post Road I realized I was overly optimistic on my plan to bike before breakfast. Downtown East Greenwich and the EG Diner were at the far limit of a comfortable ride for me but it was not a quick ride.

I should probably double back and get the car, I thought. I peeked over my shoulder back the way I came. The road was momentarily empty. No one could notice me.

"Let's try something else," I said to the road. I slammed into stoptime and leaned into the pedals. I rounded the bend and threaded through the motionless traffic. Low over the handlebars, I sped downhill through red lights past the waterfront condos. The buzz of my tires on the pavement hit my ears as a dull whuff in stoptime. I chugged up the sleight uphill into downtown East Greenwich.

"Holy shit, it wasn't a dream."

East Greenwich, pronounced Eats Gren'ich if you were local, had one of those downtowns that screamed "New England" to the rest of the world. Places like this made heaps of money every summer just because they looked like ye olde postcards. The town knew it and enshrined the look in law with the threat of kneecappings from the old ladies of the Historical Society. The broad sidewalks were adorned with old timey lamp posts. The storefronts sat in buildings older than most of the country. The only building the historical society biddies would not touch with a ten foot pole was the dirty stainless steel exterior, circa 1952, was the EG Diner.

My pedals still huffed through the motionless traffic a block and a half away from the diner when I started to feel light headed. My vision went fuzzy, so I grabbed hold hard of the threads of my magic. I cracked a smile thinking of it as magic for the first time and not just some weird ass fever dream. The grip on my magic slipped. The world jolted into motion. The front bumper of a Jag lurched into my leg. The bike went out from under me.

I lay motionless with my eyes screwed shut. I waited for the thump of Giulia Street Pizza.

It never came.

I peeked my eyes open from the hood of the black Jaguar. I sprawled out on the car worth more than I would make in two years. Some wide eyed yuppie was scared right out of his popped collar. In my panic, I grabbed hold of stoptime again before he killed me. Speed limits were for suckers and tourists in Rhode Island so even in the tiny downtown I did not stand half a chance versus two tons of money. My pulse echoed in my head. My hands and feet felt like they were floating away from my body.

Stoptime was going to kill me.

I rolled off the hood of the Jag. 'Roll' was generous. I flopped off it and barely kept my feet under me. I dragged my body and my bike off the street and into the nearest alley way. Time flashed into motion in a spastic staccato beat as I rounded the corner. Behind the building and out of sight I relaxed my magic. The squeal of rubber on pavement echoed through the downtown. I waited for the crunch of a fender bender. If there was an accident, someone would come looking for the girl on the bike.

No accident happened. The douche in the Jag would shake his head, swear about dumbass bikers and drive off. I raised a middle finger in his general direction. Asshole would have only cared about running me over inasmuch as it made him late for where he was going.

I hoped I scratched his Jag.

I let my body sag against the brick wall I took refuge behind. I shook my hands and wiggled my toes to get the blood flowing again. My leg would be black and blue but I was not out of commission.

My phone chirped again. It was Angie. I skipped reading the text. Another 'Where are you' message. I was a block away so I wheeled my wounded bike onward keeping out of sight of the street as best I could. When I saw Angie's tiny pick up, I threw my bike in the bed and went into the diner.

The smells of a sixty year greasy spoon enveloped me like a warm embrace. Angie looked up from her phone and smiled. I went to the table and she gave me a hug. I must have winced.

"You ok? You look like you ran all the way here," she said.

"Took a spill on my bike," I said as we sat. "Hit a patch of sand. I'm ahite." I waved off her concern with the fib. Nothing about my story of being hit by the Jag would be a useful addition to our day.

She never looked happy when I rode about all the Rhode Island traffic, but she dropped it and slid me a coffee.

"You're too good to me," I said. I dumped six sugars into my diner mug of the blackest coffee this side of Turkey. The taste was not going to be pleasant, but the sugar rush and the caffeine would keep me upright until the food showed up. I ordered the biggest pile of the greasiest fried potatoes and a plate full of fried eggs with a heap of turkey bacon. Angie ordered a sandwich what since it was actually lunchtime.

She shook her head smiling. "I always wonder where you put all that food.

"I guess magic burns a lot of calories," is what I wanted to say. "Hollow leg," is what I said.

We shot the shit about the show and compared notes on who sent us congrats. Angie told me that Manny committed to running the merch table for at least five of the shows on the tour. Jin-Wei had a cousin out of New York who'd help out over that way. Our food showed up with the lazy speed of old time diners. Angie took a bite of my bacon to make sure it was turkey and nodded to me. It had been a long time since I needed to avoid pork but some things did not change.

I dove into my lunchtime breakfast fork first. Angie did a lot of talking. In A Murphy Minute was about to start our biggest yearly New England tour ever and there was a lot more logistics than our usual one-and-done shows. This year we were expanding out of New England and into Ithaca, Albany and Manhattan. I gave her my two cents around my potatoes and eggs. I asked questions about driving times and hotels. Angie was happy to answer all of them. We veered off into opening band territory. Jin-Wei got confirmation that The Nightward and Magica Riot were going to open in our NYC show. The Bel Dammes were driving in for a Massachusetts show. I thought we should try to get the Providence Hooligans along for a show or two, even if their drummer was hopelessly smitten with me.

Our meal wound down. Angie kept an eye on her watch. She needed to log some hours at the café in the next few days before we were gone on tour. Our waitress came by again. She topped off our coffee. Angie was chatting with her about something. Over her shoulder, I saw another table get up and leave. A bunch of rich kids slumming it down here with us regular folk.

"Gonna leave a tip?" one of them said.

"She should get a better job," I heard as they passed by.

Irritation welled up inside of me. Stiff crappy service, sure, but she filled their fucking coffee a dozen times. The waitress flew around like a god damn ninja in the busy diner.

Stoptime came easy. Time was putty in my hands.

So was the guy's wallet.

He had a wad of crisp bills in a snakeskin billfold. I dropped a twenty on the table the Newport rich kids just left. I put another under my plate. Angie would not see it, but our waitress would get it anyways. I thought about yoinking the dude's credit cards, but then trouble might come down on the diner. The paper money was good enough. I shoved the rest of it in my pocket and the billfold back in his. I let time start back up again and they left.

Fuck those guys, I was the regular karma police.

Karma police. I liked that phrase. I found a pen in my pocket and scratching out some words on a napkin. I had half a song written by the time Angie finished chatting. I looked up and she had a sideways grin.

"What?"

"It's been a long time."

"Um… huh?"

"Since we did this," she said.

"Ate lunch? I do it a lot."

"No. Were normal. Talking shop. You're writing songs, randomly on napkins. I haven't seen you do that in ages."

We settled our bill. I used the rich kid's cash and tipped well. Angie slung her bag over her shoulder and we headed out. I was quiet because I realized Angie was right. We used to do this all the time going back to when we were kids. When had we done this in the last few months?

Out on the sidewalk, we walked towards Angie's truck. I hauled my bike out of the back. After fueling up on enough carbs to drown a fish, I barely felt my Jag wounds or the drain from pedaling here in stoptime. Angie leaned against the truck bed and watched me fuss with pedals, checking for battle scars from the run in with the Jag.

"What?" I said.

"What do you mean what?" Angie said.

"This whole 'I just smugly saw a friggin' endangered bird' look."

"It's just nice to see you acting like you again," she shrugged it off and turned away. "I really did think we'd lose you. I figured I'd be the one to find you dead. Pass out and never wake up or take home the wrong groupie. I just hoped I'd find you in one piece and not eight pieces of you thrown in a ditch or dredged up out of the Bay. I just..."

Angie turned and scooped me up in a big hug.

"I'm glad you can finally start to heal," she said. "I missed my best friend."

She let me go and wiped at the corner of her eye. I pretended not to notice. She pretended not to notice me not noticing.

"I'm late for my shift at the store, I gotta go."

"We'll do this again," I said.

Half an hour later, I stood among the grey headstones of Apponaug Cemetery. It was a swath of somber monoliths punctuated by the occasional bundle of flowers or tiny American flags. And that one Portuguese flag.

I shrunk into my hoodie and tried not to look around. I hated the place. I hated that my brother never came here. I hated that I could not stay away.

I felt the longing in the back of my throat. I reached for my back pocket, but there was no flask there this time.

I sighed and sat down on the grass in front of the plain headstone. I reached out a finger and traced their names in the granite. Anthony and Chiara Cesari. I chose the headstone myself. Marco fled the east coast for Portland after they died, leaving it all in my lap. I dealt with all the minutiae of death.

I tell myself Mum and Dad would have liked the granite monument.

My thoughts were gnawing away at my psyche again. I clenched a fist and shoved it in my pocket to keep it from twitching. The thought of chasing the bottom of a bottle down to oblivion was a fantastic thought. I shook my head from side to side hoping the thought would fall out of my head. I had to be strong.

Why?

"Mum, Dad, I met a girl," I said to myself just as much as the memory of my parents. "We're new. Real new. But she's pretty great. We have some amazing things in common. I feel great when I'm around her. She got in my head the moment I saw her and she won't leave. I don't think I want her out of my head. That's how it's supposed to work, right?"

I leaned forward until my forehead rested on the polished stone.

"We sang together. I think you'd like her."

I kissed the headstone. "I'll tell Marco I'm still the favorite. Angie says hi."

I stood and brushed the grass off my jeans. I left seven flowers on the grave. A red, white, and green bundle for Italy, our ancestral land. Red, white and blue for our adopted land. The yellow one was from Angie. Because yellow.

The cemetery was not exactly a happening place after lunch on a Thursday. I focused on nothing much beyond the distant drone of the city that never really went away, even in a quiet place like this.

"Are you Giulia Cesari?"

Lost in thought, I never noticed the large guy in the ill fitting suit skulking around the headstones. He was middle aged and not very good at skulking. If it was not for the crappy suit, I would have pegged him as some bouncer that recognized me from a show.

"What of it?"

"My boss would like a word with you," the man rumbled with a Russian accent. Goodie. This asshole was some stock character out of a bad movie. I narrowed my eyes at him. The Russian was unphased what since he was a foot taller than me. Was this some jacked up PI hired by someone I told off, or some run of the mill anti-punk fascist?

I decided I did not like this man. Fuck him.

"Why should I give a shit?" I asked him.

"Because we have some things in common, Miss Cesari."

I turned around and saw the voice came from a tall black woman looking sharp and professional in the cemetery. Her hair was pulled back tight against her head and she looked like she was barely holding back annoyance with me. She wore a vaguely Navy-esque pea coat over properly tailored trousers. She stood there looking uncomfortable in her own clothes. Or maybe she hated doing business in the headstones. Oddly enough, she wore heavy combat boots. I raised an eyebrow at that. She did not look like the hired goon type.

"What the hell is with suits in the graveyard today?"

She ignored me and handed me a business card. I took it by reflex but did not read it.

"Certain... unique talents in common." The woman held out a hand palm up. I felt a buzz in the air like when I stood next to Eris when she used magic, but this was a higher pitched. It made the fillings in my teeth rattle. I smelled an ocean breeze even though I was three miles away from Narragansett Bay.

A bubble of water swirled into being above her hand. She saw my eyes widen and I stepped back. She flicked the water away. It splashed across a headstone.

"Who are you and what do you want with me?" I said.

She looked at the card I did not read and frowned. "My name is Andrea Alessandra. My employer recruits people like us with 'special' talents."

I side eyed Andrea Alessandra's goon. "What about Captain Bad Suit?"

Over a Russian themed grumble Andrea said, "Dimitri's is a shapeshifter."

Part of me wanted to call BS on that. Part of me wanted to see it happen. Yet another part of me wanted to just give them the finger and go home.

I hesitated. "So you guys are the special kids in class. Big whoop. What does that have to do with me?"

"We want to offer you a job," Andrea said simply. "One where the unique things you can bring to the table will be appreciated."

I turned my back on her. "I don't need a job."

"You'll be turning down a lot of money."

"I don't need it." I sidestepped around Dimitri.

Andrea was persistent. She followed along behind me through the graves. "My organization would appreciate it if you entertained the possibility. You have a talent that comes along once a generation."

"You don't know jack about me. Do I look like the kind of girl who is big on organization?" I rolled my eyes even though she could not see me. "The punk rock didn't clue you in?"

"People like us, we live at the fringes of society."

I stopped and looked back at her.

"We live in hiding," she said. "Our abilities, the things that make us what we are, that make us who we are, hidden from the world. Why? Because we're different, eh? Do you think any of us could walk down the street as we really are? Even that parlor trick I showed you wouldn't fly in the middle of downtown. Do you think Dimitri here could shift in the middle of a shopping mall? What about you and your chaos abilities?"

This woman knew... something about me. More than I did a couple days ago. It sent a chill through my bones.

"We're going to make the world a better place for people like us," she said.

I looked at the card. It read Andrea Alessandra, Shipbreaker, followed by a phone number.

With the card in hand, I made a vague gesture of dismissal direction of Andrea and her Russian goon. I started to walk away again. They followed.

"You really should meet the organization head before making any decisions," Andrea said. I could hear the growing annoyance in her words.

I gave them a vague 'fuck off' gesture. It was pretty half hearted as far as dismissals went. I did not have the energy for these two, not in front of my parents' grave. When I heard them follow after me I slipped into stoptime. They wanted magic, I'd oblige.

The world lurched to a halt around me. With silent footfalls in the grass, I turned back to look at them. The Russian looked annoyed but had that professional look I saw on bouncers across dozens of grimy little clubs. He was all potential, waiting for orders from his betters before throwing down. The woman was locked in mid-scowl. She was annoyed with my refusal. She cared about whatever this was.

I still did not.

I walked off and left them motionless in the graves. I left my P.O.S. Benz at the entrance to the cemetery. Moving my car around in stoptime seemed like it would be a lot more effort than I wanted to put into ditching them. As an added bonus, I wanted them to know I was ditching them. I felt bold about my magic. I dropped my stranglehold on time next to my car and gave them a cheeky wave from a thousand feet away.

The Russian immediately began to pursue. The woman stood there. I could read her annoyance from that far away.

"We can find you again Giulia Cesari," she yelled across the graves. "We don't take no lightly."

I shook my head. They would not even get the satisfaction of a middle finger in response. Fuck those guys. I got in my car and left them there. When the twenty five year old diesel chugged away, I saw Dimitri in my mirror. He made up the ground between us faster than I would have expected for such a lumbering dude. Fucking Usain Bolt fast. Whatever. I leaned on the gas pedal. The Benz coughed up some diesel smoke in his general direction and I was gone.

Chapter 10 – Eris

She is here.

I felt the twinge in the back of my mind before I heard the car pull up outside. Had I thought that Hermes lied to me, had I doubted Giulia was a Paladin of Chaos before, this moment would have confirmed it. The hummingbird flutter in the back of my thoughts told me all I needed to know. A creature of Chaos walked up to my door. The feeling slid like oil down my spine, not unpleasant, but strange. It had been a thousand years since a Paladin of Chaos walked the mortal realms.

I created that last one on purpose.

I checked myself in the mirror again. The last Paladin had not made me worry so about my appearance. I tugged my short sleeves down over the bandage and stitches Dee gave me. They were barely covered. I made a face and thought about changing the look. The thought was fleeting and I kept my natural form, minus the toga, though the idea of greeting Giulia in a toga made me smile. I banished the idea before Primal Chaos could latch on to it and demand it.

Giulia should have been at the door by now. No knock came.

I stood in the Extended Stay Suite and watched the door from across the room. Each suite had its own

139

entrance to the outside. Giulia would be coming straight from her car. My eye wandered while I waited. I frowned. The suite was well furnished for a long term hotel. The seating comfortable, the bed large, kitchenette clean and the towels fresh. It was much more pleasant that some of the hovels that Chaos had nudged me towards over the years. Clutter crept into this place however.

When had that bothered me before?

Giulia's knock still had not come.

I crept up to the door and spied through the peephole.

"Get a hold of yourself," Giulia said. Her voice was muffled by the door. She fidgeted three paces from the door. She took a step toward me, hand raised to knock on my door and grace me with her presence, then stopped. Giulia fussed with her shirt.

From my side of the door, I smiled. Giulia was resplendent in a burgundy button down and dark wash jeans. I spotted the same Doc Martens from the stage.

Giulia smoothed out a phantom wrinkle.

She stopped and forced her hands to the side. A small litany of nervous curse words floated to my ears. I caught my laugh before it could escape my lips and give away my spying.

A stray lock of hair fell across Giulia's brow. I longed to reach out for it, if only the door had not stood between us. She tried to tuck it behind her ear, but it was too short to hold.

"Fuck." Giulia fussed with her hair.

I eased the door open and stood with a lean in the doorway.

"Well that is certainly an odd way to greet a lady," I said.

Giulia stopped in her tracks like the victim of a gorgon's glare. A sly smile spread across my face.

She forgot about fixing her hair. "I thought it was pretty good."

I let the laugh escape my lips this time. "Smooth, Giulia. Very smooth."

Her stance relaxed. "I sure thought so."

I stepped out and pulled shut the door behind me, still uncommonly disconcerted by the clutter in the hotel suite. I took her hand in mine and twined our fingers together. I kept my left side and Dee's stitches away from Giulia. We walked down the path back to the parking lot and the row of cars standing as sentinels. My skin prickled with warm little sparks when our magic touched.

"So, where are we going?" I asked.

"It's a surprise."

I gave her hand a squeeze. "That is my favorite. How did you know?"

"Lucky guess." Giulia gave me a coy smile of her own. She stopped in front of a car and opened the passenger door for me.

I gave her vehicle a once over and hesitated.

Giulia caught it.

Giulia's Mercedes was an old beater showing stains of black diesel smoke around the rear end. I could not be sure if the tan color was intentional, paint that aged like ivory, or a lack of cleanliness. The leather inside was sunbaked and cracked, though clean. University of Rhode Island stickers cluttered the cracked back window. The car appeared to be on the wrong end of a hailstorm at one point in its life.

"I can drive if you would prefer." My borrowed Crown Vic was nearby. The recent damage from Salem did not look that bad. The Vic came from hearty government surplus stock. With the toe of my boot, I prodded the Benz fender nearest to me. It made a crinkle sound.

"Uh, careful. That corner is really just duct tape and spray paint."

I raised an eyebrow at Giulia.

"Hey, Germany's finest *shisse* may be falling apart but you're a wizard of chaos. This may or may not get us anywhere. It's Shroedinger's car. That's right up your alley."

I hesitated again. This was not a good way to start off our night. "There's Chaos and there's mechanically unsound."

"But-"

I placed a hand on her arm to stop her. Our magic crackled like static.

"Chaos is unpredictable, Giulia. It is the very essence of unpredictable. That can make it dangerous with all the speed of the modern world."

The same uncertainty and turmoil I felt in me, I saw flash in Giulia's eyes. With a flourish, she took my hand in both of hers. Giulia's magic wrapped around us and the world slowed to a stop. Sound died away. Giulia's whisper echoed around me.

"Eris. On my honor and my vow, I swear by the very moments of time we stand between… I will keep you safe tonight."

I stood straighter in surprise. A vow given to a goddess was no trifling matter. The ambrosia now within her veins would burn from the inside out rather than forgo a vow given to an immortal, regardless that Giulia thought I was merely a sorcerer and not a goddess. It became a formal matter.

My voice took on the echo of Olympus. "On the honor of the darkness of Nyx, do you offer your vow freely and without coercion?"

She looked into my eyes. "Yes."

I nodded. It was a curt motion. "Very well, Giulia Cesari. I will be safe in your hands." I stamped on the ground three times and the air hummed around us like the last echo of a bass drum.

I slid into the passenger seat of the Mercedes. Time huffed into motion again when our hands broke apart. The car's old leather was a soft comfort around me.

Giulia stood there with an odd look on her face. She did not know all the levels of what just happened. I smiled and winked. New was cute.

She hustled around the car and scrambled into the driver's seat. I heard the quick plea to the "Gods of Internal Combustion" before she turned the key. Giulia's car started on the first turn. By the look on her face, I suspected that was not a common occurrence. The Benz coughed out a wad of black diesel smoke. Giulia flashed me a smile. It was infectious.

Giulia's Mercedes rumbled like a champ through the main drag of Warwick and hit I-95 pointed towards South County. The car lumbered across a few lanes of the highway, weaving in and out of evening traffic exiting Providence for the day. She made it to the fast lane with minimal swearing.

"I am just going to close my eyes." I settled down deeper in the seat and let the engine rumble become a relaxing rhythm.

"I only gave one person the finger though."

"And called that old lady in the Fiat a bag of dicks," I said.

"Well, who obeys speed limits in Rhode Island?" Giulia said. "Fifty five in a fifty five zone will get us killed. I gotta keep us safe, right?"

"No worries, Giulia." I peeked out of the corner of my eye and spied a smile on her face. "You vowed to keep me safe. I am not worried about traffic or obscenities," I said. "I want the surprise of where you are taking me to be total."

"Good. Because we just passed a Masshole."

I could picture the gestures that went with it.

I heard Giulia fuss with the cable I spied sticking out of a hole in the dashboard where a stereo should have been. She wired an USB cable direct into the car's speakers and the result was tinny punk music spilling out of the back speakers. The Vandals came on random selection. I was partial to that band since I had known actual Vandals when I was young before the Romans got pissy and turned their tribe into a word for miscreant.

We made small talk about punk music and shows during the drive. I kept my tales to concerts on the other side of the world. Stockholm, Tokyo, and the ultra underground scene in Burma. I did not want to slip up and tell her about concerts she would know were before she was born. Giulia still thought I was a wizard. I needed to come clean about that. I felt a stab of guilt about deceiving her, regardless of what decision Chaos fed me. For now, I would have to let Giulia think I was well-traveled for age twenty-nine, not five thousand.

While we talked, Giulia took a long, looping exit ramp off the highway. I swayed with the turns as Giulia drove the Benz through... a city? A town? It was hard to tell with old New England streets. Cow paths upcycled to streets meant a lot of stop and go and zero logic to the traffic flow.

Eventually the car stopped and Giulia shut it off instead of inching up to a red light.

"Have we arrived?" I asked, still not peeking.

"The traffic gods have smiled on us today, Eris. We even scored a good parking spot."

"I will make sure to thank them when I see them next. Shall I open my eyes?"

Giulia got out of the car. I tracked the sound of her footsteps around the Benz. She opened the door and took my hand to help me out like I was royalty. I kept my eyes closed but could not help the smile. It had been a long time since anyone treated me like this.

"You said you wanted the full effect," Giulia said.

"Charmer."

She positioned me just so. Her hands lingered on my shoulders. Her touch was reluctant to leave.

"Open your eyes."

The night time lights of the Newport wharves spread out in front of me like diamonds cast upon the water. The yachts of the well-to-do bobbed in the harbor around us. Newport was as old as a city could be in America and old money danced along with the tourist trade. It was a quiet city down on the cusp of the Atlantic. A jazz band played in the distance.

"There's some nice restaurants. And Newport Grand Casino isn't far if you want to play cards. Or maybe a walk along the wharves. It's nice out. The weather, I mean. If you don't-"

I slid an arm around her in a side hug.

"I love it. This is a wonderful surprise. It is like you already know the best way to a girl's heart," I said. "Let's go."

I felt Giulia release the pent up nervousness she held in her muscles. She took her hand in mine and we walked from the car in the direction of music and food. I watched my date, my unknowing paladin, as we walked. The city lights made her skin glow. The ocean breeze set a lock of hair free and it tumbled along the curve of her jaw.

She caught me looking.

I wanted to kiss her.

"What restaurant do you want to go to? There's obviously seafood, but also Chinese, sushi, and a great barbeque place a couple-"

"Shh. We will let Random Chance point us in the right direction." We stopped on the corner of the street. We were far from peak tourist season, but a few New Yorkers still mixed in with the local foot traffic.

"Do you feel that, Giulia?"

She was quiet for a long moment.

"Come on, let yourself relax," I said. "I can take my hand back if it is distracting you."

"Mind reader," she said. Giulia squeezed my hand and left it right where it was. I liked that. Our magic buzzed in feedback.

"Just obvious. Relax."

A steady stream of people flowed around us while we stood there hand in hand.

"What am I feeling?" she asked.

"You have magic now. Reach out for it."

The world slowed to a stop. The pedestrians became a score of statues. The slow moving traffic in the street became immovable hulks of metal.

She opened her eyes, halfway surprised that that she pulled us into stoptime.

"Close," I said. "But not exactly what I meant."

Giulia frowned. "Am I doing it wrong?"

"Olympus above, no." I took her hand and we walked between the silent people. "This ability you have is extremely unique and very powerful."

"So that's good?"

"Quite. But it is like... standing in the front row of a concert," I said. "The music is so loud, it drowns out the voice next to you."

I watched her bite the inside of her lip while she thought this over.

"So, there are more subtleties to this magic thing than just stoptime, I just need to concentrate."

"Exactly." We stopped and I took both her hands in mine. I held my wrists up so she could see my tattoos, the polyhedron dice on my left and the Magic 8-Ball on the right.

"Let go of your hold on time," I said. The world came to life around us.

"What if someone saw us?"

I shook my head. "People see what they expect to see. Unless we appear directly in front of them, it is unlikely anyone will notice a couple on a date." I squeezed her hands in mine. "Now pay attention. The whims of Chaos will pick a direction for us."

She started to ask a question, but I shook my head. I pulled ambient chaos energy from the city around us. Chaos is an omnipresent force of the universe. Tapping into it just requires the wherewithal with find it and draw it in. The damaged hex on my left arm still hampered my magic, but it no longer felt like a noose.

I focused the energy to the 8-ball tattoo. The blue triangle in the answer window spun steady on my skin.

"I feel it," Giulia whispered. She looked down at my wrist and my spinning tattoo.

"Go ahead," I said after a moment. "Ask it."

"Um. Where should we eat?"

I felt the spark that meant primal chaos made a choice. Giulia jumped too. The Magic 8-Ball tattoo spun down to a stop.

TURN SOUTH

We turned in that direction. It was farther down the wharf, closer to the Atlantic.

"I don't see any place to eat that way," Giulia said.

The wharf was a pleasant pedestrian way that led to a host of yachts and nautical shops closed up for the night. It was old money nice, but without much going on.

I looped my arm with hers and marched us jauntily down the way.

"We asked and chaos provides."

"But, all the nice restaurants are back that way..."

I shrugged. "This is how it works, Jules."

I could sense her reluctance as she dragged her feet. I leaned in close "Trust me."

We walked to the end of the wharf. There was nothing further south except for a couple of yachts bobbing on the tide.

"Well, I guess we could be pirates," Giulia said.

"Yar. Careful what you say. Greeks have a thing for boats."

We laughed as we rounded the corner to the western side of the wharf. I spied a cluster of people around a food cart.

"There. Our dinner awaits."

"A taco stand? Really, Eris?"

"Food trucks are the wave of the future. The trendy new thing. They are not just for sad hot dogs anymore."

"It's a cart, not a truck."

"Semantics. Let's go."

Giulia was reluctant as we queued up behind a bearded and beflanneled hipster.

"Relax Giulia," I said after I ordered for us. I asked for their specialty without looking at the menu. "I do not need a table and chairs to be impressed. You are the important part of the evening, not our seating arrangements."

We sauntered back to the quiet side of the wharf with a tray full of tiny street tacos. They were piping hot and jam packed full of cilantro.

Under the warm glow of a wrought iron street light, we sat together on a bench and watched the lights of Newport and the moon rise over the water.

I leaned into Giulia and stole a kiss. "See? What more could you want? A perfect evening."

Chapter 11 – Giulia

Side by side, we enjoyed our oceanside street tacos. An ocean breeze carried a cool saltiness though the air. We watched people enjoy the sights and sounds of the chintzy tourist shops and old architecture.

"Beautiful," I said.

"What is?"

"All of this. The night. The food," I said. "And I've never been on a date with someone so beautiful before."

The butterflies flip flopped in my stomach once the words left my mouth.

Eris took my hand and kissed it. "Flattery is not needed, but will get you everywhere."

I blushed.

I held her hand in my lap and traced along the edge of her tattoo with a finger. The eight ball ink felt warmer than her bare skin.

"So how do they work?"

Eris sighed and I felt bad immediately.

"That's ok if you don't want to talk about it," I put out there as fast as my mouth could form the words.

She waved me off. "No, it is ok. You should know. It would not be fair to you otherwise."

Eris stared off at the boats and I let her have a moment.

"It took a long time for me to put into words," she said eventually. "I am… older than I seem because of my nature. For years, it never even occurred to me to try. My chaos is me and I am my chaos. Not even the most philosophical of us Greeks ever tried to put our existence into words like that. My kind are not known for being introspective."

I reached out and squeezed her hand. I brought her out of that faraway look and she smiled at me.

"My magic is an addiction, Jules."

"But if it's always been a part of you…"

Eris gave me a sad shrug. "It works just the same. Every random occurrence, every scrap of chaos I cause, or I am a part of, each decision that is taken out of my hands, they will give me a fix. They will keep me going a little bit longer. I can build it up, make decisions to weigh against the chaos inside me. The small decisions are easier since the scales need to always be tipped towards the random."

"What happens if you don't get your fix?" I asked. I did not think I would like the answer and I did not really think Eris liked to talk about it either. We both needed it out there though.

"My body starts to breakdown," she said in a whisper. Eris took a deep breath. My new magical sense felt something waver in the air. Did she just make a big decision? She seemed sad.

"My cells start to breakdown…" Eris continued. "There is no pain like having your body rebel against itself."

At that moment, Eris did not look like an all powerful sorceress. She looked like someone lost and ashamed of things she had no control over. I wanted to kiss her and tell her what she was did not matter to me, just who she was.

My thoughts headed off down a thought train after that, tipped off by what Eris told me before. I stared at the empty wrappers of our street tacos. Eris gave me the space to think.

"So that's why you did this to me?" I asked. "Am I just some magical fix for you?"

"Giulia, no." She took my hands in hers and looked into my eyes. "I swear by everything Olympus ever stood for that is not the case. It was chance our paths crossed the first time. But it was desire that kept me coming back."

"It's ok," I said. "I swear it is. I guess I self-destructed long before I got any magic. I'm getting my soul back together now." I reached out and took her hand in mine. I laced our fingers together and gave her a squeeze.

A seagull swooped by with a caw. It eyed our taco wrappers. A fit of giggles burst out of me. I felt like such a dork. Giggles, who the fuck giggles?

Apparently, I did now. But Eris did too. Which made it funnier.

I shooed the bird away and realized I forgot something. I slid us into stoptime. I snuck over to the taco cart and snagged some extra napkins. The restaurant came back to life after I got back to my chair.

"This thing you gave me, even if it was built upon the random whims of the world, even if I am still trying to understand the strange new layer to the world, it's amazing," I said to Eris. "Thank you."

Eris beamed at me. "That is the best thing you could have ever said to me, Giulia."

I clapped my hands together. "Now that we've gotten all the heavy shit out of the way for the day, let's tell each other silly stories about ourselves that double as thinly veiled get-to-know-you talk."

Eris concurred that this was a fantastic idea.

I told her about discovering punk rock via old Ramones vinyl in Angie's attic when we were kids. I told Eris about the first time I got that stage high with my first high school band, The Handbaskets. Eris wowed me with a tale of an actual Ramones show in England.

"Punk rock, in its rawest form, is musical chaos," she told me. "Look at any of the greats. Look at the raw movement in the middle of a mosh pit. You had an affinity for chaos long before you had any magic. It's how I was drawn to you. Chaos begets chaos. Punk rock is one of the best things to happen to me in a hundred years."

We finished our food and then let our feet carry us along Newport. I had the vague notion of heading to the Newport Creamery to introduce Eris to the Awful Awful. We skipped through traffic in stoptime and wandered along the wharves. With her head leaned up against me, we watched the nighttime tides lap against the city in a quiet corner of the wharves surrounded by tourist shops closed for the night. The yachts in the harbor bobbed up and down on the waves.

"Hundred years, huh?" I said. "Magic makes wizards live a long time then?"

"Something like that," she said. "Bet you cannot guess how old I am."

I leaned back and took my time looking Eris up and down. She made a cheeky pose and I couldn't help but smile.

"You don't look a day over a hundred and four."

Eris laughed and I felt the lovely flutter at the sound.

"Not even close."

"So do I get a consolation prize even though I guessed wrong?"

Eris turned to me and caressed my cheek with a light touch of her fingers. "It may take some convincing."

I looked into her eyes. I wanted to fall into her gaze and never crawl out. "Oh yeah?" I slid my arms around her. "I like convincing."

Footsteps clattered off the sidewalk somewhere off to my right.

"How far away did we park?" she asked.

Another set of footsteps shuffled behind me.

"A few blocks away," I told her.

"Mmm, I do not know if I can wait to get back to Warwick," Eris said. "Where is the nearest—"

The footsteps turned into a run. I looked up and saw a woman dressed in black like someone's bad idea of a cat burglar running right for us. A fizzle and a pop and we were surrounded by the smell of ash and molasses. The woman in black reached out and shot sparks out of her hands at us.

Eris swore and took off her jacket in frantic motions. She threw the smoldering garment to the ground.

"What the fucking fu—"

A pile driver struck me from behind. I hit the pavement hard and the air was driven from my lungs. Sharp hands grabbed me by the hair. I gulped air and rolled before I was pinned. I looked up at an ugly fucker. His face looked like it was squished together with leftover parts. A lupine snarl spit all over me. I reached for stoptime. Being blindsided by Ugly made my hold on it slippery at best. I pulled my hair free and rolled out from under him before my hold slipped away.

The thing that attacked me did a double take when I was not where he expected. It recovered to its feet in a flash. It stalked me in a low stance, nasty looking hands tipped in rough, yellow claws held out in front of it.

"What the fuck is your problem?" I yelled at the thing in front of me. I saw Eris and Ugly's partner scuffle off to my left, but with those wicked eyes on me, I could not move. She's a wizard. She can handle herself, I told myself. Still. That other bitch was too. The scents of ashes and apple blossoms fought in the air. Sparks tumbled across the pavement.

"I liked that jacket!" Eris cursed the wannabe cat burglar.

A railing and a drop off into the Atlantic Ocean was behind me. I inched to my left towards Eris. The ugly thing mirrored me, keeping us separated. I closed my eyes and took a breath.

"Just like a mosh pit," I whispered to myself.

A boot scuff on the asphalt. I snapped open my eyes. It lunged. I stopped time, darted to the side and let ducked out of stoptime again. Its momentum carried it. I kicked my boot out at its knee. It went down, hard.

The lupine thing rolled. Its hands flashed in its coat. A knife flew out at me.

I felt the bite of steel before I could grab hold of time. My hold on my own magic power was sloppy. The knife cut through my shirt and a sliver pierced my shoulder before I stopped time. I plucked it out of my skin. The fucking thing burned. The steel looked like the sort of cheap crap that came from the Miscellaneous Wannabe Asian Junk store every shopping mall came standard with. Some design was etched in the blade. It looked black and oily.

Time fell out of my hands. I kicked the thing while it was down. It wheezed out its breath and covered its face.

"What kind of fucking asshole are you?" I kicked it again closer to the edge of the wharf. "Prick." A third kick tipped it off the edge of the wharf into the ocean. It flailed around and went down under the dark waves.

I turned and saw the cat burglar's back to me. Her hands were surrounded by a yellow-orange glow like embers of a fire. She faced off with Eris, who had rage etched across her face. A purple glow leaked from her eyes.

The cat burglar-mugger-whatever-the-fuck-she-was was spouting out a speech, manifesto style, at Eris in some hard edge language I never heard before.

I punched her in the back of the head.

"Shut up."

She dropped like a sack of potatoes.

Eris stomped up and kicked her in the head.

I grabbed her about the shoulders. "Woah, hey. Fuck these guys, but they're just some punk ass muggers. Roll them, sure, but don't kill 'em."

"They dare to step up to a goddess! An immortal! They made their choice. Let my cousin on the other side of the Styx have them."

I heard sirens in the distance becoming not-so-distant. How the hell did we make a scene? There was no one here to see any scene. Maybe they were not coming for us, but I did not really need Newport PD finding me next to an unconscious person who clearly got her ass kicked. Warwick was not the only city PD in Rhode Island that kept an eye on the local punk bands.

"Leave them, Eris. Please."

She looked at me. In those eyes, I saw the ancient power she held onto, not the date I shared street tacos with.

I kissed her.

I took her head in my hands and dropped all my pent up passion into that kiss. "There are better things we could be doing."

The anger fell away from her. She staggered into me and grabbed hold of my coat to stay upright. Eris looked up at me and broke into a smile. I was relieved.

"Let's go," I said.

She steadied herself but shook her head. "Not yet." Eris knelt down and rifled through the pockets of our attacker.

"What are you doing?"

"Information is power," she said holding up our magical attacker's wallet. Eris stood and stumbled into me. I caught her. "I am ok," she said to me. She shook her head.

Eris kissed me. That was all the encouragement I needed to get out of Newport.

We ran across the Newport streets like a couple of giddy teenagers sneaking out behind the bleachers. We stopped short at the edge of the parking lot where my Benz waited.

A trio of goons loitered around my car.

"Shit, they're waiting for us aren't they?" I said.

Eris nodded. "I feel their power in the air. They mean business."

I turned and saw that look come across her face, the one that meant "I'm a badass with magic up to my elbows, what the fuck do these skeezers think they're bringing to the table?" But she looked unsteady on her feet. I reached for the strings of time. They tried to slip though my fingers. I must have used up more power than I thought throwing down with the other two. I hammered down on my seventh sense and forced time to a halt.

"We need to make this quick," I said to Eris.

She turned to me and it looked like she was moving through molasses. My new senses strained. I was getting worn out by all this.

"They'll never know how we ditched them," I whispered to Eris. She held back a laugh. I tried to shush her but started laughing myself. I clamped a hand over my mouth to restrain myself. The Benz behaved and we took off out from under their noses, speeding out of Newport. The night air was chilly coming off the ocean. I put a hand on her knee. She snuggled up close to me along the bench seat. Her head leaned against my shoulder. I breathed in her apple blossom scent. I smiled and drove a little faster towards home.

"This was a much better idea," she whispered to me.

The city shrank in my mirror. Going back over to the West Bay, the Newport Bridge lights twinkled above our heads like a thousand fireflies taking one last swoon of the season.

"It is beautiful," Eris said.

With the wind whipping around us, I leaned over and kissed her.

We almost missed our stop.

Chapter 12 – Eris

Giulia leaned into the accelerator and her car huffed up the arc of the Newport Bridge back to the mainland of Rhode Island. The lights of the bridge still sparkled up close. I felt giddy unlike any feeling I held within me for a generation. It may not have been an epic for the annals of history, but I stood to battle with my paladin. I stood to battle with someone amazing.

I held her free hand in mine. Giulia was tense. Focused on the empty road.

"Thank you, Giulia." I leaned across the center console. "It's not often I can count on someone to stand by me like that."

"I...it was... different," she said as she cruised past the toll gantry. Clear of the four dollar fee, she kicked the old diesel engine into high gear.

"You were fantastic. You handled yourself and your new power very well." I ran my hand up her thigh. "In all my years I have never seen anything like it."

Giulia drew in a sharp breath. I let a lazy smile creep across my face. "By all that is sacred in Olympus, you are amazing Giulia Cesari."

I made the conscious decision to lean over and kiss Giulia on the neck right below her ear. It drained the reserves of chaos energy inside of me. The leftover pieces of the hex burned into my arm still kept a chokehold on my magic. Zeus be damned, I did not care.

I kissed her again.

"It's… um… a lot to process." Giulia had trouble with words.

"I have got all night," I whispered.

The old Benz screamed through red lights and screeched around corners through Warwick. Giulia skidded the car to a halt in front of her building. Running through the halls was a blur. I clamored up the spiral stairs behind Giulia.

She fumbled with the keys to her loft. I pressed my body up against her from behind and kissed the back of her neck. Her knees trembled and she almost dropped the keys.

"Not helping."

I ran my hands down the bare skin of her arms. The electric touch of our magical feedback left goosebumps across her skin. "Was not trying to." I nipped at her earlobe.

The key took and we burst into the loft. One of us kicked the door shut behind us. We stopped and stared at each other. I did not know if we fell into Giulia's stoptime or not. The rest of the world ceased to exist. Giulia quirked a smile at me. I felt a warm happiness in the pit of my soul. Butterflies in my stomach flew figure eights. I reached out to her and ran my fingers through her hair.

We kissed.

Giulia's lips tasted of fire and energy and a spark of magic. She tasted of home. My hands were all over her, a flurry of motion across her skin. She leaned into me with a desperate hunger. Giulia pressed me up against the back of the door and trailed kisses down my neck. I threw my head back with a moan.

My hands found the hem of her shirt. It went up over her head. I threw it aside. It stopped in midair as the strands of time got caught up with us. I admired the view for half a heartbeat before Giulia leaned in and planted a kiss on my neck in the same spot I tormented her with. My knees felt weak. She grabbed my butt with strong hands and held me close.

"Bedroom," I whispered. "Now."

"Oh, is that not helping?" Giulia kissed that spot again.

I moaned against her shoulder.

Giulia snaked a hand under my shirt. Her fingers danced over my skin to cup my breast. "How 'bout this? This helping any better?"

I did not have any coherent words for her.

"Good thing I'm not trying to help."

"Bedroom," I said with more urgency. I ran my nails up the small of her back along her spine. I felt fire on my fingertips from the energy between us. The passion from our first night magnified a hundred fold now that our magic intertwined with our bodies. It stole my breath and curled my toes. Giulia shuddered in my arms. She felt it too. Nerve endings across my entire being tingled. I was ready to melt together.

"Bedroom," we both said.

Giulia said some wordless sound of agreement which I smothered with a kiss. I stole her breath away and left Giulia gasping for air.

I leaned back against the door. "Go on then," I said to her.

Giulia shook coherence back into her head. Time started up again and her shirt fell to the floor.

She turned and sashayed across the room. I was drunk on the sway of her stride.

Until I saw the birthmark on her right shoulder. An apple shaped birthmark, a golden-bronze color on her skin. The golden apple. The symbol of my godliness. On her skin. I let out a yelp.

Giulia stopped. She looked over her shoulder before I could compose myself. My brain was three steps behind my sex drive.

"Are you ok?"

"That bastard did not tell me you were marked." I paced in a frantic little circle in Giulia's kitchen. "By Cerebos' hairy balls, that asshole did not tell me you were marked!"

Giulia took a step closer. "My pants are wondering if this is the best time, Eris."

I went up to Giulia and turned her away from me so I could look at her birthmark closer. I moved her bra strap over so I could run my finger along all the edge. I felt the spark between my finger and her skin. When I touched the golden apple in the center, the shock stole my breath away again.

"Ya know," Giulia said around catching her breath, "it doesn't need to take this much effort to get me out of all my clothes."

Her words barely registered.

"That satyr fucking asshole," I snapped. "How could Hermes not tell me you were marked?"

"Who the hell is Hermes?"

"Messenger God my ass. By Hera's left tit, I will bury him with his Uncle Hades for a generation for this."

"Eris! What the fuck are you talking about?"

"Your birthmark. Here." I said.

"So what? Weird little piece of skin. That's why I don't like wearing off the shoulder tops, thank you very much. Go back to the other part. Gods and Hermes and shouldn't we be fucking right now instead of talking about my embarrassing skin blemishes?"

"Please, Giulia. It is important."

She stilled and I felt time grind to a standstill around us.

"It is shaped like an apple," I said.

"Um. Yeah. Kinda I guess. I can't exactly see it well. What about it?"

"A golden apple." I put emphasis on golden.

My fingers still traced around the mark on her shoulder. The Golden Apple of Chaos gave off a faint glow while she had time in her grasp. Giulia shrugged her shoulder beneath my touch. "Where are you going with all this? Why is it so upsetting?"

"The color. It glows when you use magic. I didn't see it with your shirt on and last time you had your shirt off... we were otherwise occupied."

Giulia turned her head to try to see what I saw. She could not so faced me instead. Giulia kissed me. "We could be occupied like that again. Right now."

I did not kiss her back.

"That is why I was drawn to The Vault where you would be."

"I have no idea-"

"Was the mark always there?" I interrupted her. "When did you first see it?"

Giulia turned away from me. "I dunno," she muttered.

"What do you mean you do not know? How can you not know!?"

"Jeez, I just don't. It's not something I'm fucking proud of, a fucking weird shape on my skin. If you must fucking know, it is a weird birthmark that just showed up when I was a teenager and some fucking doctor was confused as fuck about it. The damn thing didn't hurt. It was like it was always there. It was like-"

"-magic," I finished.

An icy finger trailed down my spine. The goosebumps on my skin were not from impending sex anymore.

"Eris," Giulia said slowly, "is there something that you're not telling me?"

I could not meet her eyes. I felt a tear in the corner of my eye. "I am sorry. By the darkness of my mother Nyx, I am sorry. I never meant for you to be drawn into the life of an Olympian."

"None of this makes sense. What does this have to do with anything? Why does my birthmark have you so upset?"

"It is not a birthmark. Or a scar. Or some other blemish. It has a piece of the Golden Apple of Chaos in it. The ambrosia. I should not have bled all over your home. I should have known it would be a problem."

"Wait. Wait. That crap that almost killed me? It-"

"Was my blood. The ambrosia of the gods."

The look in her eyes said that some piece of Giulia broke right at that moment, never to be repaired.

"You had an affinity for chaos already. My ambrosia sought it out. Latched on to it. Latched on to you," I said. "Hermes told me you were my paladin-"

"Your what?"

"Paladin. A holy warrior made by the gods."

"You're not just some wizard named by hippie parents, are you?" Giulia said just above a whisper.

"No, Giulia." I stood straight and spoke with the voice of immortality behind me. "I am Eris, Goddess of Chaos, Holder of the Golden Apple, the Triskter of Troy, daughter of primal Nyx from which all took form." I sagged to a slouch once I got through the formal title. "I am not some wizard, and my mother is most definitely not a hippie."

Giulia staggered back a step and collapsed into her kitchen chair. "You chose me for this?" her voice cracked, "To be some fucking paladin?" Giulia wrapped her arms around her middle like she was going to be sick.

I winced. "Not just a paladin. You're marked. My... my ambrosia, my blood. It got in you. You have a piece of me inside you. A piece of a god."

Giulia just stared at me.

"You are a demi-god."

She got up from the chair and paced the room. "What the hell does this all mean? You just made me into some magical guinea pig?"

"I was not even there, Giulia," I shot back. "You said it appeared years ago. I do not know what happened to cause it. I did not even know there was enough belief left in the world to create a paladin let alone a demigod. When Hermes-"

"-that wingfooted motherfucker."

"Yes. The wingfooted motherfucker. Hermes told me when he appeared to collect your soul and bring you into death, that he was so shocked to find a paladin, my paladin, that he left you alone. Olympus has not seen a paladin in generations! None of us believed it was possible anymore. Not enough belief in us to give any Olympian the power to create one. The thrice cursed Hermes most definitely did not tell me you were a demigod."

"Created by you."

"Yes. By me."

"So I'm some sort of magical leftovers?"

I ran my hands through my hair in frustration. "I cannot choose someone for this even if I wanted to.

Even if I thought it was possible. My Chaos magic does not work that way."

"So all of this," Giulia waved her hand to encompass the space between us, "all of this was completely random?"

"That is who I am," I said with open arms. "It is who I have been since civilization was young. Five thousand years has not changed that. Like it or not, I cannot help it."

Giulia sat there looking at me without any words.

I felt a hole open up inside of me. It should not hurt this much. I was a goddess. After five thousand years, I should have been immune to the whims and feelings of mortals.

But I liked Giulia.

And Giulia was not fully mortal anymore, either.

It felt like the world opened up beneath me even while my two feet were firmly planted on the floor. I was all too aware of Giulia sitting there, staring at me in shock, waiting for me to say something, anything, to make it better. I opened my mouth.

Nothing came out.

She stood and stomped away from me.

"Giulia, wait!"

I reached out after her but she did not look back. Giulia grabbed a hooded sweatshirt and stalked away from me through her living room and into the bedroom. In the corner of the bedroom was a ladder bolted to the brick wall that led to a trapdoor, presumably to the roof. She threw the hoodie on and climbed up away from me.

I heard footsteps clatter on the ceiling above me.

I paced around Giulia's flat.

"What in the seven hells do I do?"

I felt a buzz of chaos magic at my wrists. The Magic 8-Ball and the twenty sided dice were ready to pluck a direction out of chaos and give me a hit of energy. I covered them up and refused to look.

"No. Not at her expense," I insisted as if primal chaos cared one way or the other. I felt my energy drain out of me like a sieve. I still ran on fumes thanks to the hex leftovers. My arm burned under the bandage I wrapped around Dee's stitches. My body was a hair's breadth away from breaking out in withdrawal shakes.

I reached into Giulia's nearest cupboard without looking and pulled something out. I threw it out the door of the loft into the band practice space. It sounded like a box of macaroni crashed opened on a drum kit and scattered about.

Creating even the smallest bit of random chaos gave me a hit of magic. Not a lot, but enough to stand still without shaking and get my thoughts straight.

I needed something bigger if I was going to have a serious conversation with Giulia. Where in Olympus' name was I going to find something big that would not damage something of Giulia's?

I buzzed around Giulia's flat while my mind raced. Tossing Giulia's groceries about would not last long. I needed a hit fast.

Outside Giulia's bedroom window, I saw the street outside. Traffic was light after dark, but I saw a delivery truck approaching the awkwardly shaped rotary.

Before I could think about it, I focused my magic on the truck.

"Sorry," I muttered.

My view of headlights turned to taillights as the truck looped around the rotary. The truck hit one of Rhode Island's ubiquitous pot holes. The latch opened and the roll away door rolled away. Boxes tumbled into the street and the truck carried on.

Chaos rippled outward like a rock thrown into a still pond. From the truck driver who would have to deal with the lost delivery to the grocery store waiting for its delivery. The people driving down the street who had boxes of produce to dodge. The mom at the market who would have a few less fresh vegetables to choose from. Little Johnny Snider would not get any lettuce on his sandwich for lunch that week because all the fresh lettuce was in the street now. He did not like lettuce-less sandwiches and would trade it for a slice of elementary school pizza on Tuesday. Onward and onward and onward, the ripple effects from my one twitch of magic fed my soul. Good or ill did not matter, just the randomness.

I felt calm. I felt centered.

I had no idea what to do.

I looked to the ladder that led up to the roof hatch in Giulia's ceiling. It must have been leftover from when her building was still a warehouse. I had to go up there. I did not choose for Giulia to become my paladin. I did not choose for Giulia to bear my mark and become a demigoddess. Nor did she. Nothing in Greek dogma said I was bound to her as a being of my creation. I could just leave her like so many in my pantheon would.

"But I want you in my life."

Saying it out loud cost me a piece of the chaos reserves in my soul. I did not care.

I crept up the ladder through the open hatch. Giulia had some old camping chairs circled around a portable metal fire dish. A small campfire crackled in front of her and an open cooler on the roof next to her. She sunk into the chair and a fifth of bad tequila dangled from her fingers.

"Are you ok, Giulia? Do you want me to go?"

She did not say a thing or even seem to hear me. Giulia took a long drink of the liquor. She finished it off and pitched the bottle over the edge of the roof. The glass shattered on the pavement below. Giulia rooted around in the cooler next to her and took out a beer. She cracked it open and threw the cap into the fire.

I sighed. Giulia did not want anything to do with me. The rejection hurt way more than it should have, way more than someone I knew for a couple days should be able to hurt a person. Especially for someone who lived for five thousand years. I started back to the hatch.

"I never really believed it."

I stopped. "In what?"

"In the magic," she said. "I did it. I could fucking do it right now. But the last couple days never felt real.

Like I would just wake up in a ditch somewhere. Like it was all some hangover dream in a bad fucking movie with a lazy screen writer that didn't know 'It was just a dream' is the reason why he flunked out of film school."

I walked back towards her carefully until I stood behind her. "Not many believe anymore," I said. "It is hard for modern people to believe."

"You really are someone out of myth, aren't you?"

I sat down next to her. Giulia still watched the flames dance along the logs in the fire dish.

"I am not a myth," I said. "I am here next to you."

"And you're in charge of all the completely random events? The bona fide goddess of chaos, straight out of my story books." Giulia rambled with a flat tone to her voice. "You're in charge of all the random events in the world. Like the one that killed my family?"

"It is not like that." In my head, I sighed. I doubted the words sunk in. They never did the first time. "My relationship with primal chaos does not work that way."

"There's no patron saint of drunk drivers. There's not a god of faulty airbags. There is no spirit of slow ass paramedics who don't fucking feel the need to hurry along." Giulia drained the rest of her beer and fished out a new one. She opened that one and threw that cap in the fire too. "They said it was a freak accident. A stack up of random events. Just chaos. That's you."

"Damnit, that is not how it works Giulia!" I snapped. "If I had full control of every completely random event, they would not exactly be completely random, would they? I hardly make my own decisions. I live every day bound by the flip of a coin."

I saw the moment all Giulia's anger slithered away from her. Giulia sank deeper into her chair. She stared into the fire.

I was losing her.

"Look, Giulia, I like you. You give me a fluttery joy every time I see you." I reached out and placed a hand on her arm. She flinched but did not move away. "Does it matter how our paths crossed? It only matters they did."

She drank.

"I'm not some divine responsibility of yours?" she asked.

"The history of my kind is filled with one night stands and not giving a fuck what happens in our wake. The stories passed down to modernkind are not even the half of them. Yes, I could duck and run out on you. I could fuck you again and walk out of here without a single look back. Like any good Greek, I would sleep soundly with my decision. Except not anymore. Now I have met you."

"I understand how you feel," I continued. "I have lost a lot of people in five thousand years. I cannot define myself by the loss. I define myself by how I carry onward."

I hoped beyond hope that my words would sink in to Giulia's heart. She stayed quiet for a long moment. Her eyes watched the fire.

I lost her.

With a sigh, I stood to leave.

I lingered for a moment and started to go. Giulia stopped me with a hand holding a cold beer out to me. It was a step at least. I took the drink and sat back down next to her. Giulia kept watching the flames. I scooted the chair closer to her and leaned my head against her shoulder.

Together, on the roof of the building, we watched the flames burn down.

Chapter 13 - Giulia

My head throbbed, and it felt like someone stuffed a bale of cotton inside my head. I clamped my eyes shut against the day and rolled over-

-just to slip off my couch and land hard on my ass.

I let out a surprised 'whuf' and just sat on the floor for a moment. I looked around with squinty eyes. I was alone. I wracked my brain for what happened the night before. I remembered kissing Eris against the door, her hands all over me. Then the yelling. And the roof. There were flashes of memory after that, but they were fuzzy. Empty bottles. Flames. Her curls and tears in her eyes.

I pressed the heels of my hands into my eyes. "Maybe it's better I don't remember fuck all how I got on the couch. Alone," I whined a little bit to myself.

I fucked up, I figured. I must have fucked up. Even the groupies usually stayed 'til morning.

The more I blinked, the less the light hurt my eyes. Only a level four hangover then. I looked around the living room of my loft for any signs of company. The clutter sat in familiar locations. I was fully clothed. There were no strange clothes or boots within sight on the floor.

"Damnit," I whispered to the room and flopped my head back against the couch cushions.

I can hold it together, I told myself. But I decided I could hold it together better with a drink. Not seeing anything in arm's reach to fix that, I staggered to my feet. I grumbled while I plodded my way around my clutter and banged into the coffee table on my way to the kitchen.

I stopped short when I saw my refrigerator door open.

Eris poked her head out from behind the door with a slice of leftover pizza clamped between her teeth.

"What?" she muffled around the food. She chomped the bite and closed the door. "Cold pizza. It is the food of the gods."

She sat down at the table looking pretty proud of herself with a plate of pizza in front of her. The coffee maker chugged along on the counter with two mugs on standby. Eris wore one of my In A Murphy Minute t-shirts, the red one with the quarter sleeves. The shirt looked much better on her than me. I saw that bandage wrapped around her bicep poking out from under the sleeve.

"Good morning, Jules," she said.

I usually hated when people called me Jules, but from Eris, I felt a squiggle of affection every time she said it. The scent of coffee fought against my hangover to get my thought train chugging along at full speed.

"Um. Morning." I sat down at the table across from her.

Eris took a luxurious bite of pizza. "I can count on one hand the number of places on earth that make pizza better than Rhode Island." She savored another bite of my leftover pizza. "And three of them are in Italy."

Her curls were pulled back, though some were already starting to escape. They had a "Quick, my hair is mussed up and I must tame it fast" look about them. Under the table, she rubbed her bare feet against mine. She wore my clothes and had the sly look of a cat in a sunbeam.

"Um. Did we..."

"Did we what?" Eris was being far too innocent for it to be genuine.

"Did we, um, finish where we left off?" Eris made me shy and mushmouthed so easily. Morning after conversations about fucking were not often hard to come by.

Eris laughed as the coffee maker beeped and she got up to prep it. "No. You are a sweetie when you are drunk. Insisted on the couch and assured me that since you are a proper lady, you could not jump into my pants until the second date."

I sat with my hands in my lap. I felt my face flush and stared at the table.

"Relax," Eris put a mug of coffee in front of me. "I am not going to storm out of here because you did not put out. I had to stir up a lot of trouble to stay with you. If I wanted a quick lay, I would not need all the trouble."

"What do you mean?" I asked.

She snapped her fingers.

A lightning bolt lit off in my pants and went straight for my brain. My breath came in gasps and every nerve ending in my body ached for release. In an instant, my body became a coiled spring of hormones. My head could not focus. I just needed. I desired. I craved. My vision focused down to a point. Eris. She was all I saw. I was ready to leap-

Eris snapped her fingers again.

I sagged back into my chair, spent. I put two coherent thoughts together. Sort of.

"Fuck. Me."

"That was the plan." Eris took a casual sip of her coffee. Mine spilled across the table, probably when I was halfway across the table myself.

"You should bottle that." I cleaned up the coffee and grabbed another cup out of the pot. My limbs had an after-sex limberness to them.

"No thank you," Eris waved the idea away. "That kind of magic is not really my game. But it is not often a goddess gets denied sex, especially on grounds of good manners."

I stared into my coffee. Eris seemed happy to let me have a minute to think. She was busy with her third slice of cold pizza breakfast.

"So it's all true then?" I asked her. "Well, the parts of it I can remember. They're all true?"

She raised an eyebrow at me. "You need another example that I am a goddess even after I just set your pants on fire?" Eris closed her eyes and pointed out in a random direction. Her finger aimed at my counter where my toaster sat there being an innocent appliance.

"The hand gestures are all for show." She rolled her wrist around and flicked her fingers towards my toaster. "But it is not often I can show off among mortals anymore. I like the show."

A thin stream of purplish light swirled around like a light fog from Eris outstretched hand across my kitchen. It coiled around my toaster. I felt the magic in the air like a distant thunderstorm. The air popped. The mist flashed.

A confused looking cat sat on my counter.

The orange tabby padded across my counter, sniffing along the way. It made a face when it got to the dishes in my sink. It looked to us and leapt across the space to the table. My former appliance gave Eris a familiar nuzzle. It padded over to me for a curious sniff. The furball apparently decided I was ok and expressed itself via a headbutt of love. It coughed, a dry hacking sound better fit for an 80-year-old smoker. The cat hacked up a tiny brown square and then jumped off the table. It sauntered across my kitchen and found a sunbeam in my living room like it owned the place.

"Still makes toast," Eris said. She picked up the crouton sized square and ate it. "It needs jam."

"I... um... I guess I should be glad you didn't point at my microwave."

"So yes, Giulia, it is all true. Eris is my honest name given to me by my mother Nyx, the essence of night and nothingness. Civilization was barely even a thought. I am a proper immortal from Greece. My powers and domain are a paradox, vast and constraining at the same time. A series of random occurrences played out in perfect succession to give you a true piece of me. You had an affinity for chaos and now you *are* Chaos in a small way. Or a large way. It is all random."

I set my mug down very deliberately. "I forgot that part. I'm a deity?"

"Not quite. A demigoddess. Think Hercules, but not an asshole."

I looked at my hands and felt stupid for it right away. "I don't feel any different."

"Why would you?" Eris plucked a pepperoni off the top of her pizza and ate it. She slid over the grease stained take out box where one last slice waited for me. I picked at the toppings but did not really have much of an appetite. Too many thoughts rolled around in my head.

"Are you ok with all this?" Eris asked after a while.

"I guess I have to be," I shrugged. "It's a lot to process though."

"Why? You have magic powers. You handled the ability to stop time. Is it that much of a stretch that I can exist too? That all the gods can exist out there in the world around you?"

"That I am one too?" I replied. I looked away from her. I felt stupid saying things like that aloud. "I never believed in magic."

"Really?" Eris deadpanned. "Leaving aside that you can do magic, it is still all around you. Everywhere. You never would have been marked if you did not have an affinity for it in the first place. And you are saying you never crossed paths with magic before? Never seen something that the rational world could not explain before?"

I shook my head. "Not like that. And now I'm sitting in my kitchen eating congealed pizza with a goddess. And a cat that used to be an appliance I bought to make breakfast. Not really how I would've expected it to go."

"Expected what?"

"You know. Meeting a deity. In my grimy kitchen eating skanky food of questionable freshness. You don't really have the look of a goddess."

A scowl lit across Eris' face. Oh crap, I stepped in it this time.

"You know. I mean…" Words stumbled out of my mouth looking for a save. "You look more like a runner than a goddess. Like one of those gym trainers or something."

"Oh really. And what, praytell, is a goddess supposed to look like?"

I would have expected… ya know…" I made the international sign for big boobs.

I felt a hum and pop of magic in the air and smelled the scent of apple blossoms in my kitchen. Eris took on the proportions of a Barbie doll. Her curls were blonde and smoothed out to a light wave. She looked taller and so top heavy that she was about to fall over. The shirt of mine she wore strained to hold it all in.

"Is this better?" she snapped. "Being a goddess does not count without giant tits?"

"Pfft, no." I made a vague and slightly embarrassed gesture in the general direction of Eris' breasts. "Mattel can keep the Barbie look. They look… unwieldy. I like you as is."

"Good." Eris started to cross her arms before she realized that was not going to help at the moment. "Leave that shit to Aphrodite. She makes a bad name for all of us, you know. Non-Greeks too. Aphrodite and her frigging renaissance painters have a hard on for the Swedish Women's Volleyball team painting any and all goddesses like this. How many blondes have you seen in Greece?"

I held in a laugh. "Not a lot."

"Damn right, not a lot," she said.

Eris saw me holding in a laugh. She cracked a smile and that was enough to let loose the floodgates. I busted out laughing and so did she. All my stress and doubt burned away while laughing with Eris in the kitchen.

The cat/toaster looked at us from the other room like we were crazy.

"I think we both needed that," Eris said once we were able to breathe again.

I fought down some more giggles and nodded in agreement. Eris came around to give me a hug, but the Barbie boobs got in the way. We laughed again. She snapped back into her body, the way it was supposed to be shaped.

"Much better," I said to her.

"Good," Eris said with my hands in hers, "because I want to see you again." I felt a twitch in her hands that carried a hint of magic with it. "But I need to head home for a while."

"Busy day ahead?" I could not help but be a bit disappointed. Sure, I had plenty of stuff to do too, but I would rather blow it all off to spend the day with Eris. Band practice was the only thing I could not shirk, but after last night's duet, Eris could just come too.

"Busy enough. Things I should not rearrange. But I want to see you again," she reassured me. "It shall not be so bad. I will be back later tonight." Eris plucked a set of keys from thin air.

"Um. Eris, I picked you up. We took my car."

"Yes. Yes, we did." She pressed the button on the key fob. A car started up. I looked out the window and saw Eris' Crown Vic with the DC plates sitting in front of the auto parts store across the street. I must have made a face. It delighted her. "Magic," was all she said.

Eris leaned over to give me a kiss on the cheek. I turned it into a kiss on the lips. I snaked my hand around Eris and pulled her close. "Let's spend the day together," I whispered in her ear. "Show me your world. Teach me. Wherever the day takes us, I just want it to be with you."

"Mmm... done." Eris grabbed my hand and we dashed off to her car like a couple of teenagers skipping class.

Chapter 14 – Eris

I parked the Crown Vic in front of the Extended Stay Suites and led Giulia into my temporary home.

"Come," I said to her. "We will not linger much, but I have a few things I would like to bring with us."

Giulia did not see inside the suite when she was over before to pick me up for our date. She tried not to be obtrusive while she was looking around.

"It looks so normal," she said.

I went into the bedroom to gather some things. I liked wearing Giulia's shirt, it carried her scent, so I did not change. I grabbed a backpack and tossed some clothes in the bottom. For later. Should the need arise.

"Why would it look anything but normal?" I called out to her.

"I dunno." It sounded like Giulia was in the kitchenette now. "Cause, ya know. Five thousand years old. Powers over primal chaos."

I had some magically infused items around the bedroom. I grabbed the magical knickknacks. As an afterthought, I grabbed Hephaestus' lighter. Smith of the gods, his deal was fire. It was the kind of thing that came in handy when the whims of Chaos left me in the wilderness, even if it was mostly useless in cities.

"Giulia," I said walking back into the kitchenette, "I lived generations without plumbing. Athens smells much better now than it did when I was young. I am more than satisfied with the comforts of the modern world."

"Um. But you hate canned goods?" Giulia stood in front of an open cupboard. Two shelves of blank cans stared out at Giulia, the labels all peeled off. She plucked one down. "How do you know what you're going to eat?"

I took the can from her and gestured for her to sit down. "Lesson one in the life of the Goddess of Chaos. I rarely choose my own meals."

"Why would you do that?"

"Because of how my magic works," I said while I fished around for the can opener. "I told you last night that I cannot control chaos. I am beholden to the whims of Chaos just as anyone else is. More so, in fact." I opened the can and got a sweet citrus smell. Pineapple.

"How can it be more?"

"Magic is like a drug, but it doesn't work that way for everyone," I said anticipating the question Giulia was about to ask. "It does for me. My body runs off chaos like yours does with food and water. When I create chaos in any form, I draw the energy into me. It powers my magic and my soul." I put the pineapple in a bowl and placed it on the table and sat across from Giulia. "I once went a week on the battlefield without eating, a nonstop blur of motion."

Giulia whistled under her breath.

"That was long ago."

"But if you don't need food, why all the cans?"

"To create that much chaos in the modern world would draw unwanted attention. Even during my youth, times like that were the exception rather than the rule. It can be dangerous for myself, not that I was concerned with that back then. Now, I fuel myself bit by bit. A random breakfast gives me my first hit of chaos a day."

Giulia picked at the pineapple for a long moment. "What happens if you run out?"

"Withdrawal," I said in a soft voice. A feeling nagged the back of my mind. I did not often talk about my weaknesses with anyone. "My body will start to break down. It is… it is not pleasant."

She reached out and laid a hand on mine.

"Come," I said, snapping out of the moment. "Today is a day for learning and discovery and you," I pulled Giulia to her feet, "are the newest divine in the pantheon and there is a new world waiting for you."

I took a bite of the fruit and walked out of the suite leaving Giulia to follow. We got in the car and meandered through the streets of Warwick. My magic felt the best it had since Wodanaz's pocket Irish witch, but was still sluggish. I let primal chaos choose our route rather than pick a direction.

We ended up at Goddard Park on the other end of town, rolling green fields and pockets of trees leading to Narragansett Bay. It suited my purposes. I walked with Giulia through the park looking for an out of the way place. We found a small rise away from main paths. Giulia spread out a blanket repurposed from the hotel suite as a picnic blanket.

While she was doing so, my phone buzzed to life in my back pocket. I hated the Titan cursed object, necessary as it was to modern life. Computers have always been things of order, inherently opposed to my nature. The pocket sized smart phone was doing its best to get my attention.

"Thrice damned thing," I muttered while I poked at the keypad repeatedly. It never unlocked for me on the first try.

There was a text message from Dee. And another. And a third. Then a fourth. I shoved the phone into the bottom of the backpack.

"You're not going to answer that?" Giulia asked?

I shook my head and sat down across from her. "Modern phones are not reliable around me, nor any other being who relies on Chaos."

Giulia frowned. "I noticed my phone was acting up earlier."

"Computers represent order. Bytes and bits and numbers and what-have-you." I waved my hand dismissively. "Pieces of code carefully put together in exacting fashion. One wrong number in all that code and..." I gestured to the backpack where we still heard the echoes of incoming text messages.

"So it isn't important?"

"It is Dee, the Ora-" I stopped myself from saying 'Oracle' out of habit but there was no need. If Giulia was to open her eyes to the new world she lived in, she would meet Dee soon enough. "Dee is the Oracle of Salem."

"Massachusetts has Greek oracles?"

I smiled at her surprise and was relieved Giulia did not ask about the texts. Dee must have been worried about my stitches. There was no way Giulia had missed the bandage over the hex stitches, but she did not ask and I did not want her to worry. "Yes. Dee was one of the earliest transplants from the Old World, the Norse explorers notwithstanding, and one of the few to stay in one place. I shall introduce you soon. Many of us old gods are... somewhat transient."

"So you're not stuck to wherever in the world..." Giulia rolled her eyes at herself. "And I just realized that is a stupid question. You can't be stuck in Greece if you're here with me."

"Not an ignorant question at all," I assured her. "It all depends on the mythos."

"So all those old myths are true?"

"Some things have been lost in translation over the generations. Some... have just been lost."

I was silent for a long moment. Giulia took my hand in hers. I shook my head out of my ancient memories.

"It is rooted in the original belief, though," I said. "Most of the old deities can walk where they will on the earth. A creature such as a dryad cannot. Their mythos binds them to their trees."

Giulia stared at the ground between us. She bit her lip while she thought it over. I ignored the muffled buzz of my phone coming from the backpack again.

She looked back up at me and beamed. "So... that means I really do get to be a fuckin' wizard!"

I laughed along with her infectious delight. "It is such a treat to see this world with new eyes."

Giulia jumped to her feet and launched us into stoptime. "It's god damned amazing is what it is. I mean, look at this..." She trotted over to a lone jogger ignoring us from a dozen yards away. She jumped around in front of him, waving her arms like an angry gorgon. The jogger was motionless to us while we were in between the seconds. Mid-stride, he had both feet off the ground. Giulia waved her hands between his feet and the ground like a magician proving she did a trick. "He's got no idea."

I indulged her wonder.

She came back to the blanket and sat across from me again. Giulia fidgeted. "I can feel where I was when I turned on stoptime. Almost like a divot in... time?"

Giulia settled and time started back up with a rush in my ears. The jogger chugged along without the slightest hitch in his stride. Out of his way, we barely registered in his mind to begin with. He never saw Giulia jumping around like a woman possessed.

"I didn't notice the divot before."

"Well, it might only be noticeable if you are returning to where you started."

Giulia thought on that for a moment. "I suppose. Makes sense. Is that how it always works?"

One bark of laughter snuck out before I could smother it. "Giulia, I have no idea."

"But..."

"I am the spirit of Chaos for the Greeks, born of Nyx and none other. I have seen war and strife. Empires have risen and fallen under my personal watch. I have seen things ignored by the chroniclers and forgotten to history. But you, my dear Jules, are unique."

"No one has done this before? Ever?"

"Not as a being of Chaos. Chronos has his domain, of course, but never has mine and his come together."

"Chronos? Like time travel? How does that happen?"

I shook my head. "The two of us are both agents of the primal force, not its masters. We are as much subjects to its whims as players in its domain."

Giulia could never be a good poker player. I watched her thoughts play out in the small motions of her expression. I let her think on it.

"Come now," I said before Giulia's thoughts went too far down the rabbit hole. "You need to learn about your abilities with stoptime if you are to live with them."

"Yeah! Being a wizard is going to be fucking cool."

I resisted the desire to kiss her.

"It is not so simple." I said. "There are hundreds of types of magic out there from just as many pantheons and domains. Chaos magic manifests itself differently in each person or deity. It is instinctual. There is no book I can hand you to study. You have to study within here." I tapped her chest over her heart. "You need to find your zen to get in the right headspace to follow your instinct."

Giulia closed her eyes and I felt the world slide to a stop. She let go of time and snatched it back under her control. Back and forth, the distant joggers moved in a staccato beat out of a herky jerky old movie. The jumps in and out of stoptime smoothed out as she went.

"See? Your bond with Chaos is like a muscle. It needs exercise."

Giulia opened her eyes and watched the world with a goofy grin while it jumped to her whims. Her grip on time faltered and the world carried on.

"Clear your head. Zen, Giulia, zen. In time, it will be as simple as breathing. Something you can do with barely a thought."

"Why all the zen, Eris? That's eastern. You're Greek."

"And?" I replied. "You are not Greek but it matters not. The ancient world was a lot more connected than the history books remember. I am five thousand years old. I have spent time in the East. I have spent time all over the world." A sigh escaped before I could reign it in. Giulia raised an eyebrow. "Between the Romans, Christians and Ottomans, my homeland has not always been a good place for us ancient ones to stay. Few from the pantheon you have joined stayed in Greece all this time. Besides, the nature of Chaos gives me wanderlust."

We spent the afternoon in the park. Giulia made a game of stopping time with joggers mid stride while we sauntered along behind them. She laughed with delight every time she stopped them mid air. We walked with our toes in the beach sand, Giulia flexed her magic and rearranged confused crabs between the water lapping against the shore.

And when Giulia's new senses tired, we stood in the warm sand and kissed.

Chapter 15 – Giulia

I felt... fluttery coming back to the loft with Eris and then promptly cursed myself for being such a girly girl. Tough, punk rock chicks didn't feel fluttery.

But I did.

And I was ok with that.

"So how about 'Time waits for no man, but it waits for this woman' to start the chorus?" Eris asked as I went to open the door. It was locked even though the rest of the band was supposed to be coming over to practice. I would have thought that was odd, I should have thought that was odd, but me and Eris were talking out song lyrics since we left the park.

"Yes, yes, and then Ric can drop in and do his thing." I air guitared my way in to the practice space.

The place was empty. Jin-Wei was not fussing with his cymbal arrangement. No Angie tuning the new bass strings I bought for her. Ric was not waiting around with a glower for me showing up late.

I was perfectly ok with that last one.

I missed what Eris said while she threw her backpack on the futon.

"Are we early?" I asked. "Fucking around with time is screwing up my watch."

Eris looked around the practice space for a clock that we didn't have. She fished her cell out of the backpack to check the time.

"No. We are a half hour late," she said. Eris tapped away at her phone, looking a bit distracted.

Something felt wrong, like a single plucked bass string tuned all out of whack. The wrongness shook inside of me.

I took out my phone and checked for any messages. Just a bunch of crap, nothing from the band. Nothing from Manny or the rest of the Zannetti clan.

"This isn't right. They should be here…" My fingers flew over the screen to call Angie. Straight to voicemail.

"Damnation to the shite side of the Styx. That was Dee calling me earlier." Eris was upset.

I gave her a look.

"The Oracle of Salem. Predicts the future. Urgent messages saying Wodanaz is on the move and 'See to your new allies." Eris grumbled. "Love her like a sister, but Oracles and their cryptic words-"

"Wodanaz? Who the fuck is that?"

A beat passed.

"Ill news. Dangerous news."

A fist pounded on my door.

I jumped. Eris dropped into a ready stance.

She put a finger to her lips and gave me a slow nod.

My blood thudded through my veins. I grabbed for stoptime. With zero focus, I missed it. I closed my eyes and forced my heart to slow. I snatched the strands of time. I still crept to the door on my toes. I held my breath when I looked through the peephole.

I let go of my breath, the tension, and my hold on time in one big go and whipped open the door. My neighbor, Carl, stood there.

"What?" I snapped.

"I... er..." he looked around me and saw Eris. "Is this a bad time?"

Not his fault, I told myself. "What's the matter?" I said in a less shitty tone.

"The plumber," Carl blurted out, still off kilter.

"What about them?"

"Um. I'm waiting for them to unclog my sink. Just. Yanno. If they knock on your door by accident. Because they're late."

I rolled my eyes. Carl was harmless but the most nervous individual I've ever known. Hell of a painter though. "If they knock on the door that says 'Giulia' I'll point them at the door that says 'Carl."

"Ok then." He gave me an awkward half wave and went back down the hall to his own studio.

I turned back to Eris. I felt her drop the current of chaos she held at the ready.

"Who is this Wodanaz guy and why is he bad news?"

Eris paced in a frustrated circle. "Wodanaz. He is another deity. We have had... run ins of late."

"Ok so some guy I've never heard shit about. Doesn't sound Greek."

Eris shook her head. "Pre-Christian German thunder god, and asshole, among other things. Almost as old as me."

"Is he a problem? Why would the Oracle woman warn you about him at the same time that my friends are missing?"

"I do not know the significance," Eris said. "There may not be one, Dee's messages are from when we were in the park."

"But there's no connection, right? Asshole thunder fucks shouldn't care about Angie or Jin-Wei or Ric."

"I do not know," she said while trying to make a call, presumably to Dee. "I am immortal, not omniponant."

"But what about-"

THUD.

THUD. Thud. Thud............

I spun back to the door. "Damnit, Carl," I yelled. "I don't have the fucking time. Stop pouring that shit down the drains and you won't have-"

I opened the door and lost my words as someone slumped against the door and slid to the floor at my feet.

"Manny!"

The Zannetti cousin mumbled something quasi coherent. He was a soggy mess. A puddle of water, tainted pink with blood, spread across my floor.

I grabbed Manny under the arms and dragged him to the futon not far from the door. Eris checked the hallway before swearing in Greek and slamming the door shut. Manny was dead weight in my arms. Eris had to help keep me from dropping him on the floor before we made it to the futon. I fell to a crouch beside him.

"Manny, can you hear me?"

He gurgled something. His eyes were bloodshot and barely focused. His hand clenched around something vaguely like a billiard ball. I tried to move it, but his fingers would not budge.

I tried to remember all that first aid crap from Girl Scouts but all I did back then was hustle side deals on cookies in the off season at huge markups. Eris ran upstairs and came back with a first aid kit and took charge of the triage.

"How did you summon that?" I assumed it was magic.

"It was under your sink." She pointed where to hold the bandage so Manny would not die on my couch.

"How did you know it was there? I didn't know it was there."

"I have used your bathroom before, Giulia. I knew where to look. Hold that there."

Eris handed me a bandage for a nasty little head wound. Manny had been sliced across the forehead. It still oozed red.

"Why aren't we using magic mojo superpowers to heal him? Can't we just... yanno... bzzzzt ... and Manny's cool again?"

Eris shook her head while checking Manny's ribs for anything broken. She used a light touch in case any were. "Chaos magic is unpredictable. Even your power, which seems pretty consistent, is rooted in fucking things up for the status quo." Eris frowned at one of the ribs she prodded. "Healing the human body is too delicate of a job to risk it. Human healing for human bodies."

"Then we should go to the hospital."

"He still reeks of magic, Giulia. Can you not feel the essence of the ocean about him?"

"Why in fuck's name would an ocean smell be odd? We're in the friggin' Ocean State."

"And miles from the sea. He shouldn't smell like low tide." Eris said. She wrapped a splint around Manny's fingers, the ones that were not clenched around the ball. "Let go of your human senses and open yourself to your new ones, to the magic around you."

Eris moved my hands away from Manny's head wound. She muttered something about stitches. I sat back out of her way and closed my eyes. A smell of sticky sweet mangoes left to rot where they fell layered with a hint of a fish boat out to sea for a day too long clung to Manny. Something else nagged at the edge of my perception. It buzzed about Manny, like the clouds before a storm. Worry for my friend shoved it just out of reach.

"We need to go to the hospital," I blurted out.

"And tell them what? He got pummeled by magic? Just help me stop all this bleeding."

"I don't know first aid!"

"He cannot bleed to death if time does not move."

I felt like an idiot.

Time stopped at my will. It was hard to hold on to the moments of time with worry for Manny pounding away at my concentration. Eris bandaged in double time. I could barely concentrate and let go of stoptime as soon as she was done.

"What about this thing he's holding?" I asked. "He won't let go."

I reached for the ball he held-

"No! Watch out-"

Eris swatted my hand away but we both touched the sphere. A flash of magic knocked me flat on my ass. A beam of light projected an image of some Euro trash looking asshole with a spear in hand into my flat. I scrambled off my ass onto my feet. I bounced on my toes, ready to fuck this guy up the business end of my fist. Eris caught my eye and shook her head though. The guy in the imaged looked down his nose at me and turned to Eris.

Oh yeah, I wanted to punch the smug right out of him.

"Eris," the man said.

"Wodanaz."

They glowered at each other.

"What's with this R2D2 shit?" I blurted out.

Wodanaz chuckled, a haughty thing that rubbed me the wrong way even if he hadn't been barging into my home with whatever in crap's name he did.

"Andrea Alessandra told me you had a new plaything, Eris. I thought you were due for a boy toy this time."

"Hey, fuck you. I'm standing right here," I said.

"Agreed," Eris said. "Go make yourself cozy with the business end of Cerebos' three pronged dick."

"Hrm. You two are quite eloquent together." Wodanaz leaned on his spear like he was chatting with an old friend. "As amusing as this witty repartee is, you should perhaps place your priority in listening, as this projection is powered by the life force of your friend that Andrea delivered to you for me."

I snarled something incoherent and lunged at Wodanaz. Eris held me back.

"Bide our time, Giulia. He is not really here."

Wodanaz laughed. "I am close to my endgame, Eris. Closer than I have been in a hundred years. I need you for the final piece of the puzzle."

"What the fuck is he talking about?"

He feigned shock like some ham actor. "Eris. *Mien ketzchen.* I am hurt you did not tell your new toy about me. Then again, she does not seem to be much of a conversationalist."

"Wodanaz, you are-"

"Julliet is it?" Wodanaz cut off Eris like she was not there anymore. "No matter, you and your friend are merely a means to my ends, but I will indulge you. I seek to bring magic back to the forefront of the lives of humanity. I have seen the rise and fall of civilizations and you people live in squalor. You scurry about the

Earth in meaningless circles. I remember when you had a purpose. Magic in service of the greater good gave your lives purpose. Humanity has forsaken its roots, forgotten magic in favor of other things. I will bring that back for you. I will give meaning to the meaningless. And you-" he leveled the end of his spear at Eris "-the Lady of Chaos, represent the final piece of the long puzzle I have put together over the generations."

"You do not need me for any of your machinations," Eris said. "Go find Apep. Or some variant of Coyote. Or Discord, that horrible mimic. I do not care for anything you have to offer."

"Only you-"

"Get over your fixations, Wodanaz. I shall not help you in any manner."

The image of Wodanaz scowled. His spear wavered. "I need you as a part of this."

"How can you say such things after what you have done over the years? You and your pissant cohorts, hounding me across the globe. Why would you think I would help you in anything, you delusional nobody?"

Wodanaz winced.

"You are forgotten," she said.

Wodanaz scowled.

"Not a single one of your schemes shall come to fruition," Eris said.

"Yeah, and fuck your face too," I added for good measure.

Wodanaz lowered his spear. "So be it. I was hoping you could see the wisdom in combining our talents like we once did centuries ago." He turned his back to us. "But you are with us or against us. There is no neutrality in this conflict, Eris. There are no innocent bystanders."

The projection's view of Wodanaz widened. The same Russian guy from the graveyard stood behind three people bound on their knees. Angie, Jin-Wei, and Ric looked worse off than Manny, half dead on my couch.

"What have you done?" I roared. I lunged at the projection and swiped through the image, hitting nothing but air.

Wodanaz chuckled. He pointed his spear at Eris and a jagged finger of lightning struck Eris through the heart. She screamed. I caught her and the jolt burned me and we fell to the floor together.

"Be at the LA Tavern in two hours," Wodanaz said. The image blinked out. The sphere clenched in Manny's hand went dead and rolled to the floor.

"Eris, are you ok?" I untangled myself from her. My fingers burned from Wodanaz's lightning where I caught Eris. She waved me off, pale and scorched.

I crawled over to Manny. He was still breathing. Not well though.

Chapter 16 – Eris

I waved off Giulia. She saw to her friend, who may have been alive still. My connection to primal chaos was next to nil. An ache formed deep in my mind and a shiver stole over my soul. Hera's tits, I hurt, I thought.

Giulia rushed to me before I could flop to the floor and I realized I spoke aloud. She murmured comforting nothings in my ear as she laid me down.

"Please, help me with this," I asked Giulia. I raised my still bandaged arm. My sleeve slid down my arm. The bandage was scorched from fire and amber with dried ambrosia from my veins.

My demigod paladin frowned but held her tongue for which I was grateful. I kept a straight face against the pain as the bandage peeled free of my raw skin. My razorblade slash opened up again, bleeding fresh ambrosia. Dee's stitches burned away. The hex carved into my arm was whole again though, and stifling my magic.

I sat up, ignoring the unsteady feeling.

"You look like death warmed over."

"I shall introduce you two at the next family gathering," I said.

"Seriously," Giulia protested. "Manny might die on my god damned couch. Literally damned by gods. Or whatever the fuck Wodanasshole is. And now you look like hell. Didn't think immortality would be so rough."

I showed Giulia the hex. The bleeding ambrosia slowed to a creep as the wound clotted. The smell turned my stomach but was leaps and bounds better than the magic stank Manny carried of Wodanaz's Poseidon wannabe lieutenant.

"A... gift from one of Wodanaz's lackeys," I said. "It blocks your Lady of Chaos from the very force which makes up our domain. My body is running on fumes, so to speak."

Giulia sat down and slid close to me. I laid my head on her shoulder.

"So we're going to rescue them, right?" Giulia asked.

"I am."

"We are," she said.

I shook my head. "It is too dangerous for you Giulia."

"And you look like you lost twelve rounds with a Mack truck. You need back up."

"I just need some rest to recharge. Wodanaz and his crew are far too-"

"Bullshit, Eris." Giulia turned and glared at me. "You told me yourself that I'm a part of this world now. I'm not going to turn all chicken shit now that you need me. I don't give a crap what Wodanaz is-"

"He is a thunder god. An immortal of the Germans. His age is almost as great as mine," I said.

"Well I never heard of him. Who the fuck knew the Germans had gods?" she asked.

I smothered a laugh. "I shall be sure to tell him you asked that."

"I'll tell him myself," Giulia said defiant.

I lifted a hand to caress a stray lock of Giulia's hair. "You are under no obligation to do this. I brought you into this without meaning to. I will make things right."

Giulia held me close and gave me a tender kiss. That kiss tugged at my old and bitter soul.

"I said we will do this together," Giulia's voice was hard edged steel. "That fucker hurt the only family I have left. He threatens you. My circus. My monkey."

We clasped hands. "Then we shall prepare for battle." I could not hide a grin. It had been an age since anyone stood by my side when facing down the maw of conflict.

The two of us got to our feet and Giulia made sure Manny was no longer on death's doorstep, I requisitioned a nearby laptop. It came to life with barely a hitch, a sure sign the aura of my chaos magic was nowhere to be found.

"Whachya doing?" Giulia sidled up behind me.

"The Internet is truly one of humanity's greatest achievements," I said as a typed 'LA Tavern' into a satellite map program. "Second only to air conditioning."

"Amen to that," she said. "Hey, I know that place. Lower Arctic Tavern. That place wishes it was good enough be a dive bar. One of those 'the neighborhood died a generation ago when the mills left and all we do now is drink' kind of bars."

"Typical," I snorted. "At least we will have some familiarity with the place."

I watched Giulia's reflection in the monitor pace around behind me. "So I just sneak in like a ninja. Stop time. Grab everyone. Then we're done. Right?"

"Too obvious," I shook my head. "Wodanaz is antagonistic and delusional, but he is not dumb. Nor is his Caribbean muscle. One or both is likely present which means some sort of defense. Even should you waltz in without notice, three trips in would require an excessive feat of stamina from you. One slip, and your friends will be the one who pay for your mistake."

"Well what then?"

I clicked around some new programs on the laptop.

"You downloaded Skype?" Giulia said. "How the shit is that helpful?"

"A good general always marshals her allies, however few they may be," I said before shushing Giulia. I made a call. "I am calling my one true ally on the East Coast of America other than Dee," I said while the call rang. "She is a Roman, but I assure you she is good people. We have known each other since Italy back in-"

"AA Imports Exports. How can I help you?" It came up voice only.

"Annona, there is much you can do." Though my words and upcoming requests were quite serious, I said it with a smile in voice. Annona Augusti, Roman goddess of the immortal city's yearly grain taxes and imports, was my truest friend in the corporeal realm.

The screen flashed to video. Annona sat at her desk, piled high with stacks of paper and clutter. Boxes with Chinese characters were stacked behind her. She looked somewhat professional today with her dark hair pulled back away from her soft features. The video feed caught a glint of the gold cornucopia pendant around her neck.

"Did you trash my car again, Eris?" Annona pointed at me through the laptop screen. "Last time I let you borrow one of my government surplus specials, I got calls from the Gary Indiana Police wondering why my car was half submerged in Lake Michigan."

"It was not that bad."

Annona folded her arms. "Eris. The other half was on fire."

I dropped the matter because it was factually true. I had avoided Indiana since the Gary Incident.

"Annona, my friend, I need your help." I bit my lip and hesitated. I knew the magnitude of what I was about to ask of her. "How fast can you get to Rhode Island from DC?"

She did a double take and frowned. "I have not left my new city since the 70s when we had that unpleasantness in Arizona."

"I am in deep, Annona, or I would not ask this of you." I rolled up my sleeve. The burned hex was healing slow. The cool air stung the raw skin.

Annona muttered a string of Latin curses.

"I am in a century's worth of trouble," I continued. "My power is almost nothing and Wodanaz has me backed into a corner with that Caribbean one off lieutenant of his."

"Fuck." Annona saved 'mongrel tongue' curses for special occasions. "I knew we should have killed him back in the 1700s before coming to America and-" I saw her eyes dart over my shoulder where Giulia hovered. "Who in Romulus and Remus' name is that?"

Giulia slid onto the seat with me. I looped an arm around her waist to keep from being pushed off the edge of the chair. I would have wrapped my arm around her anyway. I sat a little straighter with Giulia pressed up next to me. I did not know if the laptop camera let Annona see the affection.

"Annona Augusti, Goddess of the Grain Tax, meet Giulia Cesari, Paladin of Chaos by ambrosic virtue."

"I...what?" Annona leaned away from her screen on the DC side of the conversation. "Eris, in the four hundred years since our paths crossed in the middle of St. Peter's Square, I have never known you to-"

"I know."

Annona sighed. "I feel like there is a lot to this story I have yet to hear."

"We can swap tales over amphorae of wine later. I need you to bring me the Vestments," I blurted out.

"Shit, this is serious." I could see Annona half turn away from us where I knew she had a second monitor on her desk.

"Careful, keep talking like that and everyone will think you're American." I could not resist the ribbing.

Annona made a face, but it was half-hearted and she did not look away from her second screen. "My mother tongue will never die." She spoke it in Latin but switched back to English, her lingua franca whether she liked it or not, "Flight time from Dulles to Providence-"

"Hope you're not flying to Providence," Giulia interrupted. "You'll miss the airport by seven miles."

Annona gave her a blank stare.

"Cause... the airport. It's in Warwick. That's not Providence."

"Anyways," Annona said as I did a poor job holding back a laugh. "The flight time from Dulles to wherever the plane lands in Rhode Island is only an hour and a half."

"Fantastic!"

"But the next flight isn't for an hour."

I felt my shoulders slump. "Is that the fastest? There is no one who might get you here faster? Washington is littered with gods and fae."

Annona shrugged. "Technology is faster. At least faster than anyone who would help us out." Nothing short of a boon would get Hermes to give a Roman a lift, and he already had one in his pocket from me. His Roman counterpart, Mercury, considered 'second tier' gods beneath him and barely acknowledged Annona's existence. Ancient history meant the Romans were not well liked among the other old European expatriate gods that may be in Washington. Any modern fae we knew were bound by similar limitations.

"I understand. I appreciate what it means for you to leave your new Rome. We can manage until you arrive." Giulia gave her directions from the airport to her building. It was all of two miles away, but nothing was ever in a straight line in Rhode Island.

I ended the call with Annona and shut the laptop. The sudden silence in the room was oppressive.

"Fuck it," Giulia said. "We're on our own."

Chapter 17 – Giulia

A half hour before Wodanaz's ultimatum expired, I sat in my car, tucked into an alleyway behind a sketchy as hell thrift store with eyes on the LA Tavern. We idled just off Washington Street, West Warwick's main drag, though the Tavern itself faced away from us. I listened to the tik-tik-tik of my Benz's engine cooling while Eris fretted in the seat next to me. My crappy car fit the neighborhood. The Lower Arctic Tavern was the poster child for dive bars in forlorn ex-mill towns. Other neighborhoods in West Warwick may have resurrected themselves back to respectability but the town's Arctic neighborhood had yet to shake off its rough edges. The LA Tavern was the town's most ragged edge.

"It's odd not seeing any daydrunks out front waiting for the bar to open," I said.

"We are committing to battle while blind, Giulia. I worry about more than a bunch of local sots."

"The band's played sets there before. Big square room. Not much to it. It's a right proper shithole. It's been a while but I doubt they even washed the floors since then."

"That is not proper recon," Eris said. "Sun Tsu, we are not."

I shrugged. "Whatev. You're immortal. A goddess."

"One with a tourniquet around her powers. I do not know what this means for me or my safety." Eris put her hand on my knee. Her hand was warm though my denim jeans. "Nor your safety. We are greatly lacking in magical ammunition."

My hand covered hers and laced our fingers together. I watched the dice tattoo on her wrist flicker into motion. It stopped and jumped again with no pattern. Eris stared out the windshield at the LA Tavern across the corners of Pond and Washington Streets.

My free hand fiddled with one of the magical gizmos Eris had stashed away in her pack for my Intro to the Real Fucking World 101. I would've called it a Zippo before I was a paladin. I stilled called it a Zippo, just now with the adjectives 'Magical Fucking Something Or Other' in front of Zippo. I could feel the magic static in my fingertips when I held it. The thing smelled like dead campfires and sulphur.

"We got this," I held up the Zip.

Eris made an honest to goddess scoff. "A parlor trick made by a relative of mine. Hephaestus gave them out on holidays back in the 30s when smoking was fashionable."

We lapsed into silence. The air in the car grew stale. I watched the clock tick over another minute closer to Wodanaz's deadline.

"Maybe I could call in a favor from-"

"Fuck this noise," I blurted out.

I got out of the Benz and slammed the door shut behind me. I jammed the Zippo in my back pocket and stalked around to pop the trunk. Eris scrambled out her side of the car after me. I pulled out a tire iron and marched into the sun towards the LA Tavern.

"We're gonna kick in the door and I'm gonna be a stoptime fucking ninja."

Eris fell in step with me. "Wodanaz is a cocky son of a whorespawn satyr, but no fool. He will have defenses. What if your stamina is not up for it?"

I stopped in the middle of Pond Street waving around the tire iron while I talked. "We are creatures of Chaos, right? You're the Goddess of Chaos and I got a piece of you inside me too." I threw my arms in the air. "Fuck it, we'll make shit up as we go. All that Chaos will make us stronger or something."

I stomped the rest of the way across Pond.

Eris laughed. I could not help smiling at the sound. "Too true. You are catching on fast." She tried the handle on the LA Tavern's side door. "Locked."

We stood together a pace away from the door. Eris took out a switchblade from somewhere. I held the tire iron in both hands.

Eris turned to me. "You know this is likely a trap, right?"

Together we kicked in the door. Our boots barely dented the steel, but a door is only as strong as wall it is built in. The door jamb splintered and the door snapped open.

"Meh," I replied.

We rushed in.

Old, crappy tables and chairs filled the main room with the bar off to my left. All the lights were on, making them look older and crappier. The walls were stained from the decades pre statewide smoking ban. Wodanaz's crew was scattered about the bar, mostly screwing off. I recognized the wolfish looking thug, and that bastard I pitched into the ocean in Newport. Across the room, on the Tavern's pathetic excuse for a stage where we used to play music, a leathery looking boogeyman and a fucking pixie, flanked the band. I was in some sort of fairy tale throw down.

Angie, Jin-Wei, and Ric were bound in place on chairs on stage. The boys had hoods over their heads. Angie sat in front of the others. I saw a welt across her face and dried blood scattered across her shirt.

No one in the room expected us early. They startled and turned to us. In the long heartbeat before anyone reacted, my eyes met those of my best friend across the room. Hope flashed in Angie's eyes.

"Help me," she said.

All hell broke loose.

I grabbed hard at the strands of time in my head. The dive bar ground to a halt. The prick I pitched into the ocean sat with his feet up at a table in front of me, dicking around on his phone. Between the seconds of time, his face was locked into a derp of surprise. His head halted mid-turn to see what was going on with all the door kicking commotion.

The tire iron came across in a wild swing I connected hard with his shoulder. It rattled out of my grasp and clattered across his face and then to the floor. The fuckhead I hit jolted. To him, I kicked in the door, disappeared and he was about to have his shoulder caved in. Even without a timeflow to give him bloodflow, the hit looked nasty.

My "weapon" landed under a table. I was fully aware of the irony of not having time to go find it.

"Fuck it." My voice fell flat in the timeless air.

I rushed the stage. I planned to get Angie and the boys free, drop back into the timestream, then get the hell out while Eris shanked those other goons to cover our escape. Maybe I'd swat the pixie while I was up there because reasons.

My foot crossed a chalk circle drawn in the grime of the LA Tavern's floor. Runes? Scribbles? Some magic shit drawn in its borders flared with light. I felt the air stolen from my lungs. My blood, with Eris' ambrosia in my veins, burned under my skin. I gasped for a breath and stumbled into a table. My hold on time slipped away and I crashed to the floor.

The world came alive to me again but I landed on my side with my cheek pressed against the unwashed floor. The asshole I bashed fell to the floor not far off. He faced me, his brown eyes wide with shock, then recognition. They danced between hate and fear until some synapse in his brain misfired and his eyes rolled into the back of his head.

A cold emotion danced in the back of my head but I shoved it aside for later and staggered to my feet. Eris squared off with the other two. Her stance was low and the knife held out before her. The steroid guy kept a hand pressed against a bleeding wound across his stomach. Eris had the upper hand. Five thousand years of taking care of herself had seen to that. Rushing the stage and getting the fuck out was still the best plan, even if I could not hold onto time.

I turned back to the stage and saw Andrea Alessandra. The tall, black goddess pressed a pistol to Angie's temple.

"Stop."

She did not raise her voice but we all stopped as if I grabbed hold of time.

Eris shuffled a few paces closer to me, keeping one eye on stage and one on the muscle. The bleeder took a step away.

"Really? Firearms," Eris scoffed. "How uncouth. That is beneath a proper goddess. You might have a sense of honor if you were part of a proper pantheon and not just a dead sailor's imaginary friend."

Andrea Alessandra's face twitched in a grimace. The gun barrel jerked against Angie's head. She tried to lean away from the goddess, or whatever the fuck kind of spirit Alessandra was.

"I've bested you before, Chaos," Alessandra said. She pressed her lips in a thin line for a moment. "I have the hostage and the advantage. Again."

The room fell quiet.

"Terms?" Eris said in a low voice.

Alessandra's remaining muscle relaxed half a step but I only kinda saw that out of the corner of my eye as the two started talking. I didn't listen to a damn thing they said. Didn't matter. Eris bought us time.

Angie pleaded to me with her eyes. She was scared. She needed me. Sweat beaded on her brow and trailed down her face like tears. The boys had not moved.

...they had not moved? Huh? Alessandra put hoods over their heads but they could still hear. I tore my eyes away from Angie and looked at her brother. Something nagged the back of my brain, that prickle in my mind that showed up along with Eris and magic.

Ric wavered like a reflection in water.

Something was wrong.

I spotted a small sphere under his chair, the same kind of object Manny clutched in his hand on my doorstep.

"They're not here," I blurted out.

All the heads in the room turned to me. Except "Ric" and "Jin-Wei."

Eris raised an eyebrow at me. Alessandra gestured with her gun and the others crept closer to me.

"They're illusions," I said as I backed away. "You never meant to play square with us."

"This one is real though," She shoved Angie and stalked forward. A predator grin spread across her face. "And the boss only needs Eris alive. Said nothing about you."

I backed up against the bar. Nowhere left to go. I reached back and grabbed a bottle. It was open. I jammed a cocktail napkin in it and lit it with the

Hephaestus' lighter from my back pocket. The bluish alcohol flame would not last long.

Alessandra laughed. It would have been a pleasant sound if she was not trying to kill me.

"I am The Shipbreaker! A goddess born of the ocean and sea. What makes you think a flame will save you?"

"This is the fire of Mount Olympus," I held out the improvised Malotov. "I'm sure it will do something."

I slammed the flame down between us. The godfire spread across the floor and ate the old wooden boards. Alessandra jumped back. She turned back to Angie and fired off a shot.

Time stretched as I reached for that magic in my blood. The wards sucked away my power. Time lurched forward a half moment. I jumped over the flame and hipchecked the wolfish fucker out of my way.

My blood burned.

Time lurched in a staccato pattern as it slipped through my grip. I saw the bullet in the air. I saw Angie look death in the face. The air pulled at me. Time felt like pushing through wet concrete.

Time moved. The bullet blurred. Angie closed her eyes and turned her head. I grabbed at time. It burned like hellfire from within. I reached for Angie. Time stopped one last time. The bullet kissed the side of her neck.

I tackled her as I lost my hold on time. We went down in a tangle of limbs. The bullet shattered a window behind us letting in a rush of air, feeding the flames. The building was engulfed faster than any mortal flame. Distant shouting was drowned out by the roar of the fire. The air, not magic, burned my lungs now.

Stoptime was out of my reach. The wards in the floor burned away and could not strangle my power anymore, but I had nothing left to give.

We were going to die.

I held my best friend tight, the closest family I had left. She said something to me I could not hear over the rush of the flames and the dive bar dying around us. Didn't matter. The sound of her voice was a good thing to die to even if I did not know the words.

"I'm so sorry," I had no idea if she could hear me either. "I'm sorry for all of this."

Apologies were good words to end on.

Something grabbed my arm and pulled me away. Fuck that, I was done. I tried to shake it away.

"No! Hades will not take you today."

Eris dragged us out of a fire exit in the back of the building. Behind the LA Tavern, rough gravel bit at my singed body. The goddess of chaos collapsed to her knees. Angie looked up to the sky and gulped down the cool air muttering praises in Spanish. Sirens called out in the distance. The West Warwick Fire Department was not far. My burned hands made getting up a struggle.

We got to the car and obeyed every speed limit on our way out like a rubbernecking local as the first firetruck rolled up flanked by the cops.

Chapter 18 – Eris

I drove. Giulia was in no condition to do it herself and Angie sprawled across the backseat of the Benz. In truth, I was not in better condition than either of them. With the tourniquet around my touch to primal chaos, the melee with Wodanaz's underlings left me drained. Taking a circular, chaos 'chosen' route around the city fed my reserves by a small amount and took the edge of the shakes. No one appeared to be following us when I parked the car behind Giulia's building.

Annona, thank Nyx for her soul, had arrived while we were gone. She was in triage mode before anyone of us said a word. She sat the three of us down on the futon with Giulia in the middle. I was glad to let her. I put my hand out on Giulia's lap. She tried to twine her fingers with mine, but winced at the burn.

"Where's Manny?" Giulia asked.

"Upstairs. Sleeping." Annona rooted through one of the half dozen suitcases she had piled in the middle of the floor. She pulled out three small bottles, each the size of an energy shot.

"Annona, she does not know about our world."

My Roman friend looked Giulia in the eye.

"Bullshit. You told me herself she is a Paladin of Chaos," Annona said. "You know I'm not blind to Greek magic. It pours out of her."

I shook my head. "Not her."

We both turned to Angie. She had the open mouth look of disbelief I saw a thousand times since the world abandoned the old gods. I felt a pang of sadness for the simpler times five millennia ago every time I saw that look.

"Oh." Annona at least had the decency to look chagrinned. "Well, time to learn." She pressed a bottle into each of our hands. "Bottoms up folks."

I unscrewed the cap and tossed mine back straightaway. The warm restorative spread through my belly.

Giulia and Angie eyed theirs suspiciously.

"Smells like rancid Red Bull," Angie said.

Annona gave Angie a look. She pointed at the drink. "Magic healing potion." Then she went around the group starting with herself, "Roman goddess. Greek goddess. Magical holy paladin for said Greek goddess."

Angie did not look relieved. I frowned at my gruff friend.

"Come on," Giulia said. "These can't be worse than some of the dive bar rotgut shots we've had over the years." Giulia drank her healing potion. After a moment Angie followed suit.

"I... I feel wonderful," Angie said. "What the hell is going on?"

"We are-"

"Wait." Giulia interrupted me. "I'll explain. I just... want to do it myself." She pulled her friend to her feet and took her aside.

Left alone with Annona, she pulled me to my feet into a hug. "Are you ok?"

I nodded. "I am not at full strength but I will be ok for the moment. Did you bring the vestments?"

Annona nudged the pile of suitcases with the toe of her boot. "Yup. Plus some other stuff I had kicking around the office and could pack up quick."

I started to feel human thanks to the healing potion. This posed a problem being a goddess. The draught left an aftertaste and I made a face. "Druidic restoratives leave much to be desired in taste."

Annona shrugged. "Best I could do on short notice. Iron druid owed me a favor. Those were the only three he had on hand."

"I want you to know how much I appreciate this, Annona. I know how tough it is for you to leave your city."

The Roman turned away and found something to fuss with in her pile of luggage. "Yeah. Well. DC isn't my real city. This country stopped calling it Rome, Maryland long ago. And Americans-" she still said the word like she had not seen the country's independence first hand, "-aren't big on the real details of history."

She stopped fussing with the luggage.

"Is it really that bad, Eris?"

"I-"

"Be honest. You haven't touched your sword since 1852. I lugged it around for you since Civil War and it's been gathering dust in my closet since that time Discord tried to steal in in '79."

"It is-"

"Because if you're in that much trouble we could skip town. Back to DC. Maine's not far. New York. Illinois. Oregon. This country has eighteen different Romes. Or we could... we could go back to Italy." Annona turned away from me again. "I'd do it. If you need me to."

I reached out to my friend.

"I could not put you through that much pain."

"But we could still just go. I can call in some more favors. We can fix your power. We could go to Greece. I'll take you up Olympus myself. We can go straight to Nyx and get this sorted out."

I shook my head.

"I would be tolerated on Olympus. You would not."

"I don't give a fuck, Eris! I don't want you to face this trouble alone. Don't play the game Wodanaz and that lapdog of his want you to play. Let's bug out. Change the rules. Bring in some allies. Play on our terms. What in Jupiter's name is keeping you here?"

My head turned to Giulia. Across the room, she talked with her hands while Angie sat in disbelief. Like a jump cut in a bad movie edit, Giulia winked out of sight and reappeared five feet to her left. Angie must have needed proof. That she jumped between moments of time without me seeing it showed how low on primal chaos my body was.

"It's London all over again." Annona said it as fact, not a question.

"It's more than that. I made her, Annona. She is not merely touched by elemental chaos. She is not some holy paladin. The blood flows through her. Giulia is a demigoddess in her own right. Now. Because of me."

"How?"

I rolled up my sleeve and unwound the bandage over the now mangled hex carved in my arm. "Celtic magic, in part. Sever the knot and…" I shrugged with my good arm. "It partially worked. I bled a lot."

Annona winced. "And the ambrosia of a primal deity punches quite a kick."

I nodded. "I should have been careful about leaving it. Living in hiding in this modern age… Annona, I miss the simpler times. When we were young we could have laughed it off and passed around another amphora of wine."

Her hand reached out to mine. "Then what happened to Giulia?" she whispered.

I shook my head again. "I am not certain. Hermes found her near death. He sensed the ambrosia flowing in her veins and sought me out. She has a Golden Apple birthmark that appeared suddenly one day."

"Take her with us. Present her to Zeus. Present her to your mother. Go to Greece and tell the last of your Discordian priests they have a new goddess in their pantheon. Draw strength from this and-"

"While we rest on our laurels, Wodanaz kills her kin," I said.

"And they can be avenged! But not if you fall to his hand too."

We took a long look at Giulia. She sat now with Angie.

My phone started ringing, a local Rhode Island number I did not recognize. The buzzing piece of technology was insistent.

"I'm going to go upstairs and check on that other kid. Dr. Augusti still makes house calls." Annona put a hand on my shoulder as she walked by. "I'm with you whatever you decide."

I nodded and felt undeserving of four hundred years of friendship.

Left mostly to myself, the phone kept buzzing away in my hand. I rolled my eyes. I hated the damn things. I took the call.

"Eris," the voice on the other end said.

"Wodanaz. How did you get this number?"

He laughed and I could picture the arrogance on his face. "*Mien ketzchen*, some of us have embraced the benefits of technology beyond mere phone calls. There is this wondrous thing known as Google."

Point. But I was not about to let him know that.

"I have no reason to continue this conversation any-"

"We can end our confrontation once and for all, Eris."

I looked at the phone with my thumb halfway to the 'End Call' button. I looked over at Giulia huddled with Angie and felt an ache in my heart.

"How?" I whispered in the phone.

"Ah. See? That was not so hard. There is no need for any more hostilities."

"Fuck your hostilities, Wodanaz. You started this."

"*Nein*. Those who have forgotten us started this."

"Oh please, we have too much of a history for you to pull the wool over my eyes," I snapped. "I am not some new thing like your lapdog Andrea Alessandra."

"And our history is the only reason I have held back, Eris," he countered.

"It has been centuries. Move on."

Wodanaz ignored that. "Come back to me, Eris. Come back for the sake of the cause. We are going to bring humanity back in touch with the real world. Remind them what they have forgotten when they relegated us all to the realm of myth."

"Humanity has moved on without us. Why have you not accepted that?"

"Said by someone who still has priests and followers," Wodanaz said. "Oh, your *Principe Discordia* and that little cadre of followers has not gone unnoticed, small as they are. You have *something*. School children learn of your pantheon in their textbooks. How would you like to be a footnote of an index of a book that has not been read in a decade? We have nothing!

"Nothing! Eris, I watched my last devotee die in my arms a millennia ago. You sneer at my ally, but Ms. Alessandra has been lacking the devotion of her single follower for years. You have never felt that hole in your heart, Eris. Help us. With our power together we can bring the myths of humanity back to life. We will take the best things civilization has created and rededicate their successes to us."

"Save your silver tongue for someone who can still be swayed," I said. "You called me. Tell me the terms it takes to end this feud."

"Ah. So be it," Wodanaz said. "Business it is. I require a source of chaos magic for my... plans to come into fruition.".

"What is this plan?"

"Ah ah ah," Wodanaz scolded. "Yours is not to wonder why, yours is merely to do. If you do not wish to truly join our cause, then you do not need to know. Just provide us with a source of chaos energy at our nexus of ley lines and be done with it."

His arrogance reminded me why I left him centuries ago. I desired nothing more than to hang up on him, but I thought of Giulia.

"Fine," I said through grated teeth. "I will play the role of a battery in your little scheme-"

"Excellent."

"-on the following conditions."

"You do not trust me?"

"Ha! I have not trusted you since the days of DaVinci."

Wodanaz sighed. "Very well."

"First, you release your two mortal hostages."

"Done. They were nothing more than means to an end."

"Second, no reprisals. Vendetta is null and void for all of your sect."

"Come now Eris, do you think so little off me?"

The silence stretched for a long moment.

"Fine," Wodanaz said. "Agreed. What else? This list is beginning to lengthen."

"My 'participation' is restricted to twenty four hours, regardless of any success you may have in awakening the world." Immortals treated time different than mortals, but I had doubts my patience with Wodanaz would last even that long. I wanted this *parlez*-and-play over and done with before Giulia or Annona could disapprove.

"*Nien*. My time table cannot be accelerated that much."

"Then we are at a standstill. I cannot think of any valid reason you need me in your presence for any longer."

"Very well, *meine Chaosgöttin*," he said. "Before we bid each other *guten abend*, please, tell me where I shall have Ms. Alessandra deliver the bodies of the hostages?"

"...no."

"No? Ah, I thought it would be a small courtesy among peers. No matter. They shall find their end in the bottom of Narragansett Bay with all the dead Mafioso."

"I swear if you kill either one of them-"

"You'll what, *mien ketzchen*? You do not have any leverage on me while these humans clearly mean something to you. You are sentimental in your old age, Chaos," he sneered.

"I shall do it," I whispered into the phone.

"Seven days."

"Three. No more, regardless of the outcome of your scheme."

"*Ja*. Agreed. I will send you the location where Ms. Alessandra will be with a car. You leave immediately."

"You are a whore-spawn bastard, Wodanaz."

He tsk-tsk'd me. "Homer's tales of the destruction you reaped on Troy are legendary. I have seen you slay dozens by your hand without breaking a sweat. A pair of nothings in my possession and you wilt like a flower in an early snow."

I hung up on Wodanaz.

I took a long gaze at Giulia.

"They are not nothing to her."

Chapter 19 – Giulia

"I still don't believe it," Angie shook her head.

I shrugged at her. "You think it's weird for you? Try living it up here," I tapped on my own forehead. "I barely feel human at this point. Fuck, I dunno if I am anymore."

Angie got to her feet and paced about. "This flies in the face of … everything!" Her accent got heavy when she was agitated with me. If I pissed her off more, she'd slip into Spanish without realizing it.

"We both had one of those magic healing drinks."

"Herbal remedy. Blue Red Bull."

"You heard Annona. And Eris."

"They're delusional."

"You think I'm delusional, don't you?"

Angie looked away.

"You saw me blink across the room with stoptime, Angie." I grabbed hold of the strands of time. With my friend frozen in front of me, I took three steps to the right and let time flow around me again. "I just did it again."

She squeezed her eyes shut. "Head trauma. Post traumatic stress. Hell, present traumatic stress."

I grabbed hold of Angie's hand and dragged her between the seconds with me. "Damnit, just look."

"This could be anything," she said. Angie looked around the room, but made no move to snatch her hand back. Our voices fell flat in the dead air of stoptime. "The room looks exactly the same."

I led her up the spiral stairs. Our boots on the wrought iron sounds like muffled carpet.

"Congestion," Angie said under her breath. "Head injury could mess up sound too."

My feet led us through my flat to where Eris' friend had Manny laid out on my bed. Toastmaster, my appliance turned cat courtesy of Eris, curled up beside him. If Manny was out cold or just sleeping it off, I could not tell. Annona hovered over him, motionless in stoptime.

I snapped my fingers in front of Annona's face. Nothing.

Angie frowned. She waved her hand in front of the Roman. No reaction.

"See?" I pleaded. "Don't you believe me now?"

Angie scrunched her face up and bit her lip. She nodded.

I still felt like shit warmed over from throwing down at the bar and then bugging out, so letting go of time felt like a bucket of cool water down my spine.

"*Filius canis*!" Annona flailed into my side table. Accumulated clutter crashed to the floor. Manny stirred in unconsciousness. The cat opened one eye, mildly annoyed at its nap being bothered.

I winced. "Sorry."

"Appearing out of nowhere. Jupiter's balls, woman." Annona checked over Manny, then herself, and collected up some items that fell on the floor when we dropped out of stoptime. "Liable to give me a heart attack and this far away from Rome... I'd make you shlep across the Styx and drag me back out."

I must have had a look on my face. Annona sighed.

"Look, not all of us feed off the primal forces of nature. Fire, water, wind, chaos-" she gestured to me "-and et cetera et cetera. I am the goddess of the annual Roman grain tax. We're a very thorough pantheon. I thrive in Rome. We are not in Rome, ergo, you could actually give me a heart attack sneaking up on a woman like that."

"Eris said you were from DC."

Annona huffed. "It was called Rome Maryland when I moved there in 1748. It counts as far as I am concerned."

A half hearted squalk came from Angie. We both turned to her.

"I just... I can't even." She turned on her heel back through the rest of my flat.

"Angie wait," I followed after her into the kitchen.

"Look," Annona said. "I'm sorry this is a shock. Most people, it messes with their head to get the truth dumped on them so much. There's just so much going on and you're knee deep in it anyways..." She trailed off with a shrug.

Angie ignored us both as she stood on a chair at my cupboards and reached into the back of the highest shelf. She hopped back to the floor with a dusty pack of Marlboros and a lighter. She tapped one out and lit up.

"I thought you quit and-"

She held up a hand to stop. Angie leaned against my counter with her eyes closed and savored a long drag. She exhaled with a huff and waved the smoke away from her head.

"Don't look at me like that, Giulia. I know about that fifth of cheap whiskey under the corner of your mattress. This isn't any different."

"Extenuating circumstances," I said.

"Goddamn right." Angie took another long drag. When she exhaled this time, she looked at the ember and shook her head like she was disgusted with herself.

"We are still in crisis mode," Annona said. "I didn't leave my city for the first time in forty years just for fun. Once we solve the immediate problem-"

"Getting my brother and Jin-Wei back," Angie interrupted.

Annona nodded in her direction. "Once we save them, I will be happy to stick around with Eris and help show you the ropes. One problem at a time, however. My city wasn't built in a day."

"Where is she?" Angie blurted out, looking from me to Annona and back. "Where's Eris?"

I had a bad feeling about this. I hustled to the door back down to the practice space.

"She was on the phone," Annona said.

I leaned over the railing, but there was no one down there. I clattered down the stairs and burst out in the hallway. One of my neighbors was out in the hall moving some boxes, but no Eris.

"Oi! Lydia! You seen anyone leave here?"

"Couple minutes ago," She gestured down the hall. "Went out the back way."

I ran past her and burst out the door on the loading dock. Eris' car was gone.

I sagged in defeat and plodded back inside. Why? Why the hell would she bug out like that? What did I do? Did I do anything? What she pissed at saving my ass like that? Was I some sort of liability to her? Was it just some cosmic whim that said 'Fuck her silly, change her life, then leave her hanging?'

Back inside the practice space, Angie had to call my name three times before I managed to look up. She was huddled around a piece of paper with Annona.

"She left a note," Angie said between hits of her cigarette.

Giulia, I am sorry. You do not deserve this. Letters scrawled out on a page are insufficient for what you have already endured and what lays on the path before you. I want nothing more than to show you that path myself.

But I cannot be responsible for causing you any more strife, Giulia. Wodanaz offered an end to this, an end that will get your kin back safe. I had to take it. Alone. Please forgive me.

I will be back as soon as I can, then we can put this behind us and carry onward together.

-Eris

At the bottom of the note was a hasty line of Greek letters.

"What does that part say?"

Annona hesitated.

I held up my smart phone. "We can just run it through a translate app."

"Eris always forgets what computers can do," Annona said with a sigh. "She hates the damn things. Used to be few and far between in the States if anyone knew what to make of a string of Greek letters."

I pointed to the letters again.

"All right, all right. She asked me to make sure you don't follow her."

"Do you know where she went?"

Annona shook her head. "Not in the least. I've never even been to Rhode Island before. Without a GPS, I can get back to the airport. Maybe."

"What do we do then?" Angie asked.

"Wait it out," Annona shrugged. "And hope Eris knows what she's doing."

Chapter 20 – Eris

At a Park-N-Ride lot, just off Route 4, I waited, per the instructions Wodanaz texted to me after our phone call. I second guessed my decision to walk over to Wodanaz's side. I felt like satyr shit just for spending the precious little chaos energy left in my cells on making a decision at all. The tattoos on my wrists tingled. The waves of primal chaos wanted to make a 'decision' for me.

I refused to look.

I leaned against the hood of my car when Andrea Alessandra drove up in a Lincoln.

The back door opened.

"Get in."

I was left alone in the back. I could barely see Alessandra through a tinted privacy screen. The windows were darkened enough that I could not see where I was being driven to. I put my hand to the window and felt the light buzz of magic. I could not place the type. Wodanaz had done me the courtesy of not sending his goons to toss me in the trunk again, but the ride was going to get boring fast.

I rapped on the privacy screen.

"Where are we going?"

Alessandra said nothing.

"Must we play this game? I am going to help your cause-"

"Under duress."

"Point. But we can be civil."

She was silent again.

I sat back in the leather seat and thought about dozing off.

"It will help you too," Alessandra blurted out. "What Wodanaz is trying to do. It will help all of the forgotten gods and spirits."

"Wodanaz is out for Wodanaz," I told her. "The sooner you realize that, the sooner you can get his hooks out of you. His obsession changed him long ago, and obsessions rarely do one any good."

Alessandra huffed at me. "You're not the first Greek I've known to scoff at something you've never known. The world still knows about your kind. You don't know what we've been through. You haven't been forgotten."

"I have lived a long time," I said. "Try me."

We rode the rest of the way in silence.

Andrea Alessandra let me out of the car in front of a cliffside estate with Atlantic waves crashing below. I guessed Newport. The Caribbean took a deep breath of the ocean air. She rolled the tension out of her shoulders and seemed more aloof near her natural environment.

I followed her through the estate. It was posh, with a 'I'm new money pretending to be old money' sense of style. We passed muscle near the door. The *oborot* that normally followed Alessandra around glowered at me. He looked singed around the edges. I gave him a cheeky wink. A couple people in lab coats buzzed across the foyer and disappeared through a closed door. Stairs took us up to Wodanaz's office. I entered alone.

Lair was a better word for the monstrosity of a room Wodanaz sat in. Dark wood paneled the walls like an old hunting lodge. Around the room, specimens sat under bell jars. Centaur hoof. Wizard's wand. Imhotep's eye. A pixie mounted to a board like a butterfly. Dead magic in this lair from a dozen other sources displayed as trophies surrounded me. Wodanaz sat behind a walnut desk the size of a Buick with his spear laid across the top. Floor to ceiling windows behind him looked out to the sea.

He stood from his desk and came around towards me. I stopped in the middle of the room.

"So good of you to finally come around," he said. Wodanaz spread his arms. I laid one finger on his chest and kept him at arm's length with a shake of my head.

"Not even for old time's sake?" he asked. "Pity."

He paced back to his desk and leaned against the front edge.

"Let us be about our business, Wodanaz."

"Come now, *mien ketzchen*, we should have a drink to commemorate our rekindled understanding. I keep a fully stocked sidebar," he gestured to a cabinet next to a shriveled foot under a bell jar. "Whiskey. Wine.

Alas, I have not a drop of ouzo but if you would like, I shall have Andrea send someone out."

"There is nothing 'rekindled' about us. If you think any such thoughts, then you left your sanity back in the Renaissance with your good sense."

The German thunder god frowned. "Andrea said you had a new lover."

I spat at his feet. "By the darkest corner of Tartarus' pit, you are dense. My affairs are none of your business and have not been in hundreds of years. You hound me like a scorned child and you think you can just- have two thousand years on earth taught you nothing?" I spat again for good measure. "Fool."

I turned on my heel to leave. "To Hades darkest realm with you, Wodanaz. Find some other way to resolve this."

"Halt."

I looked over my shoulder. Wodanaz held his spear in hand, level with my heart. It did not waver.

"A source of chaos magic for my plans was no ruse, Eris. However, those with your affinity tend to be... flighty."

With care, I fully turned back to face Wodanaz. The double door exit was at my back. I kept my hands open where he could see them.

"Our shared history," he said "meant I was able to find you with much less effort. Though, with the headache you have caused me, it is barely worth the trouble in retrospect."

"Your pocket Celt with the divination device."

"*Ja, gut.* It was not easy to find a stray hair of Chaos to act as a focus. I had to track down our old haunts in Venice. Or it was *sehr gut* until you ran her down." Wodanaz gestured with his free hand. "There is still power in her tattoos. She has not gone to waste."

A druid's tattoos, flayed from her body and mounted in a frame, hung on Wodanaz's trophy wall. A Celt dedicated to Gaia was inked from hand to shoulder to hip to the soles of her feet.

I shook my head. "When did you become so cruel?"

"When did you become soft?" he snapped.

"I faced her in battle. You were her ally."

"I do what I must for the cause! And now that you are here, you will do the same."

Wodanaz put his hand into his pocket. I tensed. He took out a phone and spoke into it. "It time."

The door behind my right shoulder opened immediately. Andrea Alessandra and a lanky lab tech entered the room.

"What is-"

"Quiet, Eris." Wodanaz gestured with his spear. "Get on with it Bodul."

The tech uncoiled wire leads attached to a medical scanner. He stepped forward and I narrowed my eyes him. Bodul hesitated, but Wodanaz's spear point stayed my hand as he attached the round pads to my neck, temple, and wrist. An awkward cough stuck in the back of his throat. He held up the fourth lead.

"I... erm... it goes over your heart."

I snatched it from him and put the lead under my shirt myself.

Wodanaz propped the butt of his spear in the plush carpet and leaned on it, watching the proceedings with a shit eating grin. It took an effort to keep my anger off my face. That I was sure he knew my effort made things worse.

Bodul's device whirred and clacked. It made tiny electronic sounds of protest.

"Mr. Wodanaz. Sir. It... um... it's no good."

"Ha," a bark of laughter escaped my lips. "Modern technology relies too much on Order to mesh well with the presence of pure Chaos."

Bodul shook his head. "No. Mr. Wodanaz, the energy scanner works just fine. The readings are..."

"Well, man, spit it out," Wodanaz said.

Andrea Alessandra leaned over Bodul's shoulder. "They're almost nil, Boss."

"What?"

"Eris barely has any magic in her."

I peeled off Bodul's monitors and pushed my shirt sleeve up. The ruinous tattoo and the jagged scar through it swelled red and raw. "And it was your doing."

Wodanaz raged. He threw the phone he held in one hand at the mounted druid skin. The glass case spiderwebbed. "If I had not already skinned that sorry excuse for a druid alive, I would do so again. I should pull her soul back from Tir Na Nog and rip the flesh from her body all over again!" Wodanaz lapsed into Old

High German curses. The guttural words echoed through the room.

Bodul cowered. Alessandra let a frown cross her face.

"Now what?" I asked.

Wodanaz pulled his spear out from the wall. "You," he pointed to Bodul. "Go prep a containment laboratory. She is still beholden to us."

Bodul was all too happy to leave.

"I am not beholden to you, Wodanaz. Our agreement is not null and void simply because whatever plan you have up your sleeve will fail to execute."

The German turned and threw his spear. True to his own mythos, his aim held true and without a strong touch ofmy primal chaos, there was nothing I could do.

His spear, the icon of his godhood, pierced my arm, split the bones in my wrist and nailed me to the solid oak door behind me.

A fire like I had not felt in centuries burned through my soul. My knees gave out. My shoulder wretched around. I screamed. The spear would not let me fall.

"I shall kill you," I spat out through clenched teeth. "By my holy mother Nyx, your immortal days are numbered."

Wodanaz sauntered by and gave his spear a shake. I screamed and clawed at the shaft holding my wrist in place. Bones cracked. Ambrosia bled from my veins. Flowed down my arm to the floor.

I gasped at air. I felt the first tremor of shock in my muscles.

The German went to a display case and withdrew an obsidian knife. He crouched down eye level with me.

I tried to stand but my strength was sapped. I slipped in my own ambrosia. A scream tore through my lungs again.

"This blade is older than me. It is older than you." He held up the jagged thing in front of me but I could barely focus on it. "Prehistoric nomads from the tundra of Siberia carved this from living rock."

He twirled the blade in his hands. The light caught the polished surface. Breathing became a struggle.

"It was buried with the honored dead and consecrated to their god. A god forgotten before you or I were even a passing thought. A god dead and gone. I will not befall the same fate."

The knife slashed down in Wodanaz's hand. I felt the hellfires of Olympus burn through my arm as I fell to the floor. My cheek pressed to the floor. I saw my hand tumble away without my arm.

A shard of cold spread through me. Chased the flames away. My muscles shook with shock.

"Take her to the labs, Andrea," I heard through the sounds of my immortal body failing. "Pry out whatever magic is left within that husk."

Chapter 21 – Giulia

The beer in front of me tasted of ashes and abandonment. The label said it was an IPA so it should have tasted like hops and deliciousness. The carbonation burned the back of my throat as I drank it much too fast then pushed the empty away from me.

"Extenuating circumstances," Angie said and passed me another.

I nodded at my friend and started on the next beer. Ashes and abandonment again. I did not bother to turn the bottle around to read the label. Angie stuffed the cigarette butt into the empty IPA bottle and lit up another.

We sat in the companionable silence of lifelong friends. Annona looked relieved to have something to do with her hands when Angie finally passed her a beer too.

"Why did she go like that?" I said.

I only realized I spoke aloud when Annona answered me.

"Friendship with Eris can be... difficult." Annona sighed and took a long drink. "It takes a lot of understanding. She comes off as flighty. Or uncaring. Or a bitch. Or a flake. It's her nature. She doesn't mean it. She is chaos. Not a damn thing Eris can do about that. You just have to ask yourself if you can accept it."

I stared at my drink.

"How did you meet?" Angie asked the Roman at the table. She saved me the awkwardness of having anything to say.

"My city. My real city, the one true Rome, before there were any pale copies here in America," the goddess at my kitchen table said. "Most of my pantheon left the immortal city for other parts of the Empire with the rise of the Christians. My power flows from the city itself. I could not just up and leave like my kintoa. There was… unpleasantness and Eris helped me escape to my new city. That was over three hundred years ago."

"If she walked out on you after three hundred years without a fucking word, I never had a chance."

"Stop that right now. Right fucking now," Annona said. "Eris is the most loyal person I have ever known. When my own Roman kin left me behind without a thought, she is the only one who gave a damn. She cannot change what she is. You can accept it and deal without predjustice or you can fuck right off."

"Why did she leave then? She changed my life. She changed me! And then she left."

"The note said she'll be back," Angie said. Annona and me turned to my friend with the cigarette. She exhaled and a haze rose up above us. "We have to trust Eris knows what she's doing."

"And if the whims of Chaos push her in a bad direction?" I asked.

"If it does, it is not her own doing. Eris is a survivor," Annona said. "All of us old timers are. Eris is loyal. She keeps her promises, even if they don't always take shape the way you think."

"I just feel like-"

The beer bottle dropped from my hand. Slipped through my fingers like they weren't even there.

A scream ripped through me.

A burning cold slashed through my hand. The frostfire feeling stole my sense. I fell to the floor cradling my hand.

Angie and Annona rushed to me. Their words blurred in my head, drowned out by the pain.

They manhandled me to the couch. I wailed anytime they came near my left arm.

Annona appeared in my vision with a needle clenched in her teeth looking for a vein in my good arm.

Angie reached out to stop her. "What the fuck kind of magic is that?"

The goddess swatted her out of the way. "Fucking morphine. Get out of the way so I can save her."

I never felt the needle. A warm medicinal blanket was thrown over my mind. I gasped at the air.

"My hand. I barely feel it."

"That's the morphine, hun." Angie held me and looked into my eyes. "Annona is full of tricks. You're gonna feel warm and fuzzy for a while."

I shook my head. The world spun. Morphine was not as fun as alcohol. "No. My hand. I don't feel it." The morphine caught up to the two beers and my words felt fuzzy in my mouth. "I can't feel my hand. Like it's not there."

My eyelids got heavy and the world faded out.

...

"-so cold. Like dead flesh on the end of her wrist and-"

...

"Still a pulse. Barely. The rest of her-"

...

"-no fucking idea what to do-"

...

I woke up to a ginger tabby breathing in my face. Toastmaster's breath smelled of burned crumbs. I shooed them away and sat up. Coming down off morphine felt just as shitty as a hangover but without my mouth tasting like the underside of a toilet bowl. Bonus?

My loft was lit by one dim lamp from across the room and the sodium orange glow of street lights spilling in the windows. Angie sat by my feet on the couch. Annona sprawled out in the armchair with a slight snore. Angie startled awake when I moved. She nudged Annona awake with the toe of her boot.

"You alright?" my best friend asked.

I made a fist with my left hand. "Sort of. I guess. Feels like pins and needles. Slow to move." There was a perfect pink line circling my wrist, a scar bracelet sore to the touch. I tried to rub the sleep out of my eyes. "How long was I out?"

"Few hours," Angie said. "Took Manny home while you were out. Annona patched him up. He'll be ahite."

I nodded thanks. Didn't need any more on my conscious.

"So what happened?" Annona asked. "Scared the shit out of us."

"Eris," I said just above a whisper. "She's in trouble."

"That's like me telling you Jupiter shits lightning bolts," Annona gave me a look. "Rather obvious."

"Really?" Angie said. "Lightning poop sounds unpleasant and not at all obvious."

"Swear to the Big Man himself. Had to source special indoor plumbing for him and it's not like the word 'plumber' had even been invented back when-"

"Listen damnit!" I shouted.

The other two stopped. Annona had the decency to look chagrined. Angie crossed her arms at me.

"Eris is in trouble," I repeated louder. "This-" I flopped my near dead hand in front of me "-is an echo of what happened to her."

"How?" Angie's one word was all business.

"I don't fucking know, some Luke Skywalker jedi bullshit. It's like bad feedback or some shit."

Angie turned to Annona and raised an eyebrow.

The Roman shrugged. "Not my flavor of magic."

Angie nodded. "So what do we do?"

I shook my head. "I. I have to do this."

"Fuck that, Giulia. We. We do this together." Angie stabbed her cigarette in the air at me. "You're not some knight in shining armor to go running off on some King Arthur Bravehart fucking Schwarzenegger quest."

I stood up and pushed the butt away. A wisp of smoke trailed after it.

I grabbed hold of stoptime and popped back into the timestream behind her. "I've got her blood in me. I am the Paladin of Chaos, so yeah, sounds like it's my quest to me."

She spun around and grabbed hold of my wrist before I could stoptime around her again. The scar on my near dead hand burned under her grasp.

"It's my brother and my lover trapped with her. We don't even know if they're alive anymore. I have to go."

"I couldn't live with myself if you got hurt too."

"Neither could I."

We were silent for a long heartbeat. Angie's eyes never wavered from mine.

"Ok then," Annona clapped her hands. "Three of us going to save three of them. I'd say it was Fate, but the Fates are a bitch and won't have a single thing to do with Team Chaos."

I turned to Annona. Angie got as far as opening her mouth.

"Don't. Don't argue. At least I'm immortal. Mostly."

I let out a huff and stalked to the kitchen. Two pair of footsteps followed in my wake.

"What's the plan, oh noble paladin?" Angie said.

I pulled a bottle of Jager out of my freezer. "Extenuating circumstances." I poured a shot in the bottom of a pint glass and knocked it back. "We need information."

Angie looked to Annona. "Is there any goddess hoodoo that you can do?"

She shrugged. "We're outside my new Rome. Wodanaz would know better than to bring her to DC. I'd know in an instant. I could make some calls but I'm out of my element here. Literally. Figuratively. Strategically. Spiritually. Metaphorically. Magically."

"Eris said something about an Oracle," I said.

"Old time prophecies? Like in Delphi?" Angie asked.

Annona shook her head. "Like in Massachusetts. Oracles are cryptic at best. They're not for the urgent."

"Last resort then," Angie said.

We lapsed into silence. Annona took a great interest in my floor tiles. Angie watched the ash burn on her cigarette butt. I watched Toastmaster the cat saunter into the kitchen and sniff about a can of tuna someone left out for him. Her? I realized I didn't know. Toasters didn't have gender and I figured it'd be rude to ask Toastmaster to start having one upon becoming a cat.

An idea came to me before my thought train derailed too far. My stomach turned at the thought. Or maybe that was the Jaeger. Or maybe there wasn't enough Jaeger in me.

"Annona," I started slow. "Who is that wing sandal motherfucker? I caught a glimpse of him? Her? Whoever. Caught a glimpse when my... change happened."

"My wing sandal motherfucker is Mercury." She shook her head. "Pretentious sack of wooly pubes. You're wing sandal motherfucker is Hermes."

"Could he help?"

"Could he? Sure. He's a messenger god. Psychopomp. Finding people is what he does. Would he? Eris is the only Greek to ever give me the time of day."

"Do you know anyone who could get a hold of him?" Angie asked.

Annona shrugged.

"I know how." I took the cold bottle of Jaeger and poured half a pint into the glass. The fingers on my left hand barely felt the frosty bottle. I chugged half the licorice liquor in one go. My stomach turned and I felt a rush to my head.

"The hell are you doing?" Angie reached to take the Jaeger but I stepped back, closer to Annona.

"I saw Hermes." My tongue felt fuzzy already. I drank more before I could convince myself the whole idea was fucking idiotic. "When I turned into... whatever I am now. He came to me. Found me. Over there." I pointed to my bathroom.

"What does that have to do with getting drunk?"

I slid down the counter until the sink full of silverware was at my back. "I got Eris' blood in me."

Angie gave me that big sister look. She knew I was stalling.

I turned and faced the sink. "Eris' blood almost killed me. When it got in me. When it made me into this. Hermes was gonna take my soul away. It's what he does. So I need this," I chugged the rest of the Jaeger and put the glass in the sink. "Because I know how bad this will hurt."

Angie lunged at me and stopped as I fell between the seconds of time. Half a bottle of Jaeger and fucking magic hit me like roundhouse to the side of the head. The world fell. Or I did. I took a deep breath. Opened my eyes wide like that'd help being drunk. Held onto the sink for dear life. Or balance.

Picked a steak knife outta my sink and squinted at the pizza stains on the blade. Whatever. I slashed my thumb open.

Delayed reaction.

Blood seeped all over my hand before the dull ache hit me. Crimson blood and the honey gold of ambrosia mixed into an amber liquid that came from my veins. Should hurt more, I thought, looks pretty now though. I turned to Annona. 'Bout to hurt a lot more, I thought back to myself.

Annona caught on slower than Angie. She didn't move before I stopped time.

"Sorry for this."

I took the knife covered in my blood and pressed the metal to Annona's thumb. It pierced her skin. The

Roman ambrosia in her veins was sluggish in stoptime and a richer yellow color.

I clasped my bleeding hand to hers.

And let go of my hold on time.

No power in the universe could stop my screaming.

Chapter 22 – Eris

"Be calm, my child. All is not lost."

"Mother?"

Out of the darkness and turmoil in my mind's eye, a figure cloaked in the purest black of creation took shape in front of me. Primal Nyx threw back her hood. I looked the most like Mother of all her children, a mirror image save her fair skin, never to have seen the sun since before such a thing existed. I saw her eyes, black orbs offering a glimpse into the pure Void. She took my right hand, my only hand now, in hers.

Even on the dreamscape my left hand was missing. I shied that arm away from Mother.

"You have faced a long trial, daughter, but your salvation is near."

The hope in my heart flared for a moment and crumbled away. I turned my head from her. "Aloof platitudes do not help me. Even you, with all your power, cannot know what the Fates have in store for me. The very nature of the existence you gave me means no immortal nor divine can ever know."

A diffuse light rose around us. The black of the Void faded to inky blue to dusky grey. Mother faded with the Night.

"It is not your fate I watch, dearest Eris."

I tumbled out of the dreamscape.

"Who do you see?" I shouted to Mother.

A surgeon's lamp glared in my eyes. A laboratory tech sheathed in white stood over me, needles and tubes in hand. I tried to move away from him (her?) but my muscles strained for nothing. Heavy straps bound me to an operating table.

I screamed and struggled at the bonds.

The tech hesitated again near the stump of my left wrist. "The subject is moving too much," the female voice said. Her eyes, the only part uncovered by surgical scrubs and masks, looked away from me across the room.

Andrea Alessandra leaned in the doorway, arms crossed, ankles crossed, frowning at me.

"Girl is strapped to a table, it's not rocket science."

I snarled at the lab tech and summoned the god voice. "I swear by the Golden Chao, that I will-"

"For fuck's sake." Alessandra stalked across the room and shoved the lab tech aside. She snatched the heavy duty syringe from the tech's fingers.

I tried to lurch away from her, but the operating table's straps held. The buckles barely rattled. Alessandra frowned at the messy bandage around the stump of my wrist. The syringe was traded for a scalpel.

"Hey wait-"

Alessandra sliced the bandages.

My heart lurched. The cotton wraps came off clean.

I relaxed. Alessandra picked up a syringe and I thought better of it.

"What is this, amateur hour?" she said.

The lab tech stammered.

"Look at this? What kind of suture is this?" Alessandra prodded the heavy duty stitches where my hand used to be. "Get out before I get the boss."

The lab tech scurried away and left me alone with the other immortal. She took out a pair of surgical scissors and cut away the stitches. The golden ambrosia in my veins oozed slowly out. Alessandra collected it in a vial and set it aside. She summoned an orb of water around her hands. The antiseptic smell of the room was replaced by the sea. My forearm was enveloped by the salt water. My skin stitched itself back together.

"Water mages make for good healers," I said to her as she ran an IV line near my elbow.

Alessandra cast a glare at me.

"Fine. Water deities make for good healers."

"Better."

She worked in silence. I let her.

"That should heal with no scar," she said when the IV line was done.

"Why?"

"Like you said, water deities are good healers."

"But not good at understanding questions," I said. "Why did you bother?"

Alessandra turned away. "I don't like leaving a job done poorly."

"And centaurs shit roses. Why did you really do it Andrea Alessandra?"

"I did it to help you!" she snapped. A faint nimbus of magic circled about with her emotions. Salt lay heavy in the air.

I rattled the straps holding me to the operating table. "I can think of better ways to assist me than cosmetic surgery."

The other woman sighed and sat with care on a doctor's stool. "I... would not have done what Wodanaz did."

"Do I detect dissention in the ranks?"

"It's not like that." Alessandra pointed her sharp eyed glare at me again. "He is going to save the world for our kind. We all will benefit."

"Tell that to my left hand. Or your druid nailed to his wall."

She frowned.

"Do you not see beyond his façade?" I asked. "He speaks like any petty dictator, all plush words until the knives come out."

"You don't know what it's like," she snarled. Alessandra leaned over me. I saw the hurt in her dark eyes behind the steel. "I saw my last believer, my only believer, fade away and die and there was nothing I could do to stop it. His soul was a wisp in my hands blown away by the breeze. I drifted, no more bound to reality than his soul, but forever trapped here on Earth. I hold a rift within me, Eris. A void you will never understand. The Iliad. The history books. The revivalists. Your precious Discordians. You live in the hearts of men and women still after thousands of years. I had fifty. Fifty years with one soul who truly believed in Andrea Alessandra, Shipbreaker of the Wind and Seas. And now an eternity ahead of me with no one. You cannot know how it feels to be denied the very stuff of belief that makes us."

"You sound just like Wodanaz."

Alessandra leaned back and crossed her arms. A smug grin flashed. "Good."

I shook my head, which was about as much as I could move. "He spun his silver tongued tale for me. Once. Long ago. Noble goals corrupted and twisted by the rot in his heart. Do not let his pain taint your soul too."

"Spoken like someone who has never known the kind of hurt we have."

"You think I do not know pain?" I snapped. "Do you not think that in the course of five thousand years I have not been a victim of immortality such as you? There is a bare trickle of belief left for me out there in the world where there was once a torrent. The dying spirit in the desert is thankful for even a drop. This is not the way to sate your thirst for belief, Andrea Alessandra! You said you would not have done to me as Wodanaz has done. You know what he does is wrong. Wodanaz, the once noble god of thunder, spinner of tales, leader of a proud pantheon, has replaced his pain with poison. Do not consume his poison for your own."

There was a long moment where we stared at each other. The smug look long fled from Alessandra. She turned around and busied herself with the medical supplies.

"How do you know poison isn't better than starving to death?" she said under her breath.

She hooked up an IV drip bag to the line strung into my arm. A narcotic numbness spread into my veins.

"I never knew Wodanaz's people. We met much later," I said just above a whisper. "I was old by the time he was dreamed up, driven underground by the Romans. But I cannot believe that those who once revered him would hold him dear to their hearts now. His obsession has corrupted him." The sedative filled my head full of sand. "Would that last wisp of a soul you pine for recognize what you do today?"

She had no answer for me.

The last thing I saw before falling into a narcotic void, was Andrea Alessandra shaking as she fled the room, leaving me to whatever Wodanaz had in his corrupted mind.

Chapter 23 – Giulia

I woke up in my bed with yet another wicked hangover making my brain feel like it was a size too big for my skull. Conversation from the kitchen was enough for my head to start throbbing.

"I gotta stop passing out twice a day…" I groaned to myself.

My left wrist was still ringed in pink scar tissue, harsh and ugly against the healthy hue on either side. I poked at it. My hand still felt like plastic, but not so raw anymore. The rest of my body felt tingly and energized like I just had really great sex. It felt just like the last time I-

"Oh shit, it worked."

I flopped out of bed and shuffled into the kitchen towards all those voices as fast as my pounding head would let me.

"You're awake. Good." Angie jumped up from her spot around my table and gave me her seat. I was grateful to sit again. She slid a half empty Dunkin' Donuts coffee my way. I hated the stuff, but held my breath and made it happen. Caffeine would help me in my time of need.

"So the problem child awakes," said a haughty voice.

"Nice to see you when you are actually awake."

Across the table from me sat two strange men. They looked like they could have been cousins cast in a dumb sitcom called "Look how different these guys are!" The man on the left looked like he came straight from a Hawaiian airport gift shop, all super tan with the loudest tropical shirt ever made. Tropical shirt guy was drinking one of my beers. His lookalike on the right had on an expensive suit vest and pristine white button down dress shirt. He looked displeased to touch anything in my flat.

Annona was very sullen.

"So my plan worked," I said.

"Could have told me what you were going to do," Annona said.

Shame welled up inside of me. "I'm sorry. I-"

"Have more important things to do, so if you care to explain yourself?" the suit said.

"Which one is that?" I stage whispered to Annona.

"Giulia Cesari, meet Mercury, my sandal winged motherfucker. The one drinking your beer is your sandal winged motherfucker, Hermes."

"Keeping company with Americans for so long has made you so uncouth, Miss Augusti," the prim and proper one said.

Hermes tipped his beer in my direction but said nothing and went back to drinking it.

I pointed at Hermes. "I get why he's here. Repeat of last time. Which is what I was going for. But why are there two of you here instead of just one?" I asked.

Mercury scoffed. "Roman blood called to me on the brink of death. I came to take you to the Elysium Fields, however," he glared at Hermes, "someone came and brought you back to health."

"Roman blood? I'm so sorry Annona. I never thought I would be putting you at risk. I swear I didn't know."

"Ha!" Mercury laughed. "As if Miss Augusti here had the spiritual wherewithal for the Elysium Fields." Annona shrunk in her seat.

"Then why are you here?" Angie asked.

He pointed at me. "Roman blood."

I put up my hands in front of me. "Woah there. American. Now some Greek I guess. But no..." I trailed off when I saw the bandaged thumb held out in front of me.

"How can you deny Roman heritage with a name like 'Cesari?'" he said and rolled his eyes. "Americans always forget most of their nation hails from elsewhere. Although there are some within my pantheon who wonder how one marked such as you could happen without our notice."

"Pay more attention then," I snarked. Mercury got under my skin already.

The Roman frowned. "I fail to see-"

"Hold, both of you." Angie leaned across the table between us. "Giulia. He didn't take you to Roman Valhalla so don't give him shit."

Angie turned to the wing sandal duo and make an awkward half kung fu bow half Catholic self cross. "Mr. Messenger Gods," she started.

Annona's face turned red in embarrassment. She looked like she wanted to melt into the floor. I thought about it too.

"We need to send a message. It's extremely important."

"I hear FedEx guarantees overnight delivery now," Hermes snapped.

"In this, I agree with my underdressed counterpart. We are not common errand boys," Mercury said.

Angie shot me a glare, anticipating the remarks on the tip of my tongue.

"We need to send a message to a goddess."

Hermes frowned. "I think I see where this is going."

"And I do not care where this is going," Mercury stood from the chair and turned to me. "We may see each other again, little cousin, if you associate yourselves with a better class of god, but I rather hope we do not." He vanished on a gust of wind that rattled through my kitchen.

Annona spat on the floor. "Asshole." She turned to me and I winced from the look on her face. "Give a girl some warning for crap's sake. There are a thousand different things we could have done without bringing that proper bastard here."

"How the hell was I supposed to know almost killing myself, again I might add, would bring two of them into my kitchen? It's not like I'm an expert on all this."

"Which is why you should have some patience! Jupiter's hairy sack, woman, I am your expert, you just didn't wait and listen. You are just like Eris."

"She is literally part of me, so yeah."

Hermes set his beer down on the table. The clack of the glass on the scarred wood stopped us in our tracks. "I do not want to get snared into Eris' problems. They have a tendency to magnify for all involved."

"Wodanaz has been stirring this up for over a hundred years," Annona said. "Eris did not start this."

Hermes shot the Roman a glare and did not say anything.

I got sick of sitting there doing fuck all to help. I leaned across the table and waved a finger in his face. "You're already involved Hermes. I saw you the night all this started."

"Bullshit."

"You have distinctive footware."

I took his grumble as concession of the point.

"We have to find her as quickly as possible," I pressed.

Hermes pinched the bridge of his nose. "This is going to be Troy and her damn apple all over again. I do not want to get any further into a classic Eris mess. Again. I don't even know who this Wodanaz guy is."

"German thunder god," Annona said.

"Real prick," Angie added.

"See?" Hermes threw up his hands. "An interpantheon mess is even worse. You're alright," he pointed at Annona, "but a barbarian pantheon and Mercury? Out of my pay grade."

"We just need to find her," I said. "Then you can get out of dodge. Call it a favor for the new Greek on the block."

"You're only alive because I owed Eris a favor. Otherwise you'd be on the wrong side of the Styx right now."

"Then Eris can owe you one."

"She already does."

"Another one then!"

"You don't get to speak for her."

"Call it whatever is going to give you a warm fucking fuzzy feeling, but it needs to happen." I snapped.

"There's nothing you can offer that will get me roped into this," Hermes said. He got up from the table. "I am in farther than I want to be already."

"Mercury's caduceus," Annona blurted out.

Hermes stopped dead.

"I can get it," Annona said softly. "I know where it is."

Angie looked at me with a question in her eyes. I shrugged. I had no clue why they were talking about Mercury's staff thing.

"How?" Hermes asked.

"It's my nature to know everything that goes in and out of Rome."

"Christians took it from him a thousand years ago. Why would you betray your pantheon like that?" Hermes asked.

Annona gave him a look. "Cause he's a prick. Are you honestly saying to me that you like every single Greek out there?"

Hermes laughed. "Done." He struck his own caduceus on the floor three times. "Information on the wayward chaos goddess in exchange for procurement of one Roman artifact."

He blinked away.

Chapter 24 – Eris

There has never been any true chaos in a laboratory, not on purpose. Laboratories are fortified against the likes of me, carefully arranged to distill the essence of the world into pure order. Like being crammed into a sensory deprivation chamber, it felt like roaches skittered under my skin.

I kept my eyes closed against the white walls but the fluorescent lights beat against my eyelids. What was left of my arm worked back and forth against the restraints holding it in place.

"You have one fatal flaw," I said in Greek.

With a tear, I pulled my arm free. I clenched my teeth against a scream. Immortality still came with pain receptors.

"Your restraints were designed for hands."

Half the bandage of my left stump tore free. I bled on the table. Wodanaz's science types had too much of my blood, too much of my chaos to force into order. I shook my head while using the stump of my hand to fumble around with the other cuffs holding me in place.

Let my veins spill more ambrosia for Wodanaz, I thought, he cannot have me.

Freedom from my restraints gave me the barest trickle of chaos. The itch in the back of my mind told me

Wodanaz was smart enough to keep my element at bay. Corrupted by his own dreams, yes, but not foolish.

I lurched to my feet. Wodanaz broke his word. I needed escape, but to free of his shadow, I needed to get in touch with my basest nature.

There was little in the room left for me to disrupt order with in the lab. Locked cabinets. Stainless steel counters. The exam chair I just broke free from. A specimen refrigerator hummed quietly in the corner.

I placed my hand on the locked door. The coolness within seeped into my skin.

"How much of my ambrosia is in there?"

The lock was sturdy and every cell in my body felt withered. My frown spread into a smile when I spied the power cord snaking from the fridge to the wall.

"Even the mighty walls of Troy can do nothing-" I felt a surge of chaos when I pulled the plug, "-if you leave the door open."

The smallest jolt of primal chaos. The little shake up in the world hit me like a shot of ouzo on a cold day. My hand felt steady, tired, but steady.

Good enough, I figured. It was time to leave.

The exit was locked and with no time for subtlety, I forced a glob of chaos magic through the door handle. Metal parts clacked to the floor. I pushed through the door and found a standard issue hallway. Utilitarian cinder blocks and I had a vague feeling that I was underground. I did not think, just reacted to the flow of chaos and went left. I hustled though the narcotic haze that still hovered around my body.

Through the door at the end of the hall, stairs only went up. With no windows and no idea which direction led away from Wodanaz, up I went. Rounding the first switchback on the stairs I heard a noise from above.

I halted my scramble up the stairs. The door above me drifted closed. There was no urgency in the pair of footsteps coming down towards me.

"So didya get those TPS reports done for the boss?"

"Don't even get me started on those. Three-oh-seven had a bad reaction last night. Almost lost the whole experiment."

"Really? I thought Three-oh-seven was taking the DNA graft well."

"The chaos blood brought out some recessive genes in the subject. By the time I dealt with that, those reports took me til eleven."

The science types above me chuckled like human/deity experiments happened in every office. Experiments with the ambrosia from my veins.

Zeus' puckered asshole, they were already at it!

An immortal fury crept up within me. The gall of some mere mortal to think they can toy with the fabric of the gods. It was a gift bestowed from the Olympians, not a puzzle to be decoded. The essence of chaos would not be confined!

The righteous indignations grew but my hand started shaking. Withdrawal found me like a cold drop of water between my brows. Clarity. The scientists were almost down to my level.

Fight or flight?

I looked to the Magic 8-ball tattoo on my good wrist.

Flight.

I ducked through the door on my landing before the two people chittering away about TPS reports could realize how close they had come to a messy death. Flight was more urgent now though. Surely they would raise the alarm soon and all the hounds of hell would begin pursuit in earnest.

One floor up from the laboratories and the building was like a different world. Carpet. Wooden walls. Soft lighting highlighting accent tables and art work. Important decisions were made on this floor with the dirty work performed below. I slowed my roll. This was the land of management. Techies staying late to finish reports were not management.

Safe for the moment, I leaned against the wall to catch my breath. Across from me, lit like a museum piece, was a renaissance painting of St. Boniface felling the Dawn Tree. The patron saint of Germany brought Christianity to the men and women Wodanaz once watched over. Often at the tip of a sword. I shook my head at the painting. I knew that feeling down in the bottom of my soul, most of us old time Europeans did.

The only thing that made Wodanaz's pain unique is that most of us did not keep reminders hanging on our walls.

"Inspiring, isn't it?"

I spout out a litany of Greek curse words.

Wodanaz leaned on his spear like he had not a care in the world. "Do not even ask how I snuck up on you," he chuckled. "You stumbled upon me, *mein ketzchen*. And you are more the fool than I remember if you think you go about this place unmonitored. The modern world has eyes everywhere, Lady of Chaos."

I did not even feel furor anymore. Weariness settled over me. I cursed the whims of chaos that sent me down this hallway. I sagged against the wall I leaned on.

"Are you accepting modernity all of a sudden, Wodanaz?"

"No fight left in you, Eris? Are you going to join me of your own volition now?"

I rolled my eyes. "You avoid my question."

His smirk slid like oil down my spine. "As do you."

My weary scowl turned into an annoyed one.

"Very well," Wodanaz always got theatrical when he was enjoying himself. "Most of our kind falls into one of two camps, *nein*? There are those who reject the plague of modernity. They go to ground, retreat to the farthest corners of the earth to live like the old days.

"But they are the old days for a reason! Eris, the unspoiled parts of the world shrink every day. Like the locusts descending on the lone scarecrow, standing as a wall against the tendrils of the modern world is futile." Wodanaz paced back and forth across the hallway, punctuating his points with the end of his spear.

"Eris, did you know that even the steppe nomads where the Mongols once roamed now use cell phones to get the best free market prices selling yak hides? A hundred miles from the nearest town and the yak herders strap solar panels to their pack mules to participate in the global economy with pocket size computers. The farthest reaches of the world are not a refuge anymore. Humanity has tried to put our kind in the footnotes of history, a history that we remember, a history that we helped to forge! Those who retreat from the world will wither and die. I do not intend to do that, Eris, nor do any who flock to my banner.

"Nor will we be mollycoddled into mere survival like you and yours are so keen to do, because survival is all that it is. You keep your head down low and live off the scraps of humanity. History's footnotes will not let you survive forever, Eris. You Greeks, and the Romans, and the-" he spat on the floor "-bastard Norse. Embraced as fairy tales by the modern age. Fairy tales become footnotes and then you will know the pain inside that we feel. It is a matter of time before the masses of humanity forget about you too Eris. Relegated to the dustbin of history. Just ask them, Eris! Ask your precious humankind if they know who started the Trojan War. Do they even know that it was your golden apple that sent thousands of Greeks to battle?

"They forget, Eris! They have already forgotten me and the tales of my people."

Wodanaz stabbed his spear into the painting of St. Boniface, piercing the man through the heart. "The Christians do not even remember their own history of putting my followers to the sword. I will bring magic back to the world and make them remember."

I shook my head. "All these years and you have yet to change. Destroying progress will not help any of us."

Wodanaz laughed. "Who said anything about destroying progress, *ketzchen*? I work to marry the best of the old ways with the bits and baubles of the modern world. The gods of this Earth made humanity and humanity's own toys will be used to make them remember what they forgot. The final pieces are coming together, Eris, with you at the center of it all. We can open the floodgates. Let magic flow for the whole world to see with their own eyes. Then the masses will have to believe!"

"You will drown the world!"

"Adapt or die, *nein*? What the humans forced on to us shall be fed back to them."

The primal chaos around me trembled. The forces of the universe quivered at the thought Wodanaz put out there. It would be the biggest shake up since the earth was born of the Titans. Every cell in my body shook in harmony with the primal chaos. I fought down the tempest within.

"No."

"No?" Wodanaz laughed. "Your body betrays you, Lady of Chaos. You think I do not know how you crave it?" He leaned in to my aura. "Your very nature yearns to turn the world on its end."

My eyes lost focus and my stomach wretched. My body rebelled at the biggest decision in a thousand years with nothing left within to offset it. I stepped away from him. "This is not the way, Wodanaz. Subjection is not belief."

"It is better than the alternative!" Wodanaz screamed. "It is better than another thousand years in the dark, waiting for my turn to fade into nothing."

He stalked to me and grabbed me by the arm. Wodanaz pulled me and my head felt dizzy from withdrawal. I grabbed for the chaos around me but the primal force rebelled. I tried to use my magic within me. My body burned with the fire of Tarturus without any power left to drawn on.

My body failed me.

I collapsed where Wodanaz dismissed me. I threw up bile onto an office floor. My hammered senses said it was vaguely less opulent and much smaller than the office Wodanaz severed my hand in. He rummaged around a desk and pulled out some baubles my eyes refused to focus on through the pounding in my head.

"Holy amulets plucked from a frozen grave in Scandinavia," Wodanaz ranted. "Who did they honor? Who did they worship? Lost to the frozen ground, Eris. A thousand years before you or I woke to the world, this god was already forgotten and gone. There is no mythos left to protect and preserve this one. Every year our stories dwindle farther into the past we become more like this one here." He threw the ancient pieces of copper and stone across the room at me.

"Or this one here." Wodanaz held a necklace of animal teeth and bone carved with runes. "Plucked from a museum storeroom. 'Unknown Saharan artifact' it said. Who died when we forgot about this one? I refuse to go out that way and you do not have to either, Eris." He held out his hand to me. "Let us put this quarrel behind us. Together we can steal what civilization has built and marry it to what we have in our bones. Show the world what they have refused to see is in front of them for thousands of years."

"And when the world burns?" I hissed through clenched teeth. "When your story becomes one of fear and hate?"

Wodanaz frowned and let his hand drop to his side.

"So be it."

He raised the spear over his head. I moved. Not fast enough.

The spear cut through sinew and bone, pinning my leg to the floor. I screamed. I tried to twist around to grab the spear, but the weapon of a god is not easily broken. My leg tore with agony.

I fought the animalistic urge to rip my leg free. Wodanaz frowned at me like he would a misbehaving dog.

"Vladimir," he said into a cell phone, "Bring a containment team to my office. And tell Rhonda she wins the pool for when Eris would try to escape."

He made a second call.

"Andrea. We're moving up the timetable. Eris has forced hand. ... ... I don't care! We go to Gould Island tonight and you better be there."

Chapter 25 – Giulia

We sat crammed into Annona's rental car on the street in a posh neighborhood of Narragansett. The sprawling house we watched sat on the shore of the Atlantic Ocean. With Eris being completely off the grid, and her abandoned car being devoid of any leads, Annona guilted (and I threatened) Hermes into giving us this second lead as a freebee.

"How long do you think we can get away with sitting here before the cops come trolling us? We stick out like a sore thumb," Annona said.

"Nah," Angie waved her minty toothpick in dismissal before clamping it back in her teeth. The smell wafted around the car. "Blend in with the beach tourists and college kids. Only mostly white neighborhood, not ultra-white."

"Wouldn't think Wodanaz's head goon would be so... domestic," I said from the back. "It's the height of well to do suburbia out here."

Annona shrugged. "Hermes knows what he's talking about. It's his thing."

I rumbled in frustration. "Whaddya mean it's 'his thing?' I don't know what the hell you're talking about. Everyone acts like I do."

Now Annona made a frustrated sound. "His thing. What he does as a god. I know about what's going in and out of Rome. That's my thing. He's a messenger. Ergo, he knows how the fuck to find people."

I crossed my arms and sunk into the back seat. "He couldn't find Eris."

"Interference by someone else's thing."

Angie interrupted our bickering. "You two sound like you're arguing over a bad porno."

Annona glowered at Angie now. "If Hermes says Andrea Alessandra is in there, she's in there."

"So let's go," I said. "Before we annoy the crap out of each other. Stakeouts aren't this boring in movies."

"Creative editing," Angie said.

"Fuck it. Doing it." I said. I got out of the car and stalked down the street towards the waterfront home.

I heard swearing and footsteps following me. I spun on my heel back at Angie and Annona before they could say anything.

"We've been here two hours. She's in there alone for whatever reason she has to be home on a weekday at lunch time. I guess being a goon means weird working hours. Whatever. Sitting around here isn't going to change that Alessandra is in there alone. Sitting around here isn't going to save Eris. I'm sick of inaction. I'm going to-"

"Fine." Annona put up her hand.

"Wait huh? You're ok with barging in now?"

"You're right. Sitting isn't going to save Eris. Just let me get my bag of tricks." Annona went and took a duffel bag out of the back of the car. She rooted around and tossed me some keys. "Elvish skeleton keys. Opens any door."

Annona pulled out a baseball bat and passed it to Angie. She held it tight in both hands. I could see her knuckles straining. I worried she wasn't coping well under the cool façade.

"So is this like, carved from some immortal tree imbued with magical powers?" Angie ran her thumb across the carved lettering. "Does it go all Gandalf if I say magic words?"

Annona just looked at her. "Wal-Mart special. You hit things with it."

"It's good. It's fine," I stopped anymore questions about whatever Annona had in her weird Tardis bag. "Grab a shoulder, each of you. We're going in stealth mode."

I stepped between the seconds with both of them in my own personal bubble of stoptime. The air felt thicker than when I was in stoptime by myself. Pulling them along for the ride took more out of me. In the most awkward jog ever, we trotted up the driveway to the side door of Andrea Alessandra's Martha Stewart looking home.

The Elvish skeleton key opened the door into a clean kitchen. Big picture windows opened on an ocean view. The smell of salt water lingered in the air, even in stoptime. Ocean magic or just the Atlantic, I could not tell. A stack of dishes sat in the sink, waiting for soap. It was way more than one person's breakfast dishes. I tensed. Were there more people here? Should we have waited longer in the car? Too late now.

Andrea Alessandra was in the next room. Couches flanked a big tv in the living room. Toys were scattered all over the room. Alessandra was bent over picking up a doll and a video game controller.

"What the hell?" Annona's voice fell flat in stoptime. "Some kinda stay at home mom?"

I shook my head. The world did not quite keep up with my head. Three people in stoptime left me shaky on my feet already. "Questions later. Can't do this all day."

"Right." Annona pulled a set of manacles out of her bag of tricks. I wanted to snark that they were the 1800's special, but she'd probably snark back they were 1700's.

Angie dragged a chair over and we manhandled Alessandra into the chair as best as we could while keeping us all in contact and in stoptime. It was the worst Twister game ever.

"I feel like an idiot standing in front of her like this," I said. Alessandra was bound in a rolling office chair. The game controller was still clenched in her fingers, now behind her back and cuffed.

"She's still in her pajamas..." Angie said.

"Remember this bitch almost killed all of you." Annona said

"Right. Hard ass faces on," I said.

I dropped us out of stoptime.

I don't know how tough we looked, but Alessandra jumped so much she tipped over the chair into a pile of kids' toys.

"What the actual fuck?!"

The smell of saltwater grew thick in the air.

Annona snapped her fingers in response and I heard a rattle of chains. "Cut the magic. Those cuffs can cut your hands right off with one more snap."

I hauled Alessandra back upright.

"Ok, fine." She held her head high, looking proud. Not exactly an easy task while wearing pajamas. "You got the jump on me. I know how this goes." She closed her eyes and tensed.

Angie bounced with a nervous energy. She brandished the baseball bat with two hands. Her feet planted in a half hearted ready stance. I couldn't blame her so I stood back. She waited. Shuffled closer.

"I can't do it," Angie screamed and kicked out at the chair. Alessandra's chair rolled back on the hardwood and hit a sideboard. Angie stomped off in the other direction, throwing the bat down.

Annona and I rolled Alessandra back to the middle of the room.

"Revenge looks a lot different when it's right in front of you," the water goddess whispered.

I slipped into stoptime and spun her chair around to face me. Her eyes went wide. In her timestream, the movement didn't happen, it just was. I let a smirk creep across my face.

"So how did it feel when you took Eris, hm?"

"It's not like that." Alessandra turned her head away from me.

I blinked back into stop time and turned her chair back to face me. I crouched down to look Alessandra in the eyes.

"So tell me how it is? What slight did Eris, what slight did we, do to you to earn this?" I paused a beat.

"I-"

"Oh wait. You're not even the one running the show. You're just a hired hand. Annona, what should we do with another hired hand?"

From behind me Annona said, "In DC the hired muscle finds their way to the bottom of the Potomac."

"Water goddess might like that, though-"

"Ocean goddess," Alessandra interrupted.

"Whatever," I said. "I'd think an actual goddess wouldn't be a lacky to some cut rate Eurotrash. Maybe she's not even a goddess. Maybe she's just a poser."

"Cut the bullshit," Alessandra snarled. "I know what's going to happen. Get on with it. Just... not here, ok?"

This was not what I expected. I thought we'd have to play the hard ass game a while longer.

"It's not your call," Annona said to her.

"They don't know what I'm a part of," Alessandra said.

"Who?" Annona asked.

I saw it as Annona asked. We had tunnel vision and didn't notice before. The Martha Stewart home. The toys. The pictures on the mantle we didn't pay attention to. Alessandra in a formal evening gown with a Scottish guy in full kilt regalia. Alessandra and the Scottish guy with two kids at the beach. Grilling on the porch. The kids' school photos.

"Fuck. She's got kids."

"Step-kids, but please, leave them out of this."

"Just like you left my friends out of it?" I snapped.

Alessandra looked away. "That wasn't my idea. Wodanaz calls those shots."

"Why are you with Wodanaz then?" Annona said.

"You don't know what it's like!" Alessandra shouted. "Everyone knows about the Romans. The mighty Romans! Even a footnote like you gets recognition. Someone knows about you even if it is some scholar. I am the Shipbreaker of the Sea and Wind and I am a pantheon of one left adrift when the only man who believed in me died. That's who Wodanaz calls to his banner. The dispossessed. The unbelieved. You and Eris and the remembered wouldn't know that empty feeling. You wouldn't know what we would do to get that back!"

"And inciting a bunch of thugs to kidnapping?" I snapped.

Alessandra closed her eyes tight. "We need to shake up the status quo! If all we do is hide in the shadows, none of us ever win. The status quo is going to slowly destroy us until our kind is extinct. Shane is a kelpie driven out of his homeland. Sloane and Gregor never knew their mother. She was killed by myth hunters when they were too small to remember. They will never know the feeling of true belief unless something changes. I haven't felt it in decades. Wodanaz has a plan so we might get it back."

"His plan involves things that would make the Mafia blush," I said.

"I am desperate, not a fool!" Alessandra shouted. She glared at me with anger in her eyes, though for me, Wodanaz, or herself, I had no idea. "A flawed plan is better than no plan!"

"And what happens when he corrupts you, or better yet, decides you're a liability?"

"How else can I get my belief back?" Alessandra said. "How else can I-"

"I'll believe in you." Angie's soft words cut through the room. I hadn't heard her creep up behind us.

"What?" Annona and I both said.

"Why?" Alessandra said.

Angie shuffled over to stand before Alessandra. "Because you can't hide the pain in your voice."

"Even after…" Alessandra would not look anyone in the eyes. She turned her head like she could still see us through closed eyes.

Angie checked her pockets and looked disappointed to only find her mint toothpicks. "Everyone makes mistakes."

I raised an eyebrow at that. "I punched her in the face because she held fucking a gun to your head."

Her hands trembled taking the toothpick out of the small box and tucked it in the corner of her mouth.

The mint smell lingered between us. Angie closed her eyes. I swear I saw a hint of a tear. "I didn't say it was a small mistake," she shrugged.

"I don't like this," I whispered.

"You don't have to. Not this time, Giulia. Sometimes you see things you can't unsee. Sometimes you feel things you can't unfeel."

All the shit that I put Angie through over the years flashed through my head. All the fucking worry I caused my best friend with my self-destructive streaks. The times she covered my ass or gathered me up when I fell apart after my parents died.

All the crap I put her through this week.

I never stopped to think how fucked up "Your bestie has power over time after a hot night with a goddess out of myth" was for Angie.

"Uncuff her Annona," I said.

"What?!"

"We're gonna drop it. Find another way to find Eris."

"I don't trust her," Annona pointed at Alessandra.

"But I trust her," I pointed at Angie.

The Roman shook her head in disbelief but took off the 18th century special anyways.

Angie stayed behind, so the posse, down a woman, left Andrea Alessandra's house and walked up the block back to Annona's rental car.

"She'll be ok." I don't know if I was speaking to Annona or myself.

Annona bit her lip and looked away, busying herself with putting her bag of tricks back in the car.

"She'll be just fine," I said one last time as we drove by the unassuming home where Angie was with a goddess of questionable trust.

Annona was nice enough not to burst my bubble.

I smelled the sea as we drove off.

Chapter 26 – Eris

Gould Island was a blip in the middle of Narragansett Bay that I had never heard of before. Thrown into the bottom of a crappy fishing boat, none of Wodanaz's crew seemed like they were going to enlighten me about the place. The boat bobbed up at down tied to the dock. From the bottom of the boat, I saw feet milling about. We were not going anywhere either.

"*Wo ist* Andrea?"

Wodanaz's crew answered in non-committal mumbles.

"Cannot-" cough "cannot keep track of your people, Wodanaz?" I croaked from the boat.

The god loomed. "Now is not the time to test my patience, *ketzchen*. Once Andrea shows up-"

"I'm here." A gentle wave washed over the rail of the boat and Andrea Alessandra stepped aboard from Narragansett Bay. The water sloshed across the deck so I lay in a cold puddle.

"You are late."

"Not my night to be here."

"I have advanced the time table."

"She don't look like she's helping us."

"I am laying right here." They ignored me like I wasn't.

Wodanaz frowned at Alessandra. "The plan has changed."

"But what about-"

"Just take us to Gould Island," Wodanaz snapped. "Your role right now is to take us to the island. Nothing more."

"Years of work and now you tell me I'm just nothing more than a ferryman?"

"Years of work?" Wodanaz scoffed. "I was ancient before you were some sailor's hallucination. This is the culmination of centuries, so when I say the timetable has changed, all you need to know is run faster."

Wodanaz stalked to the aft of the boat. "Load up," he called to his people milling about. "We leave in two *minuten*, that is if Ms. Alessandra would be so kind." Wodanaz glowered and left to motivate those still on the dock.

With the thunder god off the boat, I moved to sit upright. Easier said than done with ropes binding my elbows and ankles. Wodanaz's crew took no chances this time. Andrea Alessandra watched me struggle for a moment then sighed and propped me up in a sitting position near the helm.

"Not what you signed up for, is it?" I said.

She busied herself with the helm.

Not talkative anymore. Oh well. I leaned my head back on the steel bulkhead to snatch some rest in a semi-comfortable position. The sun dipped below the horizon, but the air still held onto some of the warmth.

"I am a goddess of ship and sea," Alessandra said. "I am at home here on this deck."

I cast an eye to the woman at the helm. "That is not what I meant."

She frowned and found something boat related to busy herself with.

I shrugged my shoulders and regretted the movement. My left arm was a froth of pain, between the hacked up rune and stump of a wrist. Ambrosia began to soak through my bandage again.

"I know what you meant," she said.

Alessandra would not meet my eye when she said it.

Wodanaz returned to the requisitioned fishing boat with ten of his people. The *oborot* and a rock golem carried a crate between them that rocked the boat when it was loaded. Myths and scientists embarked alongside the German.

"Take us to Gould," he barked. "And keep us out of sight. Too many eyes on the water."

"Do not step aboard my domain and tell me how to rule it." Alessandra glowered.

Wodanaz pointed his spear at her. "Gould. Island. Now."

Alessandra kept her eyes locked on Wodanaz and raised her hands. A fog rose from the waves lapping at the boat. The diesel engine chugged to life beneath us. Alessandra snapped her fingers and all the running lights on the boat blinked off. We would be invisible on the night time waters of Narragansett Bay. The only light aboard was a crackle of electricity in Wodanaz's glower.

The boat soon bobbed alongside some military remnant on the shores of Gould Island in the middle of the bay. A concrete special of the Cold War stood out on the edge of a pier. It looked like the next hurricane to saunter into New England would wash it away.

Wodanaz leapt to the decaying pier and stalked on ahead to wherever his endgame lay. The crew went about lugging the gear on shore. I stood. With a rush to my head and nausea in my belly, I staggered against the bulkhead. My wrist bled through the bandage.

The rock golem grabbed my arm. I smacked him with my bound hand/wrist. The phantom pains burned like a thousand quills of ice. I kept my face as stony as his.

"The memory of an immortal is long," I said. "Best you start using yours."

I shuffled away down the gangplank.

"I'm not the one in chains."

Point. Not that I was going to admit it.

"Shut up, McGarry," Alessandra said "Just get the gear over to the site."

The golem grumbled but carried on.

When my feet set upon the cracked concrete, Alessandra stepped up beside me.

"What is this place?" I asked.

"Gould Island," she said as if I had not heard that part before. "A former Navy depot and a forgotten drop of land in the middle of the bay."

A barge bobbed on the water next to the fishing boat we arrived in. Near the tree line, trucks and excavators sat on old concrete pads where buildings once stood.

"Forgotten? Because I leave backhoes wherever I forget things."

Alessandra dismissed the construction equipment with a wave of her hand. "Nah, those haven't turned a bit of soil in months. They're a front. We move them just to keep appearances." She started off toward a derelict road that was swallowed up by the darkness past the tree line.

I closed my eyes and reached for the primal chaos around me. My arm throbbed. There was not much nearby, Wodanaz laid down order on this spit of land. Between the blood loss and the chokehold on my magic, reaching for the ambient chaos was like tearing through wet wool. I soaked up a spark. I reached my magic to-

"Hey now!" Alessandra swatted at my shoulder. "None of that. Come on then."

I rolled my eyes and shuffled after her. Alessandra's long stride was too much for the chains at my ankles. With a grumble, she kneeled down and grabbed the chain in her fist. A splash of water formed around her fist and split the links apart.

She strode to the road ahead.

"Fight or flight?" I whispered to the chaos around me.

I looked to the 8-ball tattoo on my surviving wrist.

Reply hazy, try again later.

I let out a sigh. To the crows with this.

"Ya coming?" Alessandra stood with her hands on her hips waiting.

"Sure, what the hell." I followed after. We strode down the broken pavement, swallowed up by overhanging trees. The sound of Narragansett Bay fell away, shrouded by the same trees that kept the moonlight at bay. Our footsteps and the chittering of night birds was all that followed us.

"Feels primal," I said. "A thousand miles from civilization. Reminds me of Greece when I was young." We stepped over a rusted storm drain. "Though the broken shards remind me of my Greece as it is today."

"Heh. Before my time," Alessandra said. "I was not born on land. Give me a sea and a sail."

"Then you would have loved my land when it was young. Island hopping. Kapsali. Kriti. Serifos. Naxos. Tilos."

A stray beam of moonlight let me see Alessandra flash a smile, but it faded fast. We walked on. I kicked rocks into the trees to break up the silence.

"Why this kindness, Alessandra?"

"I walk you to Wodanaz. It is no kindness."

"You let me walk," I said, "of my own two feet. You do not carry or drag me to my fate. You do the deed yourself rather than a subordinate. You cut my chains when I could run."

"Ha!" Her laughter was loud in the darkness. "You are on an island. Where would you run?"

"You deflect the question."

Alessandra stopped and took me by the arm, the good one. "Look. Just…"

"Just what?" I asked. "Second thoughts now that it is time to do the deed?"

"Today I saw… Eris, we've been at odds, but things are more complicated now than you know," she said.

"I live for complications."

She turned back down the path. "Yeah, not everybody does," she snapped. "Do us all a favor and just roll with what Wodanaz wants then you all get on with your immortal life. I wish you no ill. I merely want a future again."

I caught up with her and waved the ambrosia soaked stump bandage in her face. "Yes, because me and Wodanaz just plan to share a cup of tea."

Alessandra pinched the bridge of her nose. "In a thousand years, you'll forget all about this. Do something for the rest of us for once."

"He cut my hand off!"

"I am truly sorry for the way things played out Eris. There is a… zeal among Wodanaz and the disenfranchised that gets the better of them from time to time."

I snorted at that. "I have noticed."

In the moonlight, I saw the other woman frown.

"I tried to…"

She trailed off and lapsed into silence.

It was better that way. The hole she dug for herself only went deeper.

Sounds of activity drifted through the trees. After a bend in the derelict road, we walked into a clearing around another abandoned Navy building. Decades of New England winters collapsed the roof, but the empty shell stood watch over Wodanaz's assembly.

Torches staked into the ground encircled the clearing. The smell of burning pitch brought me back to a time before electricity. Wodanaz's people bustled about the edges of the clearing. Some held obvious magical items. A pair of lab coats busied themselves with a tangle of laptops spread out on a folding table. Wodanaz himself stood in the center of the clearing, at the foot of a great tripod which reached over his head. He traced lines in the dirt near his feet with the tip of his spear.

Alessandra cursed under her breath. She grabbed me lightly by the elbow and led me to the center of the circle.

"Wodanaz," she called out. "What is all this here? This does not look like the plan we discussed."

He held up his free hand. "You wait."

The spear looped and changed directions in the soil. I saw runes at his feet, but they were not Germanic. Some sort of angular interpretation of an eastern alphabet? Rare was the day I saw something truly new anymore.

"Done," he said and turned towards us.

"What are you doing Wodanaz?" Alessandra asked.

"What needs to be done, *Frau* Alessandra."

"And would you care to let me know what that is?"

Wodanaz frowned. "Does the general tell the inner workings of the battle plan to the private? Is the captain of a ship worried about the rat hunters in the bilge?"

"Since when-"

"Since now, Andrea Alessandra. Since now." Wodanaz gestured in a slow circle to everything around us. "Plans change as is my prerogative."

"So now we do this without any of the relics? Without any of artifacts or-"

"Can we just get on with this?" I blurted. "Whatever Hera damned Cerebus shit you have in mind, can we just get it over with."

Wodanaz stopped. The bastard smiled a snake oil quirk of his lips.

"*Ja.* Let us finish this, *mien ketzchen.* We shall finish this once and for all."

The butt of the spear stamped on the ground. A great spark of sound, like a thousand volts cracking to life, rose around us. Pure white light burst forth from the runes Wodanaz etched in the dirt. The runes surrounded us and filled the torch circle. My feet could not move from the dirt. The runes trapped me in place.

Alessandra cursed next to me. The light runes held her firm.

"Apologies for ensnaring you in the *Mait-reth* runes, my dear Andrea," Wodanaz said. "Without her fetters, *mien ketzchen* here could have fled."

He walked towards me in slow steps.

"Fight or flight," I whispered to chaos.

The 8-ball tattoo said nothing. It was a void in my skin.

"It will all be done with soon enough." Wodanaz ignored Alessandra and slung his spear behind his back. He produced a length of rope.

I held my head high despite the inability to do much. "Willing participation in exchange for leaving me and mine alone, Wodanaz. What happened to our agreement?"

He laughed. "That went *kaput* when you showed up on my doorstep without enough power within to light a candle. Unable to participate as promised. The agreement is null and void."

He tied the rope to the broken fetters at my feet.

"Then what are we doing here?" I asked.

"I still seek to gain the power I need."

Alessandra yelled in frustration. "Wodanaz! If she does not have the power we need, why all this? What is the point? No artifacts. No chaos. There is nothing here for us. Has there ever been anything here for us or was this some vindictive quest? Did O'Shea die for nothing? Or Henri? Or Esmerelda? Or any of the others who follow you into the breech? Why is this the way?"

Wodanaz swung a backhand at Alessandra. She blocked it a hairsbreadth away from her face. "Know your place," he hissed. "Or you might not have one any longer."

The German turned his head back to me. "I will get the chaos I need to bring the world back to light."

A clap of thunder in the cloudless night and the rope pulled me free of the runes and my feet out from under me. The world upended. I dangled under the tripod. I swayed back and forth over the ground with Wodanaz's nasty smile level with my glower.

"You have crossed the line, Wodanaz!"

Around the torch circle, assembled dregs of the magical world murmured in surprise. Their eyes locked on me and sparkled in the torch light.

"*Ja* I cross the line," Wodanaz, unaffected by the light runes, walked across the circle to where a weathered wooden chest wait. He picked it up and sauntered back. I twisted in the wind and struggled to keep him in sight. "I will cross every line you lay down before me if it means restoring magic to the earth."

He came within striking distance, though my hands were still bound. I spat at him.

"The last futile gesture of the damned since time immoral," he said.

With a gentle care, he placed the chest on the ground. From within, he removed a large laboratory bell jar. The same as the specimens in his office. Sitting in the bottom, lay my left hand.

I raged but he just laughed.

"I have been reading, Eris, *mien ketzchen*," he said. "I have learned much in the four hundred years, give or take, since you left me in Verona. Below the ashes of your Roman cousins, deeper than the shadow of the Estruscans, there was knowledge."

Wodanaz took out the obsidian knife he cut my hand off with. Rage burned in my heart.

"Almost forgotten," he said. "I saved it before it could go the way of whoever this blade once honored. It told me how to steal immortality. How to kill the unkillable."

The god voice came down on me then. "Wodanaz, I swear to you by my mother, primal Nyx that-"

"Save your breath."

I felt a fire on my skin. My neck burned. Ambrosia dripped from the obsidian blade. My lungs spasmed and the air they drew did not pass my lips. I choked on the lifeblood spilling out of me. Hanging upside down, it trickled down my face. Ambrosia filled my nose, clouded my vision and tangled in my hair. It fell to the ground. The light runes pulsed in time with every drop of my life that hit the dirt. The bell jar filled.

I tried to scream.

Gurgle. Wheeze.

Rage turned to fear. Fear turned to panic. I thrashed on the end of the rope as my strength fled me.

"What have you done?" Alessandra screamed.

Wodanaz laughed. "See, *mien* Andrea? We will get our chaos. We will complete our ritual and our calling."

With my hand and my stump, I tried to hold the ambrosia inside the slice in my neck. My skin parted to the bone. I felt my vertebrae under my fingers.

"This is barbaric!" Alessandra screamed.

My breathing grew shallow. The torrent of golden lifeblood slowed to a trickle. My limbs went limp. I slowly spun at the end of the rope. The jar below my head was nearly full. Of my ambrosia. My left hand floated in it, fingers twitching.

"Without the ambrosia in her veins," Wodanaz said, "she is mortal within this circle."

Help me, I thought. Happier times in the height of Greece flashed through my thoughts. The golden apple. The battles and triumphs.

...Don't let me go mother, please put a stop to this, Nyx...

Synapses fired and died. People and passions flew by, some barely remembered, some sung about for eons. Memories went dark. One floated to the top and held strong.

...Giulia... help me...

My vision dimmed.

My thoughts slipped away.

My world went dark.

Chapter 27 – Giulia

A chill clung to me as the moon rose over the roof of my building. I paced along the roof. I frowned at the lawn chair and the cold fire pit. It wasn't long ago I sat there drinking with Eris.

Now, instead of a lover, a pissy Roman sat there and frowned at my pacing.

"I still think Andrea Alessandra is the key to all this," Annona said.

"And I told you hours ago, I agree."

"So we go back to the original plan," Annona said, "we go to the *landica*'s house and crack some skulls. Go old school on her."

I threw up my hands. "That's a dick move now."

"And so is kidnapping Eris for fuck knows what ends."

"I know, I know. We can't go that route now. How's that any different than what they did to my friends, which by the way, we still haven't found them all yet."

"It's not different," Annona glowered. "I don't care it's not different. And neither should you."

"So when in Rome-"

"Don't." Annona leveled a finger. "Low blow."

I grumbled and paced near the edge of the building. Annona was driving me friggin' nuts. I sighed.

Maybe it was the inaction that was crawling up my spine and down again. Jin-wei. Ric. Eris. I didn't know if they were alive anymore. Now Angie was off with-

A car drove up around to the loading dock of my building and someone got out the passenger side. A rideshare dropping off one of the tenants.

Wait.

"She's back!" I ran past Annona to the hatch back down into my flat. "Angie's back!"

I clattered down the ladder from the roof. The world slid into stoptime as I shouldered my way through the door and down the hall. I burst out the back door and leapt into a flying hug and the world spilled back into motion around us.

"Holy shit Giulia!"

We were laughing by the time we hit the ground.

"You're ok," I said.

"And you scared the crap out of me."

"Yeah but you're ok."

We lay there on the loading dock snickering like we were kids again.

Annona walked up with her hands shoved in her pockets. "So the Caribbean didn't sell you out?"

We sighed in unison at Annona's buzzkill.

"No," Angie said as we got up, "she's trying to... temper, the extremism with Wodanaz's group."

Annona snorted. "That's a lot of help."

"Cause you've never made a bad choice in your life, coming from the goddess of a place she can't go home to."

Annona lunged with a right hook.

Stoptime held her in mid swing. I stepped between the seconds and between the two women.

"Stop it!" I yelled at them. "Pissing each other off isn't going to help."

"But she-"

"Don't care," I said.

"So-"

"Stop."

Annona stepped back. "You're right." She was still glaring at Angie.

"We need action," I said. "We've been going stir crazy without a direction."

Angie took out her phone and waved it at us. "I've got us a direction."

"Why didn't you say that?"

"Well, first you tackled me out of thin air and then-"

"Where is it?"

"Andrea gave it to me," she said. "an address in Newport. Jin-Wei and Ric are there."

"Not Eris?" Hurt crept in my voice at the mixed news.

"Small steps," Annona said. She started walking to her car. The Roman turned back to us when we didn't follow. "What? You said you wanted to go bust some heads. I'm gonna show that barbarian Wodanaz the might of Rome with a boot up the ass.

We flew down the road to Newport, driving like the worst Masshole tourist ever. Annona flipped off the EZ-Pass reader on the bridge toll and didn't look back.

The location in Newport was down in the nice part of town among the mansions. We looked sketchy as hell cruising around there in the middle of the night, but the cops never trolled us. With the New York plates of Annona's rental, we blended in good enough as lost tourists.

A slow roll past the address Angie had in her phone showed a wrought iron gate and security station.

"Looks empty," Annona said.

I thought for a moment and then laughed at myself and slipped into stoptime.

"Duh," I said to the flat air between the strands of time. "I can just check for myself."

Climbing out of a moving car felt wrong, even if it was not moving per se thanks to stoptime. Openly walking to the guard shack of my enemy's safehouse felt ridiculous so I crept up along the side of the building.

Empty.

And I still felt ridiculous.

A sandwich sat abandoned and half eaten next to a monitor showing camera feeds from around the perimeter. One feed locked in on the shack and caught Annona's car in frame. I spotted the camera above the gate. I mussed up my hair, cocked my head at an angle and gave the lens a dead eye stare. Time flowed for half a moment. I took three steps over and did it again.

I laughed to myself and went back to the car.

"Seven hells, Giulia," Annona yelled when I started up time. "Don't do that."

I forgot they would see me disappear. I laughed harder.

"Park here," I said after the hilarity was over. "No one there."

"So what were you doing?"

I made the zombie face at Annona. "Fuuuucking with their caaaaameraaa feeeeeed."

Angie laughed with me.

"Cute," Annona said as she got out of the car. "But let's get our game faces on."

She popped open the truck of the car. It was kitted out with some of the heavy duty cases she brought with her, not the duffle bag from last time. Annona took out a leaf shaped dagger and strapped it to her thigh.

Annona handed Angie a war club, darkened with age and covered with metal rivets. "Figure this one is an upgrade over the Louisville Slugger."

"Lighter than it looks," Angie said. "It feels... almost warm. It feels..."

"Certified magic weapon there, kid," Annona said. "Few humans lay hands on things like that."

"It's not Roman," I said while my bass player gave the club a test swing.

"Nope. Got it off an oni I found snooping around DC in '44."

"Ok," I said. "If you two are all set, let's go."

"Wait," Annona put a hand on my shoulder. "I brought something for you." She held out a sheathed sword. The hilt looked plain and the leather scabbard old. It radiated power. I reached towards it and felt an intimate energy reach back.

"It's Eris' sword," I said.

It wasn't a question but Annona nodded anyways.

I slung the scabbard for an over the shoulder draw. It was secure and comfortable, like it was made for me. I felt a spring in my step having something of Eris with me.

"I haven't the faintest idea what it's going to do for you," Annona admitted. "You of all people know how chaos magic works."

The weight of the sword felt heavier in that moment.

"What did it do for Eris?" I asked.

Annona shrugged. "I've been keeping it safe for her since the War of 1812. I last used it to slay Angela's oni," she said nodding to Angie's weapon. "It was... not what I expected."

I rolled my eyes. "And that means?"

"I have drawn that blade six times. Each time it was a different weapon. Short sword. Dagger imbued with lightning. Pole arm made of stone. Bastard sword. The claymore almost cost me my life as I am not adept with a two handed blade. Somehow it was a wooden club once."

I frowned.

Angie clapped me on my shoulder though. "Relax, it's not like you know how to use a single one of those anyways."

I spat out a laugh. "That really shouldn't be comforting."

"We've never needed a clue yet," Angie said dragging me along after her.

"We're so fucked..." Annona muttered.

Arm in arm, I pulled them into stoptime with me and we forced the locks on the guard shack to get by the perimeter. In a stumbling three-person jog, we trotted up the long driveway towards the main house. It was bigger than I pegged it from the street. I held on to stoptime as much as I could. Halfway up the lawn, my hold on time skittered and stuttered until I dropped it, gasping for air.

"Harder to use the closer we get."

"It's ok," Annona said. "Save something for inside."

She sprinted to the building.

"Come on," Angie grinned ear to ear despite the situation. "Just like tagging buildings back in school."

I huffed down more oxygen and caught up with the two of them alongside one of the mansion's tall first floor windows.

"I gotta quit drinking," I grumbled. "Or drink more. Not sure what'd be better right now."

Annona shushed me and messed with the window. "B and E isn't exactly my forte."

A faint odor of the salt spray lingered around the whole building. In between my pulse pounding in my ears, I heard waves. I rolled my eyes. Let's make the breaking and entering scenic by picking a waterfront mansion. A regular one wasn't challenging enough.

We clustered around a back door like we clearly saw too many cop raids on TV.

Angie gripped the oni warclub tight in two hands and raised an eyebrow at me. "Magic time?"

I was too damn wiped out from the dash up the millionaire lawn.

Annona threw me a concerned look. She shook her head. "Save your strength. Wodanaz is a huge *scopio*. Who knows what he has inside."

"It's a trap!" I said in my best Akbar.

Angie snickered despite the life we apparently led now. Annona rolled her eyes at us like a put upon big sister. "Come on, let's get this over with."

Annona turned the doorknob and we found ourselves in a massive commercial grade kitchen. Completely abandoned, it looked like people left in a hurry. I idly turned off a burner on a huge gas range where a pot of something sat on a low simmer. We were here for a rescue mission, not arson.

Maybe a little bit of arson later since it was the week to be trying new things.

"Smells good," I said.

"Shush it," Annona stage whispered.

"Why? There's no one here." I picked up an empty pot on a counter and banged it around. Annona looked right to fight me herself if no one came running. The silence was heavy after my clattering.

"Fine," Annona said after a long moment uninterrupted by anyone coming to see what the ruckus was about. "But let's not invite trouble on purpose again."

I shrugged. "I am chaos. No promises."

She muttered something in Latin, probably some curses, and led the way out of the kitchen. Every room on the lower floor was as empty as the last. Just as fancy as expected for a Newport mansion, and utterly empty. The only sign of life since the simmering pot was a TV left on, playing the low drone of a crappy sitcom.

"It's actually way creepier this way," Angie said after we finished our loop of the ground floor.

"You're not wrong," I said. We were in the main entryway at that point. I sauntered up the grand staircase. The other two still looked tense but I just couldn't keep up the hypervigilance forever.

"Still think it's a trap?" Annona asked.

"Well, it's gotta be something," I said back from the top of the stairs. "Pick something. Either be a bust or spring the damn trap already."

At the top of the stairs, I picked the first door I found and pushed it open. A high ceilinged office was ringed with bookshelves and display nooks for whatever rich guy doodads Wodanaz favored. A massive oak desk faced me.

"Boo." A thick Russian accent said from behind the desk. The chair swiveled around, Bond villain style, and the voice belonged to one of the musclebound goons I saw earlier at the graveyard. "We meet again."

"Ladies," I yelled over my shoulder, "I think I found the trap."

Behind me, I heard Angie and Annona clatter up the stairs. I kept my eyes on the man… monster, in front of me. Now that I knew magic was literally in my blood, standing this close I could feel it radiating off him and knew what it meant. Whatever he was, it wasn't fully human. I felt an itch in my hands to do… something. The chaos in me desired action, though what, I could not guess.

My back up ran into the room beside me. On my left, Angie made a sound halfway between a growl and a yelp. I could see the anger radiate off her.

"Dimitri," she said, low and menacing.

He gave a smug smile from behind the desk. "The little fish that got away. How's it been since the kidnapping? Your boys had so much fun after you left."

Angie started forward but I grabbed her arm.

"Where are they?" I said. "Where's Eris? Where's Wodanaz?"

Dimitri stood, still completely unconcerned there were three women threatening him. Arrogant prick.

"So many of your people unaccounted for," he tisked. "And yet I shall give no answers to your little posse." Dimitri sauntered around to our side of the desk. The sprawling room was big enough that he still kept his distance. Magical energy swirled around him while he eyed us like meat.

My creepy man alert went off in my head. No shit, brain.

Dimitri stopped and cocked his head to the side, looking at Annona. "Where do I know you from?"

The goddess on my right spat on the floor. "Vienna."

Dimitri's body rippled. It wasn't a flex, more like some sort of instant roids and a heat mirage. I heard tendons snap and muscles pop into place.

"Heh. Vienna," he said with a shit eating grin. "That's-"

-when Annona lunged with a yell, dagger out swinging for a gut shot. Dimitri hulked out. In a blink, a full on werewolf danced away from Annona's savage swing.

"Oh shit we're doing this!" I drew Eris' chaos blade and got... a spike ball on a stick. A mace? Some Dungeons and Dragons cartoon shit? "The fuck?"

Annona yelped. Overcommitted to the slash. Left a huge opening for the Russian werewolf to land a heavy left hook to the ribs.

Annona staggered back with a wheeze and a limp. Angie stepped in with a home run swing.

"Where are they?" she yelled.

Deflect. Deflect. Deflect. Dimitri's Popeye forearms shrugged off Angie's warclub again and again. He retreated a step at a time, chuckling the whole time. I couldn't take a swing with the spikey ball of death without Angie being in the danger zone.

Claws out, Dimitri stepped inside Angie's reach and shoved. She stumbled back into a display case. Glass shattered. Blood. A lupine laugh yipped.

I saw red.

Attacked with the most inelegant overhead swing. Dimitri didn't even humor me with a block. He sidestepped and my spikey ball of death thunked into the solid oak desk.

Pain shot up my leg and I met the ground hard. I turned, up against the desk and the Russian loomed over me, fangs drooling. His werewolf snout growled out "Pathetic."

"Time magic! Time magic!" Angie yelled.

"Fuck!" I grabbed for the strands of stoptime. Slippery. Hard to hold. My body buzzed from the drain. Time wouldn't hold.

Dimitri came closer in a staccato hiccup and my grip on time fluttered. My new magical muscles burned with an effort that wouldn't be good enough to save me this time. I reached up and grabbed the mace stuck in the des. With leverage from the desk, my regular muscles surged to rip the spikey ball of death free.

In the last gasp of stoptime, Dimitri's eyes went wide.

The biggest, spikiest part of the ball of death came down on werewolf foot, through flesh and tendon, pinning him to the floor.

Stoptime fell away and Dimitri howled. Angie swung for his knees with a golf swing. Crack! He couldn't step away as his legs buckled. A flash of metal, a splash of something warm and gross, and it was all over except for the limp, dead weight that collapsed on me.

"Giulia!" Angie came to my side and awkwardly shoved Dimitri off me. "Oh my god, be ok!" Panic tinted the edge of her voice.

"I'm ok… just stuck under this fuckhead." The two of us unceremoniously dumped Dimitri off to the side. Angie helped me up, getting some of Dimitri's leftovers on her.

"Oh jeez, he's really dead," she trailed off in Spanish. Angie turned away, looking green around the gills.

Annona cleaned off her dagger. "Kill or be killed with that one," she said softly while holding her side. "Nothing else to be done about it."

Angie didn't look back at us but nodded still. "This is an office. Bond villain office. Let's… look for clues or something."

We spread out. Annona was unphased by a dead body, but me and Angie made it a point to not look in that direction. The office was pretty much what I expected from a Newport mansion. Big leather chairs, a globe that probably had booze in it. Books. Tastefully lit nooks for knickknacks. My new spidey senses felt tingly when I reached a hand towards any of the display items. The chaos in my blood ached for the pure potential they held. A pair of broken glasses. A sliver comb. A shard of pottery with suspicious stains. A monkey paw with one finger still raised.

That one was a bit on the nose.

"Is he collecting magic?" I asked.

"Yes," Annona said. "Nothing I've seen on the market. Or at least nothing that's come through DC. Seems like he's gathering it all himself," she sneered.

Tattooed skin covered in Celtic patterns. A broken horn. Teeth. Blood. The goodies got grisly on Annona's side of the room.

"Guys," Angie stood behind the desk. "There's something here for you Giulia."

We gathered around. The chunk of wood I gouged out of the desk with the spikey ball of death aside, it was a very organized workspace. No computer, but everything was neatly in place. Smack in the middle was a fancy envelope. An elegant cursive spelled out "Giulia Caesari."

"Is it a trap-"

"We should-"

Annona and Angie spoke over each other. I rolled my eyes.

"Doing it." I snatched up my letter and cracked open the wax seal. The others cringed like I just clipped the wrong wire in a bad movie. "What? Herr Asshole wants me to read it. Probably to gloat, the smug bastard."

I unfolded the letter and read it aloud.

One step behind. I expect no less from Eris' new paramour, struggling to keep up with your betters. If my dear oborot *has failed me, then it remains your task to play perpetual catch up. It does amuse me to let you know your friends are not here. I sold them to someone who has a vested interest in the new world I will create. Someone in need of fodder for the mill. And you now can go to your graves knowing you failed. The time you wasted reading this could have saved out.* Gutentag. *-Wodanaz.*

We all looked at each other.

"...that's not good..." I said.

The fancy paper in my hands got hot and burst into flames as I dropped it to the desk. "Fuck!"

A sound like tin foil tearing split the air. A rift opened in the room, the other side looking like radio static made solid. Growls. Hunger. Claws picked at the rift from within, prying it wider.

I scooped up my spikey ball of death and Angie gripped her warclub tight. We tensed. The air around us rushed into the rift as something inky black poured out.

"Nope!"

Annona grabbed us both and dashed for the door. I scrambled to keep my feet underneath me.

"Annona!" I gasped as we hustled after her down the stairs. "What the-"

"Nope. Shit. Fuck no. Way above our paygrade." A whole bunch of Latin swear words spilled out of Annona. She pressed something into my hand. A battered Zippo. "Time magic. Burn it. Now."

"But arson wasn't-"

"But now arson is! Before it gets out!"

I pulled on stoptime hard. It came with a gasp. The dull ripping sound still echoed, even in stoptime.

Ok. Definitely above our paygrade.

Dried plants. Some paper tchotchke. Fuck, the flames were small. Why didn't rich assholes keep entryways full of flammable things? My soul burned from the magic strain. I grabbed some artwork off the wall and smashed the frame. Inside was a crap print made to look fancier than it really was. Dry and crumbly for the flames was all I needed.

The lighter took as my hold on time faltered. With a whoosh the crumbled art went up much faster than it should and singed my hands as I dropped it.

"Fucking warn a girl about magic lighters next time," I yelled at Annona.

The fire had spread across the carpet, hungry.

"Run now. Argue later." Annona grabbed the back of my shirt and pulled me out the giant front door.

Fast spreading flames nipped at my boots as we burst out the door. We kept running.

I took one look back once we were at the guard house. Smoke drifted out of the windows, a flicker of flame at their heart.

How bad did we fuck this up?

I felt a shadow of that chaos rush Eris told me about. Whatever the results, I caused that.

"Come on," Angie yelled at me to catch up.

I didn't look back again.

Chapter 28 – Eris

I heard a river behind me.

My teeth crunched on the grit of old dirt.

My head throbbed like something I had never felt before.

I rolled onto my back. My vision was cloudy and out of focus, but there was no sun in my eyes. I sat up with care to keep my head steady. Phantom pains from my missing hand throbbed worse than my head.

The barren riverbank stretched out to either side of me and the river stretched wide out in front of me. The grey light was too dim to see what was on the other side.

"Where in Hera's bloody asshole am I?"

Voices chattered on the wind from upstream. My ears rang, but they did not sound English. Was I still in America? The mongrel country had so many tongues running under the current of English, language was not a good clue.

The river looked like it should be familiar to me, the memory just out of reach, faded by time and clouded by the throb in my head. *I've been here before*, my addled mind pieced together, *but it was a lot different.* Crowded. That seemed right. My severed wrist warred for attention with the pain in my head and neck.

With my good hand, I pushed myself to my feet. A branch embedded in the dirt stabbed at my hand. I kicked at it. Not a branch, a bone.

A human bone.

This should bother me more, I thought. But my thoughts were distant to my own mind.

The tangled strings in my head started to tease apart the-

"*Da ist sie!*"

I looked up. A tall woman stalked across the riverbank, her flesh a mottled white and greyish blue. She pointed at me and gestured with a flick of the wrist. A pair of dark wraiths dashed ahead, low to the ground, homing in on me like a pair of bloodhounds.

I ran. The whims of Chaos be damned, I had no desire to wait for them to point me in a direction. So I ran. Away from the wraiths, or at least I tried to. My body dragged. My muscles felt leadened, stiff and hard to move, like a hundred years of grit ground through my bones.

The dry riverbank turned to gravel under my feet. My shuffle turned the rocks and sent me crashing to my hands and knees. A fog rolled in from the river. The wailing wraiths sounded from all sides. I staggered to my feet, looking through the fog for the predators. My good hand ached for a blade like it hadn't in centuries.

I crept away from where I thought the sounds came from.

"Show yourselves," I growled, but the bravado tasted false even to me.

"Ask and you shall receive," a voice like sandpaper said from the fog. In German.

My heart dropped into my belly. The woman, with limbs too long for her body and clad in scorched armor, stepped through the fog. The smell of charred bones followed her. Haljo laughed at what she saw, her sharpened teeth showed malice. The dead goddess leaned on a fire scarred cudgel, longer than I was tall, made from some ancient leviathan.

"Eris Nyxtochter. In all my centuries, I never thought to lay eyes upon you here."

My eyes darted around for anything to pick up and wield as a weapon. The riverbank rocks were not even large enough to be worth throwing. I angled the stump of my wrist away from Haljo and retreated a step.

Her shadow wraiths growled from behind me. They penned me in.

"You won't run, Nyxtochter."

I spat at her feet. "I shall not give you the satisfaction," I said in Greek, not willing to even speak her language.

"Oh, you will give me the satisfaction, bastard spawn of chaos." Haljo narrowed her eyes. "But you will not run."

The dead goddess swung her cudgel in an overhead arc. I moved left. River stones scattered where she missed me and struck the ground. The burst of movement made every ancient wound ache. I felt all five thousand of my years as I stumbled away.

A wraith snatched at my leg. Its teeth sunk into my flesh and a wordless scream ripped from my lungs into the dying fog.

"A thousand years since my realms lay empty!" Heljo brought her cudgel down across my back, sending me to the stones below. I sent a weak kick to the wraith on my leg but its brother snatched at my foot. I struggled to crawl from the wraiths, my hands clawed at the stones but found no purchase.

"Three hundred years since you lit the blaze that locked me here in the land of the dead!"

With a sharp kick, Heljo broke my ribs. I vomited on the stones, then gasped for air. I felt nothing but fire in my lungs from shards of bone grinding together. She shoved her wraiths aside and straddled over me, victorious. She leaned over me. The smoke that still wafted off Heljo's body burned my eyes.

"You do not get to look away, Eris Nyxtochter!" Heljo jammed a knuckle into my broken ribs.

I gasped in pain and my eyes shot open. Her scarred face hung over mine. She gripped my head in her hands and forced me to look.

"Three hundred years, Eris. Three hundred years I have waited for this moment, the moment when you would be mine," Haljo hissed between clenched teeth. "Three hundred years since you killed me, the very Goddess of the Underworld itself, trapping me within my own realm. My kingdom turned to a prison. Empty of followers.

"Three hundred years I walked the realms of the dead, lord and ruler of no one! Until my brother said he found a way to send you to me. When can I have the Greek traitor, I asked him. Patience, Wodanaz said. All in due time, Wodanaz said. My wraiths and I hunger! And Wodanaz said we could eat our fill on your once immortal soul.

"So I waited."

Heljo leaned in and hissed her smoky breath in my ear.

"And now begins a long eon together."

Heljo leapt to her feet and pulled me beside her. My heart thudded against my broken bones, pain came at me from all sides and fingers of panic began to clench my soul. I had no magic, no chaos, no strength left to fight. I stumbled to the first trickles of river water. Heljo laughed and tripped me with her cudgel. She stepped in the water after me to drag me back to shore.

A figure on a low boat appeared through the fog.

I let out a wordless scream, a plea for help.

"Leave this place and return to your dead," the boatman called from the water.

I crawled away from shore. The dank water washed up past my elbows and over my legs. The boatman seemed a better choice of devils.

Heljo laughed behind me. Her boot found my back. I gasped and river water rushed in my lungs when Heljo forced me below to the riverbed. Panic warred between my lungs and my limbs. I needed air but I could not break the surface. My arms felt heavier with each moment. Each grasp for the surface came a little weaker.

Mother Nyx save me, the torment was the first in a thousand deaths if Heljo had her way.

Someone grabbed my arm and hauled me out of the water. Ripped from the sweet oblivion to a world of pain thrown into the bottom of the boat. My body sang with every gasp of oxygen despite the fire in my bones.

I coughed, spat, hacked dirty river water on the sandaled feet of my savior the boatman. My arms tried to raise me up but I fell on the same feet, unsure if I should thank or curse them for bringing me back like this.

I stayed where I was, curled around my broken body, hair caked and plastered with the remnants of the muddy water. The boat rocked underneath me like a caring mother holding a babe.

"Demon witch should know better," the boatman said in a low voice. "It has been an age since anyone came to the banks of the Styx and-"

"Styx?" My voice hoarse from the drowning, my body broken from the beating, I stumbled upright.

"Aye, it is," the voice said in Greek. "And if you—Hellfire and damnation! Sister, what happened to you?"

My brother Charon rushed to set down his oar and knelt beside me. "By every thrice damned shit of Cerebus, you should not be here Eris. I did not even recognize you."

I hacked up another lung full of the river Styx. As ferryman of the underworld, Charon spent little time above in the modern world. He dismissed much of modernity except for Jane Austin novels and all things Tolkien, so without wizard robes, a toga, or Victorian skirts, it was little surprise he did not realize who was just pulled from the river. I looked out over the water. A long limbed body lay face down in the shallows and a pair of wraiths paced along the shore.

"Charon, seeing your face is the best thing that's happened to me on a very fucking bad day." I felt a grin spread across my face even though I figured I could pass for a drowned possum.

His face fell.

"What?"

Charon picked up his oar and faced away, polling the boat away from the banks where Heljo lay.

"Eris... it was not by Fortune's whim that I was present to fend off the German devil. Nor was it the fickle taste of your own realm."

Fog rolled in to swallow the far shore. Heljo and her wraiths were lost to my eyes. With adrenaline gone, my mind felt like sludge and all I felt was frustration.

"Hera's tits, brother, what are you talking about?" I said. "A bastard upstart banished me is all with some magic he dug up older than even our time."

The opposite bank came into view and I saw where Charon was taking us.

"No..."

"This is official business, Eris. You're dead."

Chapter 29 – Giulia

Fleeing to Massachusetts felt like a failure. Sure, this witch, oracle, healer lady patched us up and managed to calm Angie's grief. Sure, my home was compromised as any sort of safe house so this was the best option. Sure, we wanted to keep any other mortals from getting roped in our mystical bullshit. Sure, Annona said we can trust Dee, the Oracle of Salem.

But fucking Massachusetts.

It's not my home.

It's not where Eris is. We think.

It was nice to breathe though.

The original parts of Salem, the ones the tourists always want to see, are clustered together in a way only an old New England city can. Dee's house could have been older than the country but there was a wide porch and tall hedges around the yard to keep the rest of civilization at bay for a small corner of quiet. Dee gave Angie something to help her rest. She slept off her grief with one hand clenched to that magic warclub like Wodanaz was some boogieman who would appear out of the friggin' closet any second.

Annona assured me that he couldn't but we let Angie hold onto it even in her sleep.

I didn't have the heart to find alcohol, as nice as oblivion spoke to my soul, so I sprawled out on a wicker bench on Dee's porch with an arm over my face to keep the morning sun at bay.

The closest thing to peace I had in days disappeared in a poof when I heard a door open and footsteps walk across the porch. I hoped it was Dee. I liked her, especially with the saving all of us, but the grumble I heard meant it was Annona.

"So, what's next?" she asked.

"Fuck, woman. How in the hell am I supposed to know?" I said. "You got two thousand years of ideas up in that head of yours."

"Three thousand," Annona said. "But this isn't exactly an everyday occurrence for me." For once she came back at me with no acid in her voice. Annona sounded bone weary.

"First, you two have something to eat." Dee came out on the porch with a platter of breakfast. It smelled delicious and gave me reason enough to sit up, despite my bone weary hoplessness. Hashbrown patties, bacon, muffins, bagels slathered with cream cheese. I took a bite of a fresh muffin and immediately felt a bit better, though, hell if I knew if it was the magic of an Oracle or the magic of baked goods.

I saw the fidget which meant Annona chaffed with inaction, but she listened and took a strip of bacon.

"Turkey bacon?" I asked.

"Huh?"

I raised my hand like I was in school. "Pork does not compute."

Dee appeared with a small plate of the stuff. "A good hostess always provides."

I crunched into a piece. Charred to a crisp, just the way I like it. The Oracle could make a killing on the B+B scene with psychic breakfast predictions.

There was a moment of peace while we ate. A bird flitted onto the porch. I pitched a couple crumbs to the grakle and it zoomed off with its treasure.

"I think we need to press Andrea Alessandra again," Annona said finally.

I took a sip of the black coffee instead of responding. Burned my throat going down but I took another sip anyways.

"I don't think that's a good idea," I said. I topped off the cup rather than look at Annona.

"Unless Angela got something more from her new patron, who, I should remind you, is in the enemy camp, we have to get it ourselves."

"It's complicated and I don't want to hurt Angie more than she's already been through," I said.

Annona pinched the bridge of her nose. "Look. Giulia. I get you and Eris are crushing something hard. Great. Awesome. You two make a cute couple. Maybe come down to DC and we'll double date to the zoo or something. But I've known Eris a lot longer than you. She saved me from a Catholic purge. More than once. We've been sisters for centuries. I own her my life. I respect you want to do right by your friend," Annona's voice took on an echoing cadence that these deities kept doing when Shit Got Real, "But I swear by all the Roads that lead to Rome, by the lifeblood of the Immortal City, I will not let a single mortal stand between me and saving Eris."

I stabbed my fork into what was left of my muffin and grabbed hold of stoptime. I felt strong here. The magic came to me with barely a thought. I walked around behind Annona and let loose my grip on time.

"Good thing I don't think I'm mortal anymore."

Annona spun around in her chair. "Why do you need to be so difficult?" she screamed. "That ocean one off has information. We need information. It is a simple equation."

"No, it's anything but simple. The collateral damage is getting too high. We have to do this without fucking anyone else over in the process."

Annona rolled her eyes. "Welcome to this immortal life, then. This is what all of us," Annona used actual air quotes, "'myths' do. We fuck up and other people get dragged in. Yourself included."

I looked away and gripped the handrail around the porch in both hands. There was no way I could deny that.

"Look," Annona softened, "We'll go inside and give Angela the *affabilitas* that it's going to happen. She does not need to come with us, but then we go back to Narragansett and we finish what we started with Andrea Alessandra."

I turned back to Annona. Grim determination settled on her face and the whole argument was giving me a headache, like some ringing growing in the back of my head. She had a point, for all her bluster. Maybe Angie would understand. We were all swept up in something we barely understood, right? And Annona was our expert in the corner. She knew the rules we didn't, right?

"Ow, what the fuck is that ringing?" It pierced through the air like some mic feedback turned up to eleven.

The Roman frowned. "I don't hear-"

A whomp sounded in my head, like an explosion without the bang. The air felt snatched from my lungs. I staggered to my chair and sat back down.

"Seven hells, I felt that," Annona said.

Dee rushed out from the kitchen. "Are you ok? I felt... a disturbance?"

"I... dunno. I feel tingly all over." And it wasn't even in the great post-sex kind of way. "Like someone poured ice water in my veins."

I wiggled my fingers to try to get some heat back into my blood but instead I looked up and saw I fell into stoptime.

"It's not supposed to be that easy," I said.

"What's not?" asked Annona.

I had fallen back out of stoptime without realizing it again.

"Crap."

"Eat some fiber then and be serious," Annona said.

"No, I mean 'oh crap, my magic shouldn't come that easy." I flit back and forth between the moments and watched Annona lean back in her chair in a staccato slow-mo. "Like whatever that was supercharged me."

"Oh no..." Dee said in a small voice. Her eyes flared with a white light and her voice echoed in that sound I started to figure meant Very Serious Magic Shit Going Down.

"The Psychopomp comes for thee again," she said. "First to take your soul, then to save a soul. Now he flies to bring you a burden. You will face the lightning and the thunder, but consider the ocean a friend."

"What the hell?" I said.

Dee shook her head and the light vanished from her eyes.

"Prophecy, Giulia," Annona said. "True prophecy from an Oracle."

"Isn't that what they do, just, yanno, like every day?"

"No," Dee said. "A prophecy unbidden, unasked, and unsought means the tapestry woven by Fate will change its threads for you."

"Or not," a new voice said.

Hermes still looked like the personification of a Jimmy Buffet concert. His Hawaiian shirt was a garish yellow with pineapples and martini glasses this time.

"Dee," he nodded to the Oracle, "always a pleasure." To me he said, "Nice to see you're keeping better company this time."

"Is this about Eris?" I said, hopeful we wouldn't have to put Angie in the bad place that shaking down Andrea Alessandra would create.

Hermes winced. He tried to cover it up by flopping into an empty seat by the breakfast table and snatching a slice of bacon. "Why does everything have to be business with you guys? Maybe I just want to check in with my favorite German hunters."

"There is no such thing as coincidence in the house of an Oracle," Annona said.

"Maybe I came to collect the caduceus you owe me," Hermes shot back.

"You're here because of the prophecy," I blurted out. "It's the third time you've come to me. You're here because Fate has changed for me."

He sighed. "I'm here because Fate has nothing more to do with you, Giulia."

"Can you please make some sense?"

"I can make it official." Hermes stood and struck his caduceus three times on the ground. A golden scroll appeared before him.

"By the sacred laws of Mount Olympus, handed down by Themis, the Lady of Good Counsel and Divine Order, daughter of Uranus above and Gaia below, consort of Zeus, Thunder God and Lord of Olympus, it is my duty to inform you, Giulia Cesari, Blood Consort of Chaos, that the Rules of Succession have been invoked and you are now the presiding force of Chaos for all that fall under the shadow of Mount Olympus. Thus it has been declared."

Hermes struck his caduceus three more times. He waved away the scroll and sat back down for bacon again.

Dee held her hand over her mouth. Annona let her jaw drop in shock.

I looked between all three of them. "The fuck does that all mean?"

"The Rules of Succession..." Annona sputtered. "Hermes, do you mean what I think you mean? You can't mean that! Mine haven't been invoked in a millennia. Not since the Great-"

"I mean exactly what I said," he said. "I take no joy in it. Mine have not been invoked in two millennia. Until now."

"What the fuck does this all mean?" I shouted.

Hermes frowned. "Eris passed on to the underworld. You're the Goddess of Chaos now."

Annona sobbed beside me.

"So that disturbance in the force-"

Hermes nodded. "The death of Chaos."

"But I'm not even Greek."

A grim smirk spread across his face. "Which will certainly shake up the status quo. And I do believe that is exactly how you draw upon your power."

"No, this can't be a thing!" I burst out of my chair and paced a frantic circle around the porch. "I want to save Eris, not replace her."

Hermes shrugged. "Not my call."

"Why is this even a thing? How is this a thing? There's no logic to this!"

"In this, there is logic." Hermes waved his hand and a silver scroll appeared. "The Rules of Succession are beyond the reach of Chaos, they are enshrined in the earliest Olympian Law, beyond all save Themis. The law states very specifically that the 'surviving blood' of the fallen shall assume all the rights, privileges, duties, and outstanding debts of the role."

"Wouldn't that mean Aite is now Chaos?" Dee asked. Annona still held back tears.

Hermes shook his head. "Aite and her pure godborn siblings all have their own roles with no one new to fill them."

"Well then wouldn't that mean Nikita or Hazel or Martin-"

"Surviving blood." Hermes pointed at me. "She's the Blood Consort. Not just a consort. Olympus would be a nightmare scene of overpopulation if sex was all that qualified some newbie to true godhood. Eris' blood flows through her-"

"Dude, I'm standing right here."

He nodded to me. "Eris' blood flows through you quite literally. And since I didn't cart you off to the underworld when that ambrosia first spread to your veins, you, and more importantly, the actual blood of Eris within you, are still surviving. Ergo, you're now the Goddess of Chaos. Like it or not."

"But she's immortal," I protested.

"Clearly not anymore," he said. "Something happened to change that."

"Well what was it?"

"By the bloody balls of the titans, I don't know!" he threw up his arms. "Don't you think I wish I did? I actually liked Eris. And it's a bit of a slap to the face to find out that maybe, just maybe, we're not all as immortal as we figured. It's probably directly related to whatever shit you lot have been up to your assholes in thanks to that Wodanaz jerk. Eris has pissed off a lot of people over the last five thousand years. But I'm just the messenger. No one tells the details to the messenger."

"Can you help us?" I blurted out.

"You already owe me a boon. Eris was in debt to me."

"So you can't help, or you won't help?"

Hermes sighed. "Eris made me promise not to intervene. For your sake, I might add. She didn't want the family getting their claws on you before you were ready."

"Well, shit, I'm still not ready for any of this. I need to save Eris."

Hermes shrugged this time. "I am bound to deliver the Message to all of Olympus. The Rules of Succession dictate that I personally let everyone in the Pantheon know. I feel it compelling me to wrap this up and get on with it right now."

"No you can't!" Annona piped up. "You have to let us fix this. We can still fix this. We can! I know it."

The side eye from Hermes was epic. "You're not even one of us, Annona Augusti. You don't even have a Greek counterpart. I have to deliver the Message. Have to. You know how that works."

"We need time," Annona pleaded from Hermes, then to me. "I know we can do it. We just need more time. The underworld is just a place. We can go there and cut a deal. We can rip Wodanaz apart and trade his soul for hers. We can undo whatever immortality stealing hoodoo Wodanaz did."

Hermes shifted from one foot to the other.

"We're going to save Eris," I said to Hermes. "You can be a part of it or not. But it's going to happen. Please. Eris means too much to us."

"Alright." Hermes stood and stamped his caduceus to the ground to make it official or something. "Giulia Cesari, Goddess of Chaos, Blood Consort to Eris Nyxdaughter, Annona Augusti, exiled Blood of Rome, you shall get your assistance. But it won't be from me."

I frowned.

"Then what?"

"I am not bound to tell of your ascension to the Pantheon in any particular order. Trust me in this."

Hermes was gone in a blink.

Enigmatic asshole.

Chapter 30 – Eris

"Please don't do this, brother," I begged Charon. "This is not how our mythos is supposed to be. This is now how our stories are written."

Charon looked away. His eyes stayed with the flat bottom boat and could not meet mine.

"Some stories change," was all he said.

I struggled to sit on the bench running along the boat, using the gunwales of my brother's boat as a crutch. The pain, all of it, felt far away but my tattered remains struggled to remain upright.

"Our stories were set in stone thousands of years ago, brother," I spat out. "Those who wrote them died millennia ago and are revered as storytellers for the ages. It is our legacy."

Hands calloused from countless leagues with the ferry pole steadied me. The boatman's hands wrapped around my arm and left no room for argument, gentle as they were.

"As above does not always mean as below. Even stone wears down under the gaze of Chronos. Stories change, Sister, but my task in this realm has not." He frowned as he poled the boat away from the shore.

I turned back to watch the living realm drift farther away into the fog.

"Everyone always looks back."

Cold penetrated my bones the farther across the Styx we drifted.

"But we're immortal..."

Charon grunted. I didn't realize I had spoken aloud.

"Stories change," he repeated.

I hit my good hand against the side of the boat. "Stop saying that!"

"What else is there to say Eris? Look at us," he stopped poling the boat to gesture to us and the Styx. Out in the middle of the wide river, I saw nothing but fog. "We are relics of a lost age! The world has moved on without us and left us behind."

"You are my brother, but you have no right to talk about the world to me, Charon. When was the last time you came to the living world? I have lived it. I have lived all of it. I have watched the world change."

"Says the Lady of Chaos, the harbinger of change. When was the last time you came here?"

"It was..." I knew it but the answer was fuzzy. Out of reach.

Charon rolled his eyes. "Exactly."

"You still don't have to do this. Immortals don't die."

He sighed. His burly shoulders sagged in defeat. "I am bound by my nature. Same as you are. Were."

Being free of chaos to make my own decisions should have been... freeing? Terrifying? Natural? I felt numb.

A monolithic building appeared out of the mist head of us. Grey bricks. Grey mortar. Square block-like structure. Unadorned square windows spread along the side of the building facing the Styx. A plain door led to a row of steps down the river bank where a short dock jutted out into the river.

"There's nothing Greek about this sad excuse of architecture," I said.

"Like I said, when was the last time you were here?" He tied the boat to the small jetty.

I looked to the door. Simple. Unassuming. Plain steel with a small window of security glass. Yet a dread seeped into me standing there on the boat. In my years I clashed swords and spilled blood at Troy. I walked the trenches and smelled the gas at the Ypres. I had stared down dragons, minotaur, kraken, leviathan snakes, and on one occasion, an extremely pissed off eagle the size of a city bus. In five thousand years, I had never once pondered my own mortality. Mortality in others? It hurt to watch others fade to dust until my memories alone were all they had, but my own mortality? Never. I thought of those who would mourn me. Annona. Hermes. Nikita and Hazel. Kalliopi Kalyvas. Shehu Ebuehi. Giulia.

My heart ached.

Did she think I abandoned her?

I just wanted to keep Giulia safe. Out of Wodanaz's path. I should have just left. Skipped town. "Oh that's just Eris, fuck them and leave them." "Flaked out again." "Unpredictable and unreliable." Giulia would have cursed my name like others before her.

My soul ached to think of Giulia with hate in her heart for me.

But she would have been safe.

And I would not be staring down the steel door on the wrong side of the Styx.

I never felt so alone before.

"Ahem." I snapped my head over to Charon. He held out his hand. "No one is exempt."

What did he-

A cold rage seeped into me. I jammed my hand into my pocket and fished out a scattering of pennies that were never stripped from me in my captivity.

"Fuck you and your fare." I threw the pennies at him. I hobbled off the boat and up towards the steel door. I heard the copper coins fall to the dock and plop into the water. Charon sighed. I tried to hold my head high and let whatever awaited me on the other side know that the dignity of a goddess cannot be stolen.

But the slit in my neck let a cold breeze burn through parts of me never meant to feel the air. My head tilted and the world spun. The door opened and I was pulled through into a bright light.

I righted myself. The bright light came from a fixture in the ceiling. Fluorescent lights lit up a handful of scattered with chairs and stations that roped off lines leading to teller windows.

"I died and went to the DMV?"

"Underworld Central Processing," said a bland voice beside me. The Asian man spoke an old dialect of Mandarin.

"That doesn't make sense. We crossed the Styx but this isn't Hades."

The side door sentry pointed to the queue zigzagging across the room.

"But-"

He just pointed again.

The queue was long.

A black man in front of me spoke no language I knew. A white man behind me spoke Norse but only muttered of fjords and hellfire.

I waited, trapped with my thoughts.

Happier days in Greece fled to centuries of watching it fall. Regret when I could not help. The pain of being passed over by a humanity with a new obsession. Regret. Regret. Regret. I laughed as the Romans fell only to find regret when I saw what it did to Annona. Regret I was such a burden to my friends by my very nature, one that I could not change.

Finally, though my thoughts danced around it, regret I could not say goodbye to Giulia. Regret she would not understand. Regret I could not hold her hand and kiss her once more.

"Next!"

I stood at the front of the line.

When did that happen? There was no clock, no sun out the windows to gauge the time. So easy to fall lost in thought...

"Miss, while we do have all of eternity, you are holding up my line."

"Oh. Right..." I stepped up to the teller window. The man who was in front of me was nowhere in sight now.

"Paperwork." The teller was a skinny little goth teenager.

"What paperwork?"

He rolled his eyes. "The papers in your hand."

I didn't remember getting any paperwork, but there it was, clenched in the one hand I had left. I passed it thought to the goth and he started tapping away on an old computer keyboard.

"Name?" he said.

"Shouldn't that be on the paperwork?"

He channeled the spirit of every DMV worker who ever asked a stupid question. "Name?"

"Eris."

"Last name?"

"None."

"Eris Nun... You're not in the system."

"No, it's just Eris."

He ignored that. "Theology?"

I reflected the stupid question face back at him. "Greek."

He tapped away at his computer featuring an early 90s CRT monitor. It looked like there was a bullet hole through the side of the case. I spied 'William' on his nametag.

"So what's going on here Will? I crossed the Styx but I can't be dead-"

He interrupted me by pointing to a sign nearby that said "Please save your denial of death until after you are served."

"-because this isn't the Underworld. Where's Cerebus? Where are the gorgons, the harpies? Where are the Elysium fields, the Asphodel meadows?"

William ignored me. Tap tap tapping away at the keyboard.

"You're flagged for a special case worker," he said without looking up. William stamped my papers and handed them back to me. The ink smeared. The text blurred. My eyes didn't want to focus on the words.

"Miss?"

William was trying to get my attention? Did I zone out again?

"Please go wait for your case worker over there."

"Oh. Right." I shuffled over to the waiting area and sat down.

My thoughts fell inward again, tumbling over centuries of heroics and misdeeds, to the center of my being where I held those who were special to me. Giulia's light lit fast and burned bright.

"Eris of the Greeks?" a surprised voice said.

I looked up. A woman emerged from an "UCP Employees Only" door. Shorter than me, she wore modern, western clothes but a vague familiarity hovered around the back of my head.

"I'm Culsu, your case worker." She offered her hand to me. I felt a spark of the divine when we touched.

I bit my lip in thought for a moment. "Etruscan?"

Culsu smiled. "You remembered." She led me through the door where a room full of cubicles spread out. She led me to a central cube. Her workspace was decorated with her divine symbols, doorways and scissors. "We met at the Conclave of 1172 and that was so long ago, I wasn't sure you would remember."

"I try my best, though I am feeling a bit... out of sorts here," I admitted.

Culsu's face switched to a professional frown. "Well first thing's first, sympathies over your recent death."

"I can't be dead," I blurted out. "I keep telling everyone here that this isn't the Underworld. There aren't any government grey block offices in my underworld. Since I got off my brother's boat, I have yet to lay eyes on a single Greek. No offence, but you should be in your own underworld."

The other deity sighed. She leafed through a desk drawer next to her and pulled out a pamphlet.

Underworld Central Processing.

"It has been a long time since you visited any of your counterparts in the underworld." Culsu said this as a fact, not a question.

"I am five thousand years old. That's relative."

"At the Conclave of 1988, Tuonen Piika, death's maiden from the Finn pantheon, proposed a shared resource pool for pantheons out of antiquity."

Like most of us old time deities, Culsu danced around saying 'pantheons without any followers left.' The centuries of upheaval could still be a sore subject.

"All this," Culsu gestured around her, "was in place by '94, though there is talk that the Norse may pull out of the Agreement on the strength of their Revivalists."

"So what does all this mean?" I gestured vaguely all around me.

"Eris," Culsu sighed. "You're dead. This is your death."

"No. The Greeks are immortal. I. Am. Not. Dead."

She raised an eyebrow at me and pointed to her neck.

I brought my hand to mine. The ragged wound. The cool draft burning the wrong side of my esophagus.

"But this should not be. At worst, I should awaken on Mount Olympus from a false death. I-"

The Etruscan reached across the desk and placed a comforting hand on my arm. "We have a special protocol for fallen deities here in the UCP. That's why I've been assigned as your caseworker. To help you through this."

"Somehow Wodanaz stole my immortality," I sputtered out, barely hearing Culsu. "He had this ritual. Something ancient. Before his time. Before mine or yours."

"I can assist in filing a Form 8410 Petition for Vengeance." Culsu perked back up now that she was back to handling the bureaucracy of being dead. "As your special case worker, I can fast track the request directly to The Vengeance Department. They look favorably on fallen deities. Divine vengeance is not invoked often. Although, a cross pantheon issue will mean an extra review so-"

"Divine vengeance? Wait!" My thoughts processed Culsu's words. "No. Don't call on Nemesis."

Culsu frowned. "Clearly there were crimes against you." She gestured to my ruined throat and missing hand. "An 8410 Petition for Vengeance is fairly standard with all the antiquity pantheons serviced by the UCP." She lowered her voice in a conspiratorial tone. "Rumor from the gorgons is you were mixed up in an interpantheon mess involving some Irish-Japanese cabal."

"What? No. I have not had any deals with the Tuatha de Dannon in a hundred years."

She leaned close to me. "Was it that-" she spat to the side of her desk "-Roman who gloms on to you?"

"No," I put as much steel in my voice as I could with half the air from my lungs leaking out the side of my neck. "Annona Augusti is an immortal refugee as much as you or me. Moreso even."

The Etruscans shared a homeland with the Romans so held a grudge against them as much as most of my own Greek brethren. Culsu just rolled her eyes and did not press the issue. "Then why the issue, Eris?" Culsu was not unkind.

I closed my eyes and huffed out a breath. "I do not wish Nemesis involved."

A beat. Then two. "Oh! I forgot your sister is the Greek representative in the Vengeance Department."

"And there are... others... who I do not want embroiled in vendetta for my sake."

Culsu brightened up again. "That's a Form 624 Bequeathal of Devine Heritage. I can get that-" she trailed off. She must have seen the emotions plain on my face.

"There is no statute of limitations for divine requests," she said softly. "We'll get you into housing. You can take whatever time you need."

Chapter 31 – Giulia

"I don't think anyone's coming."

An hour passed on Dee's porch. The longest hour of my life. Three times I checked to see if I had slipped into stoptime without realizing it. My power was touchy since Hermes' announcement that I replaced Eris. Beyond that, I didn't feel any different. Just sick to my stomach with worry.

Annona nodded. "Time to get on with it then."

"Do we have a plan?"

Annona shrugged and led me inside. "Sure. Go to Wodanaz's house in Newport. Bust some heads."

I followed her through the house. "And if he's not there?"

"It should draw him out."

"… It's a pretty shitty plan."

"Ha!" Annona barked out laughter. "You're the Goddess of Chaos now. You don't do plans."

We went into Dee's garage. Annona had unloaded all the crap out of the trunk of her rental car onto the concrete floor. The pile of hard cases looked no different than packing the Murphy Minute van for a show.

"We having a garage sale?" I asked. Annona rummaged through the boxes, looking for one in particular I guess.

"Pft. Always the snark with you."

"So tell me what we're doing then."

Annona shot me a look. I knew that one well. A snappy clap back incoming. Likely laced with a cuss word or two. The tension fell out of her shoulders instead. "Right. Right. Sorry, I uh… It's just…"

"S'alright," I told her. I looked away, let Annona cover up the hitch in her voice with a cough.

"So what's in the boxes?"

"You got Eris' sword already," she said.

I was glad I hadn't had any need to use it so far, though I didn't figure that was going to last long.

"Since you're now… Since you're the main gal now, you get to wear this." Annona opened up the hard case she was searching for and, fuck me, it felt like the shining moment from Pulp Fiction and she was my Vince Vega.

"Holy shit," stumbled out of my mouth.

"Yup. The Holy Vestments of Chaos."

Chaos energy rolled off the armor like the aroma of good whiskey when the cork is popped for the first time. The intoxicating sense of chaos filled my head. Was Eris' armor that powerful or was this how she felt all the time when she was 'the main gal?' My fingers tingled at the literal possibilities.

Annona laid out the armor before me, the ancient metal regal even on a dirty concrete floor.

The metal of breastplate and greaves shone like platinum infused with its own inner light. The helmet's plumage was a deep purple. The edges of the toga were picked out in purple and gold trim. Gold inlay picked in the armor traced out Eris' golden apple sigil.

"Shines brighter than Discord's armor," Annona said, "though my cousin begs to differ."

In my head I could see Eris kitted out for battle. Wild curls flying from beneath the helm, armor glinting in the sun thought the battlefield haze... the chaos of melee swirling around her, drawn to the point of her sword-

"Strip down. Time to suit up."

"Wait what?"

Annona looked at me like I was the one that told her to get naked. "Juno rest the soul of Levi Strauss, the man may have been a genius in the world of pants, but you're not going into battle in a t-shirt and jeans."

"Unless you got some magical tequila in there, shirt stays on."

We compromised, and by compromised, I mean the armor was strapped on over my shirt. Annona cinched the breastplate up like some kind of industrial corset. After one short breath that felt like I was in a bear hug, the energy from Eris' armor seeped into my skin and the metal felt like a velvet glove. Once the grain tax goddess tightened the last strap, I felt like I was draped in liquid metal. Except one thing.

"That's it?" I asked.

"Well, Eris said she lost the shield sometime during the Trojan War so-"

"Pants," I blurted out. "My legs are friggin' cold. I don't do skirts."

"You have the greaves."

A snort of laughter came from behind us. Angie looked like her soul was held together with chewing gum under that brief smile. "Looks like a battle kilt and futbol shinguards."

I mangled a Scottish accent, "Just call me Giulia MacCesari."

I got the ghost of a smile from Angie.

Annona rolled her eyes.

"Seriously," I looked at them both. "This is drafty as hell. My butt is cold. How was this a thing? Greeks invented math but not pants?"

"Have you been to the Mediterranean? It is hot. Why would any of us invent pants?" Annona said. "Pants came from the steppes of central Asia. Horseback nomads."

"Cause Genghis Kahn's crew was smart. So yeah. I want them." Seriously, I hated showing that much skin. Embarrassment crept in the back of my head. I turned to keep Angie and Annona in front of me.

"You are wearing the Armor of Chaos, Giulia, imbued with primal magic as old as civilization. Do you notice how it fits like the smith forged it for your body even though Eris is taller than you?"

I nodded.

"The magic melded the armor to your body. Use the magic to make the armor your own."

I closed my eyes cause it seemed the fucking thing to do. I still felt a bit foolish, but I thought of the armor on my body looking like some Caesar's Palace casino extra. Bleh. I thought of pants instead. Jeans, worn in from a dozen nights in the mosh pit. And a comfy hoodie and Docs while I was at it.

A flash of chaos swirled around me coloring the space behind my closed eyelids.

I opened my eyes and I was encased in denim and cotton from this century. The hoodie was black with a dark purple stripe down the sleeves and a golden apple flash on each arm. I hugged the hoodie around me. It smelled of apple blossoms and Eris.

Annona gave me a moment before she whispered, "Let's go."

"Not without me," Angie said.

"I-"

"Sh. I want to do this. I need to do this."

Her eyes were still bloodshot from the tears, but the steel within burned them all away.

I hugged Angie close. "To the end of the Earth then."

A high pitched whine rose from the city around us.

"Speaking of the ends of the Earth…"

Steel slid across old leather and Annona drew her blade. I followed her out of the garage and into the driveway with Angie by my side.

"Wodanaz isn't the patient type," I said.

A bird of mythic proportions circled overhead, keening into the wind. Seeing as I was a myth now too, I figured the definition of "mythic" would need an update.

Whatever. The flying thing was a lot fucking bigger than a bird ought to be.

The flyer dropped to the ground ahead of us, kicking up dust. Clearly a she and not some huge bird, the myth before us stood, six feet tall. Flame colored wings arched behind her back. She rose from the cloud before us, shaking the feathers from her body. She wore jeans and a loose tunic with cut outs for her wings. She looked us over and announced something in another language.

"I have no fucking idea what you just said."

"Pardon," her voice was like flint across velvet. "Hermes said the Blood Consort of Chaos would be unconventional."

"Can someone just tell me what the frig is going on for once?"

"To the point I see." Her stony face quirked in amusement. "I am Tisiphone Erinyes, the Fury of Vengeance, Infernal Goddess of Righteous Destruction. Hermes made very sure that I would be the first of our pantheon to congratulate you on your ascension. Olympus will be… more interesting it seems."

"Why did he tell you first?" I asked.

"Because, new cousin, the need for vengeance you hold in your soul warms my heart. Your desire in this is my domain. I bring you a gift in celebration of your godhood. A gift of information you need."

Chapter 32 – Eris

Culsu swore up and down to me that ironic punishments like Sisyphus and his boulder fell out of vogue after the consolidation of ancient underworlds. There was too much paperwork involved, she told me.

Could have fooled me.

Remnants of that Irish hex scrawled on my arm had me running empty of magic for days before my... before going to the underworld. Then Culsu left me in an empty room.

Empty.

Beige walls. Floor. Ceiling. Diffused light coming from nowhere and creating no shadows. The room warmed to a nullified body temperature. Surface with a slight give. There was nothing to break up the monotony. Not thing break up the order.

Order.

Pah. Even the thought of the word left a bad taste in my mouth. Culsu said that in death, my soul was freed of my compulsion for chaos, but my body remembered the habit and protested.

I lost track of time while the monotony, the ennui of the place pressed in on me. Culsu never lost track of time though. A painful eon for me was all of a pair of hours outside the confines of my own personal hell. It was her scheduled rounds of all her charges though. Routine. Planned.

Ordered.

That fuzzy distaste in my mouth was back. I scrambled for the interaction, for the break in the monotony, but I hated myself for the desperation at the same time.

"Come to spring me, warden?" I said.

Culsu held her tongue and shuffled through a sheaf of papers. "Protocol states that as part of my routine check in I give you the following options as per your stated pantheon at the time of your passing."

"Hey, it's me. There is no need to be all business, Culsu."

She gave me a flat stare.

"I am bound by the rules of the Consolidated Underworld as well as you are. The regulations which this facility operates under are derived from two hundred and sixty eight pantheons, religions, and creeds." Culsu sounded exhausted. "Within these halls, there is little room for anything but business. If you would like to schedule an Afterlife Consultation appointment or apply for Post Life Group Therapy, there are forms which I have here you can fill out."

I stretched out my senses, reaching for any hint of chaos radiated off of Culsu. The aura of order was impenetrable. Apparently her protocol included answering questions about the protocol to the newbies. My soul gnawed away at my insides without any chaos to feed on, but I felt bad for Culsu. She seemed as much a prisoner as I did, tethered by the remnants of her Etruscan underworld folded into this... conglomerate.

In the middle of that room, I felt the hope drain out of me while Culsu droned on. She stared into the middle distance, reciting the minutae of this realm.

The Demon of Doorways was midway through listing the services allowed to me as a Greek when I felt a twitch in my soul. My eyes darted around the beige room. Culsu kept talking like nothing happened, but my body said something did. I just had not the faintest clue what.

A hint of chaos. A flash in the pan. A tremor under the earth that triggered the lizard brain while the logical, refined mind dismissed it as nothing. As a creature of impulse, I fought the urge to jump at it. My senses reached for it while praying to mother Nyx that Culsu was blind to the trickle of chaos around us.

Something far away and getting closer. Whispers rose just out of reach of hearing. Monotony filled with magic, a flavor I never tasted before but laced with such potential. Whispers became a chant, words smothered to become a sound pulsing up and down without meaning. A voice carried though the chant-

"Wodanaz!"

Culsu looked up, the spell of her bureaucracy broken when I spat out the name.

"If you want me to go back to the Petition for Vengeance, I can but..." she trailed off, looking at a point over my shoulder.

She sensed it too.

I turned around.

A point of utter blackness, pure Void, the nothing between the realms burned in the air in the middle of the beige room. I stood, reached out to the rip in the realm. Pure chaos rushed me.

Like a desert rain, my very essence soaked up all the chaos pouring out of the growing tear between worlds. My ears heard the chants, heard Wodanaz's voice thread through the magic. My starved body did not care. The desert rain turned deluge and the flash flood of chaos ripped through my body. The remnants of the Irish hex burned away with any sort of rational thought.

A thundercrack ripped the hole open between worlds.

Earth. Wodanaz, surrounded by his lackeys. My dead, desecrated body in the dirt as his feet. An altar with a bowl full of my ambrosia.

Wodanaz looked through the rip in spacetime and saw me. He laughed and lightning sparked through his hair.

"Today! Eris, today is the day you save the world!" he shouted over the cacophony of chaos. "You will bring magic back to the eyes of humans. You will give all of us a proper place in the world again. We shall not be relegated to the footnotes of superstition ever again!"

Wodanaz took a severed hand-my severed hand!- and wrapped a ritual blade in my dead fingers. I felt the cold blade in a hand that was not mine anymore.

Drop it!

Whatever Wodanaz wanted to do with my hand- no! I would not let it.

Drop it!

The fingers of my severed hand twitched.

Wodanaz snarled and squeezed a fist around my severed fingers. Thunder crackled in his fist. A wordless bellow ripped through his throat and he brought the blade down in the bowl for of my exungulated ambrosia.

It flash froze.

The flash flood of chaos became a whirlpool drawing on the endless potential of the Void between realms, drawing on me.

Chaos called to its own and I felt drawn in through the tear in the realms to whatever heinous ritual Wodanaz had spread out in front of him.

"It's your destiny *mein ketzchen*! I always knew you and I together would bring sense back to the world."

"No no no," I called out in Greek. "Fuck your delusions, I want no part of that." Punch drunk from more chaos that I had felt in an eon, a garbled scream was all that crossed my lips.

Wodanaz laughed as his ritual dragged me across the beige floor, from the underworld to Earth where my own nature threatened to overwhelm me beyond my capacity to control-

"Halt!"

On the threshold, that one word echoed out from behind me. Culsu stepped up in full demonic regalia.

"As the Mistress of Doorways, the Paragon of Pathways, I command you shall not pass!"

Power, drawn upon the underworld around us, channeled through Culsu and slammed the portal shut around me. The Void burned as the nothingness between the realms ate away at the remnants of my soul. Culsu and the underworld demanded that the realms close and I remain. Wodanaz claimed my chaos for his own in the mortal realm, his ritual, more ancient than I, pulled on me like the dark heart of a black hole.

From the Underworld side, "Stop!" Culsu called out. "The Underworld Treaties are sacrosanct! The powers that be will not stand for this!"

"I signed no treaties with you!" Wodanaz bellowed.

The door squeezed around me.

From the Earth side, a new voice, "Wodanaz you need to stop!"

Through the haze of chaos and magic, I glimpsed Andrea Alessandra. She spoke for me?

"This is too much, Wodanaz," she said. "You've gone too far, you're going to rip her soul in two! You are going to unmake her!"

Wodanaz swung the butt of his spear in a backhand arc. The blow caught Alessandra across the jaw, sending her staggering.

"So be it," he shouted over the noise to all the sycophants around him. "Her power will be mine one way or another. I will have it. I will have my resurgence. I will not let the dregs of humanity forget me again."

"And if she ceases to be? Beyond the reach of even the afterlife?"

Wodanaz spoke to his lieutenant but his lightning cracked visage looked straight to me.

"She ceased the moment she opposed me."

The water goddess stepped forward to the lightning god as close as she dared.

"What happened to the good of all, Wodanaz?" Alessandra pled as Wodanaz's crew grabbed her arms and pulled her away. "Were those all lies you sold me? This is no future I followed you for."

Wodanaz leveled the tip of his spear to Alessandra's breast. "Then it is no future for you."

A flash of lightning and the water goddess was gone, lost in the torrent of warring magic.

"Now Eris, *mien ketzchen*, we-"

A scream ripped from my lungs. "Get on with it! Fucking epic poetry gods, just get on with it!"

Wodanaz smiled.

He got on with it.

With great prejudice.

Chapter 33 – Giulia

"This doesn't seem right," I said from the back seat of Annona's rental car. The car rolled to a stop at the end of Cyprus Street, a forgotten nook of Newport sandwiched between the Bridge and the barbed wire fence of the Navy War College.

The Roman goddess and Angie were in the front seat bonding. And by bonding, I meant they were bickering over the closest we could get the car to an island in the middle of Narragansett Bay.

"Yeah," Annona said. "We can get closer from… from whatever island that is over there." She gestured across the Bay to Conanicut Island where the town of Jamestown slept.

Even with the Chaos armor-turned-hoodie pulled down low, I knew Angie rolled her eyes. Seen that look enough times to hear it.

"And we tromp through some rich prick's backyard. That'll be helpful."

"Yes. Yes it will. We can-"

"No, this is fine," I blurted out. "I mean, it's not like we have a boat anyways unless this car has magic pontoon fucking tires." I slid across the cracked vinyl seat and out the back door. We found Cyprus Street via the magic of Google. I walked out to the end of the street. It ended with a chainlink fence and an abrupt drop into the Bay. The block of houses between the highway and the Navy base were nicer than they had any right to be, but Newport was Old Money, so the city's bad neighborhood was a hell of a lot nicer than most cities'. I kept a nervous eye over my shoulder at the houses of Cyprus Street. The sounds of Bridge traffic kept us under the radar. So far. The empty dock at the end of street wasn't labeled public or private. Trespassing was the least of my problems so I just sauntered out to the end of the wooden planks jutting out into the Bay.

I caught the scent of Angie's mint toothpicks over the salt spray of the waves below our feet.

"Still trying to quit at a time like this?"

She gave me a nudge with her shoulder.

I smiled.

Annona walked up on my other side.

"Jupiter's hairy ass, we can't even see Gould Island from here."

The underside of the Newport Bridge loomed over us to the left and off to the right, farther up into the Bay, all we could see was more of the city. So technically Annona was right, I just didn't give a rat's ass.

And I told her as much.

"Calm down. It's in a straight line over that way," I pointed off to our two o'clock direction, "But this is as close as we're getting without being painfully obvious. That's the Navy War College over there. Wanna add them to the list of people we're gonna piss off tonight?"

Annona legit huffed at me.

"We steal a boat, some dingy or whatever, and sail on over like a buncha pirates, rescue Eris, and-"

"What if they're not on the island?" Angie asked.

Annona and me both shook our heads.

"Tisiphone has no reason to mess with us," I said.

Annona agreed. "Vengeance is her domain. We just need a boat and we can get on with it."

"And I picked the only fucking dock in Newport without a boat."

Annona sighed. "We just steal a different one then. There's got to be some dingy no one's looking at."

I looked to the south towards downtown. "A lot of options that way, but a lot more eyes too."

"So, we just act like we belong," Annona said.

I wasn't sold on that. "A cocky attitude won't help if we pick the dingy owned by the hundred foot hundred mil yacht."

"Let's just get back into my car and go. We'll pick one when we get there and-"

"We don't have to," Angie interrupted us. She pointed out to the water.

A figure stood on the crest of a wave and stepped on the dock in front of us. Andrea Alessandra stood before us.

Annona swore and reached for her blade. My hand shot out to hold her back.

"Dude. Hold."

Alessandra stood before us with her arms held out wide and her hands free of weapons. A welt across her jaw looked fresh. This was no aggressive act.

"How did you find us?" I asked.

She looked to Angie. "When you have one honest believer, she burns bright."

"Why did you find us?"

Alessandra got down to her knees before us. "I come to beg forgiveness. I let myself be led astray. Wodanaz-" Annona spat off the edge of the dock at the name "-has a silver tongue. His ideas were noble. Once. Before bitterness corrupted his heart. And I let his bitterness seep into mine. I... I can't do it anymore. The things he has done... I am done with him. I wish to atone."

To Angie she said, "Was your heart true when you said you believed in me? Can you trust me when I say I truly do not know the fate of your kin?"

To Annona she said, "Can your heart forgive another goddess who knows the soulache of losing every follower you came into being for?"

To me she said, "Do you have the steel in your spirit required for what lays in front of you?"

We all said "Yes" in the same breath.

"Then come with me." Alessandra turned back to the Bay and with a gesture, a boat rose from below the water. The Zodiac nudged up to the dock, covered in ocean grime with one nacelle deflated. She stepped onto the boat. Angie hopped aboard behind her. Annona looked like she was going to drop a "hell no" and I raised an eyebrow at the whole waterlogged mess.

Alessandra quirked a smile. "I was born of a shipwreck. They heed my call."

It looked about as sea worthy as an old Buick.

"Screw it." Annona jumped aboard. I sighed and followed.

With Andrea Alessandra at the helm, the Zodiac glided northwest under the cover of darkness. The gentle swell of the water hardly rocked the Zodiac and the motor made no sound as Alessandra steered northwest across the Bay. The city sounds of Newport faded behind us.

I stood next to Alessandra and stared out at Gould. The island was a black smear dancing in the reflections of the moon and the lights of Rhode Island.

"What's waiting for us over there?" I asked.

She stared ahead without turning towards me. A reflection of light caught the ragged gash along her jaw.

"Nothing good. Wodanaz uses ancient magic, older than Rome and Greece combined. He spent centuries with ancient texts to create a siphon carved into the very ground of this island. He steals the powers of others for himself. He will dry Eris into a husk."

I nodded. "So we make that not be a thing."

"Brilliant plan," Annona said. "Let me get Sun Tsu on the line."

A derelict dock at the southern edge of Gould Island was visible in the moonlight ahead.

"Plans-" even saying the word made Eris' armor chafe me "aren't gonna save the goddess of chaos."

Alessandra guided the Zodiac to the rotted wooden planks. We walked ashore like a regular A-Team. The moment my boots landed on the dirty shore,

I felt a thrum through the bottom of my feet. It vibrated through my core but every pulse of it felt wrong. A bass string out of tune.

My cohorts stepped ashore with me while the boat slipped below the waves, returning to its watery grave. Flickers of light danced off the depths of the tress on the island. Moonlight or magic, I couldn't tell. No one moved off the dock. They were waiting for me. I was waiting for...

Angie stepped beside me and grabbed hold of my hand.

We watched the island ahead of us.

"Friends forever," she said in Spanish.

"Until the end of time," I said in Italian.

I stepped into stoptime to let the moment last as long as I could. The strands of time, the chaos from Eris that flowed in my blood, were harder to reach here on the island. It wanted to slip from my grasp. I hugged the chaos armor hoodie closer to me with my free hand, literally wrapping my goddess around me. The strands of time solidified in my new senses and we stood there longer.

"We should go," Angie said after a long while staring at the treeline ahead of us.

"Mmhm."

"Get this over with."

"Mm."

"Save the world."

I held her hand tighter. "I guess."

"Save your girlfriend and get some revenge?."

"That's more like it."

"Tally fucking ho, then."

I let go of stoptime. The world rushed back to us. Eris was ahead of us. Wodanaz was ahead of us.

Chapter 34 – Eris

Wodanaz bound my soul with a thread of magic tethered to the fragments of my hand he stole and the frozen ambrosia from my veins he horded. Magic older than the Titans, simpler than my own golden apple, pierced through the essence of myself like needles of fire from Hephaestus' forge. Yet Culsu, Hades, the whole fucking Underworld Inc. demanded their due, even if their due was a magical loophole.

On the far side of the rift, Culsu struggled. Wodanaz's stolen magic outclassed her. She rallied others to her side who lent her power. The rift crackled around me.

Wodanaz used the blade grasped by my severed hand to call upon the cardinal directions and summon power from the space around him. His cohorts chanted guttural words in long droning tones. Artifacts at the cardinal directions surrounding the clearing drew upon the elements and flowed to the pure chaos of my ambrosia in the center.

My soul stretched thin to fuel the ritual. Tore to shreds.

My sister Despair took me then.

Fuck it. Rip it to shreds.

Culsu could have that part of my soul back. This other piece here Wodanaz would take. Fade the rest away into the primal chaos between worlds.

Save one bit for Giulia.

Giulia.

My heart ached in a moment Despair let her talons slip. My soul was drawn to a vision of her.

One that showed her wrapped in my armor. At the edge of a clearing. Striding forward like the nations of Greece storming Troy so long ago.

A magical shift in the atmosphere hit me with a shock. I gasped with a memory of lungs that burned the tattered remnants of my soul. Giulia was there! She came for me.

Wodanaz felt the shift in the air too. Hesitation crept into the ritual words he spoke. No. The cocky sonovabitch let a smile creep across his face. He laughed. Wodanaz was blinded by his manic arrogance. But the chaos magic he stole, the soul he ripped in two from the underworld, they were not his to steal.

They were Giulia's.

I turned my ghostly sight to Giulia. I saw fear, anger, but also steel of the mightiest blade.

I should have told her to run, to save herself. Isn't that why I ended up there, torn in two, to keep her out of danger? Instead, I pulled the pieces of my soul together and mouthed, "Save me."

The chaos summoned by Wodanaz's old magic would not bind to his ritual when the rightful blood of chaos stared right at me.

I let the fight in me go.

The chaos I held at bay away from Wodanaz turned from a trickle to a torrent.

It overwhelmed me. It burned.

Mother Nyx, save me, it burned.

Chapter 35 – Giulia

I stumbled into the clearing and the choicest of curse words dropped out of my mouth.

"Fuckcock."

There were no guards, no sentries on the island. Every one of Wodanaz's sycophants surrounded a vast hex carved into the ground. The lines were the color of void, of pure nothingness. Artifacts leaking elemental magic into the air ringed the ritual.

In the middle of a swirl of magic shit, Wodanaz laughed, and a spectral visage of Eris splayed out in torment in the center of the mess.

I reached for the strands of time to dance between the seconds and put a boot up his ass. It was like pushing through a wall of jelly though. Whatever hoodoo Wodanaz carved into the earth kept me away from stoptime.

"*Mein ketzchen*, your plaything has arrived," Wodanaz said to Eris. "And brought a nobody and a traitor with them. I guess you shall see them die before I drain your magic to the barest husk."

Wodanaz made a dismissive gesture to his sycophants and went back to his ritual. "Be done with them."

A group of Wodanaz's flunkies emerged from the shadows around the rim of the ritual.

Some scrawny fucker crept up first on the right. Angie let out a scream and cracked him with a grand slam swing with the oni warclub. The toadie doubled over. Angie put a boot to him and he toppled into one of the ritual lines carved into the island. Black flames tore through his body where the line was crossed.

Wodanaz's crew rushed us. Annona drew her Roman blade and Andrea Alessandra brought her fists up surrounded by magical water.

"Go!" she yelled to me. "We'll hold the line."

With each step and skip between the lines of nothing the more intense the pulsating blood in my soul became. I didn't know what the ever living hell I was doing, only that my body knew that with each step I was closer to Eris. Was it the magic in my blood? Was there some soul level connection with the goddess I needed to save?

Fuck it. Gonna get my woman back and put that cocksucker in the ground and if it saves the world too, so be it.

Wodanaz turned and glared.

"You are playing above your class. I am done with you."

He leveled his spear and a bolt of lightning shot forth.

A lurch of chaos in my gut and I threw myself to the right. Ozone crackled in the air and I went down hard. I skidded across old concrete. My back landed across one of the lines of nothing. Flames of biting cold danced across the chaos armor hoodie. I rolled away to smother the flames.

A voice tickled in the back of my head when I stood. "Embrace who you are now. Embrace the chaos."

I closed my eyes.

I ran.

Let my feet fall where chaos would have them.

Five strides. Ten.

Wodanaz's laugh echoed louder than the crackling of magic.

Smarmy asshole.

Twenty strides an I drew Eris' sword. I opened my eyes and a heavy machete blade was in my hands. Cold flames bit at my heels. Wodanaz set his stance with his spear.

I lurched a golf swing with the blade, catching the spear and pushing the tip over my head. I bullrushed inside his reach. Like a matador, he sidestepped my rush, stole the momentum from the crude parry and hooked my leg out from under me with the blunt end of the spear.

The ground knocked the wind out of me. A boot cracked into my chest. Bile lurched in me and another blow caused stars to cross my vision.

"You have been such a problem child, *ja?*" Wodanaz knelt down next to me.

I made an awkward swing at him. He knocked away Eris' sword with a tut tut sound like I was a bad dog that pissed on the floor.

"You do not understand. You are not worthy of her," he pointed to Eris, writhing in the crackling magic. "You are not worthy of the gods. You forgot. All of humanity forgot like we were some toy you were done playing with. But we are still here. I am still here and I remember."

I gulped down enough air to spit out "You're a dick."

Wodanaz rolled his eyes. "So like Eris to keep company such as this."

I levered up to my feet at his altar, no plan in my head beyond "Get to Eris. Save Eris."

From the ethereal plane between two worlds, she screamed.

Wodanaz's spear struck home. Pierced through the flesh at the hem of my chaos hoodie.

Stabbed in the gut, I fell across the altar.

"You are quite persistent. Under different circumstances, we could have been allies."

Fire burned through my belly. Blood burned the back of my throat. I spat at Wodanaz.

He touched a finger to the blood and then to his lips. "You have a touch of the divine to you. If you live, you will thank me for this day when I reawaken humanity to the magic they left behind. I will show them the way. They will thank me. You will thank me. And I shall remake the world the way it should have been. Or perhaps I will drain you along with your lover."

Wodanaz turned from me to Eris. She looked more solid, more part of this world. Her screams echoed louder. The thunder god drew an obsidian dagger opposite his spear. He chanted something in a harsh, guttural language that felt oily in my ears. The lines carved in the island pulsed in time with his words.

Wodanaz stabbed the dagger at Eris' spectral soul and pierced through the tattered remnants.

Raw chaos poured forth, surrounding Wodanaz. Soaking into him. A storm god with the power of stolen chaos.

I slumped against the altar.

"I'm sorry Eris."

The chaos in the air held each nerve on edge.

"I wish I could hold your hand one more time."

The hand in the bell jar. The hand at the center of the ritual. The hand that anchored Eris to the magic ripping her apart.

Cut the anchor. Break the ritual.

I reached out with one hand, fighting blackness at the edge of my vision. The hilt of Eris' chaos blade brushed my fingers. It was every blade that ever was and ever would be. It was potential wrapped onto a sword hilt grasped in my hand. I picked it up.

A butcher blade.

I smashed the bell jar. Wodanaz was lost in the ecstasy of raw magic. I upset the anchor of the ritual but it was too strong to stop. A tidal wave against a lone beach.

Steal the anchor. Steal the ritual. Take the chaos back. Take Eris back.

I lifted the butcher blade. Brought it down across my own hand.

The cut was clean. Surreal. My hand fell to the altar next to Eris, my light skin next to her sun kissed tan.

Shock flooded my system. The knife clattered to the ground. My blood, not the crimson O+ I knew, nor the golden honey ambrosia of Eris, but an amber bronze half way between, spilled across the altar. My knees buckled but I held myself up.

I grabbed Eris' severed hand.

Steal the anchor, steal the ritual, save Eris.

I held her hand to my wrist.

The world stopped.

Wodanaz, ripped from the throes of the magic, saw me and cursed. "What have you done?"

The shock. The pain. All gone. I held Eris' hand up and flexed her fingers. My fingers?

I reached across the veil between worlds, the veil that trapped Eris, and with her hand grabbed hold of her and pulled her to the land of the living. She fell into my arms.

I held her close. She still smelled of apple blossoms.

The vortex of chaos, crackled with storm energy and swirled around us like the eye of a tornado. Wodanaz shouted wordless rage from the other side of the eye.

"You saved me," Eris said.

"Course I did," tears streaked down my cheeks. "I'm half in love with you."

Eris kissed me. "I'm the other half in love."

The island rumbled underneath us. The chaos storm cloud rose around us. The ground split at our feet. Bitter cold flames spat from the ritual lines.

Wodanaz planted his spear in the ground and braced himself against the storm.

"I cannot let you stop me! I have come too far and for too long to end this here." He reached for the lightning in the storm. "I will remake the world. They will remember the old ways. They will know it was I who brought back the light."

I stood with Eris.

"No." We spoke in unison. Two souls with one voice. "You are a toxic order which I am bound to oppose."

I reached out with Eris' hand on my wrist. She reached out with my hand on hers. Together we reached for the chaos storm. Pure potential enveloped us. Lightning, winds, and thunder accepted us as one of their own.

Electricity crackled across Wodanaz's skin, jumped from skin to spear to cloud to Chaos. Wodanaz's own magic siphoned away from him to our outstretched hands.

He fell to his knees. "What have you done?"

"Steal the anchor. Steal the magic."

In that moment, thunder and chaos slammed into us. I arched my back and screamed my lungs raw.

Every atom of my being ripped forth and in that one moment, the world hung in the balance. All things were possible for one breath.

The magic burned us up to nothing, but the potential put us back together.

All was silent.

The great ritual lines carved into Gould Island burned away, leaving nothing but a faint odor of ash.

Wodanaz looked around at his grand plans come to nothing. "How could you?" he whispered. He lurched to his feet and charged in a punch drunk rage.

Eris smiled at me and raised a hand towards him. I did the same.

Thunder cracked.

Chaos roared.

Wodanaz was no more, unmade in the fury of vengeance.

Epilogue - Giulia

Italy was the land of my forefathers. America, the land of my home. Now Greece was the land of my blood and magic.

My third homeland woke me with the sounds of birdcalls and the earthy aroma of mountain wilderness. A suburban girl through and through, I never realized the woods were so loud. Camping out under the stars on the slopes of Mount Olympus National Park felt like magic.

Well, figurative magic, since I knew what real magic felt like.

I had never seen so many stars before. I wouldn't let Eris set up the tent the night before. I wanted to soak up as much starlight as I could.

A small bird covered in a mess of bright feathers made a huge racket and flitted down to land on my backpack. It looked at me like it was waiting for something. It squawked at me.

"Shoo! You'll wake her up."

Eris stirred under the double size sleeping back next to me, mumbling something in Greek in her sleep.

I kissed her forehead and she snuggled back to restfulness. I felt smooshy inside when she talked in her sleep like that.

With the first rays of sun, and the annoying bird who still watched me, came a morning breeze with the faintest hint of the Mediterranean Sea off in the distance. Greece spoke to the blood inside me, the part of me that was Eris. The cells of my body soaked up the spirit of this place, this new homeland of mine, and woke up a wanderlust in me to explore every part of this place, make every part of Greece a part of my soul.

Eris mumbled against me again.

"I don't wanna get up" was a universal sentiment in any language.

"Hey bird," I whispered, "Pass me that bag?"

The bird ruffled its feathers at me but was not particularly helpful.

"You woke me up, you owe me."

I rolled my eyes at the bird and reached over for my backpack. I got out a half written postcard for Angie with a Trinidad address on it. I finished writing about the tourist traps and the seascapes. She would still be on a boat heading south with Andrea Alessandra and her family. Just like the trip to Greece was a return home for Eris and me, the slow sail to the Caribbean was a return home for them. Andrea's kelpie family hailed from Scotland, so they had never seen the ocean she was born from either. The kelpie kids adored their Auntie Angie already.

I signed the postcard with "Friends forever" and a little doodle of a golden apple.

Turning it over in my hands, I still could not help be in awe of my two different colored hands. I traced the line where my white skin changed to Eris' Mediterranean olive. Eris said she sometimes felt the things I touched with the hand of hers I now owned. When we held our hands together, I could not tell which was mine and which was hers. The line in my skin unnerved and fascinated me still. I put that there. I did it. I raised the blade and brought it down-

I shook that part of the memory out of my head. I wished I could forget that one part.

But when I gave myself over to chaos, when I stopped thinking to just do, when I took Eris' hand for my own...

That's when I saved them all.

I kissed her hand that was my hand.

"I wonder if I can mail this when we get to Olympus?" I said aloud to the bird that was still staring at me. "Probably not. Maybe I could bother Hermes into delivering it. Messenger god and all."

"Not a chance. I'm not a post office," the bird said.

"What the fuck?" I screamed.

Eris woke up and tried to jump to her feet from a dead sleep. We twisted up in the sleeping bag and tumbled away in a tangle of limbs.

The bird turned into Hermes. His garish shirt matched the bird feathers he had a moment ago. He squatted at the edge of our campsite.

"I wondered how long you were going to sleep," he said.

Eris sat up and gave him a death stare. She seemed completely unconcerned by our lack of clothes, just pissed that she was woken up. I covered up with the sleeping back. The cool air sent goosebumps down my back anyways.

"Go away!" I yelled at him.

He rolled his eyes but turned away. "Messenger god. With a message. For you two. So you know, official business, not a peep show."

I looked around for my clothes in the grass. Eris just got up to get hers. She warned me some of the pantheon had decidedly pre-modern notions of modesty. I got dressed under cover of the sleeping bag. I couldn't help cracking a smile at Eris. She held in a laugh at Hermes' discomfort.

"So whyfor did you wake us up?" Eris said with a stretch.

"You two are missing your own party. Zeus wonders what was taking you so long," he said. "As if he couldn't guess."

Decent, I got out from the sleeping bag and felt the morning dew between my toes. Energizing more than any morning coffee. I tried to start cleaning up our campsite, but Eris waved her/my hand with a flourish of magic. The camp was packed away in our packs, though it was anyone's guess if it was put away correctly.

"We shall be there shortly," my better half said. "We are hiking up the Footpath. I want Giulia to see Olympus properly for the first time."

I gave her a peck on the cheek. "You're too good to me, love."

Hermes tried to look annoyed with us taking our sweet time to hike the long way to the top, but he couldn't keep up his jaded façade. I saw a smile before he vanished. Back to Olympus presumably.

"Come," Eris hoisted her pack and took my/her hand.

I felt the air change around us. A bone deep magic surrounded us, earthy and more primal than even the chaos I had learned to embrace these last few weeks. The magic of Olympus itself.

A pathway appeared at the far end of the clearing where we illegally camped the night. The other end of the Footpath was beyond the reach of mortals.

"I haven't been home in centuries," Eris said. She shifted back and forth on her feet. I felt a tremor where her hand held mine. "Everyone will be there. Everyone. You- us, we're totally unprecedented in Greek lore."

"It will be just like when I'm on stage," I said. "We'll wow the crowd together. Again."

We kissed.

Olympus waited for us.

But it could wait a few minutes more.

THE END

Acknowledgements

This has been a long time coming.

This book has been through a lot. Title changes. Plot overhauls galore. Giulia went through a name change and a genderflip. Hell, I went through a name change and a genderflip too. A lot of life happened in the [REDACTED] years it took to get to this point. You'd think after all this time, I'd have the Thank Yous ready to go.

A lot of people have been rooting for me over the years. Sometimes I forgot that, but it always meant a lot.

Thank you to my Mom for reading Narnia to me before bed. Thank you to my Dad for handing me my first Zelazny book. Thank you to the teachers who thought I might be on to something with my silly words. Thank you to everyone who wrote one of the (very many) books on my shelves that have kept me company and inspired me. Thank you to all the people who see me screaming into the void and scream back.

Thank you to RSA Garcia and AJ Knights, my first real writer friends. Thank you to the litany of people who have been cheerleaders, encouragers, and enablers of the best sort over the years; Suzan Palumbo, RWW Greene, Tyler Hayes, Delilah Dawson, Jen Donohue, Tonya Moore, Audley Z Darke, Katheryn McMahon,

Jasen Bacon, Ani King, Wendell Bolm, and that rando in a bar back in 2005 who's name I never knew.

There are more that have drifted away with the winds of one social media collapse or another. Life may have moved on but every nudge in the right direction meant a lot.

Thank you so much to Lauren Sullivan, cover artist extraordinaire, who brought Giulia and Eris to life and captured the moment from Chapter Seven better than I thought was possible.

Special thanks to my kiddos, O and J. You two are awesome and I'm so proud to be your Other Mother.

The last and most special thanks is for my better half, Denise. The eighty-eight thousand words in this book wouldn't be enough to tell you how much I love you.

About the Author

Katelyn Forrest exists in Rhode Island writing SFF fiction of all flavors. She went to film school, has been a radio disc jockey and a dot com prospector. She has spent way too long working on steel and isn't allowed to give blood because of that one time with the cow brains out of a vending machine in Europe. She got on stage at a Dropkick Murphys show and drank free samples of Guinness in Dublin. This gal is a descendant of a grave robber and the third in line storming the beach on D-Day. She keeps an anvil in her garage and seven different currencies stashed away. Just in case. Find her on BlueSky @kateforrest or links to all her fiction at katelynforrest.com